F₁TS HER TO ▲ T

A Novel

AL₁CE XAVANÉRO

Copyright © 2022 by Alice Xavanéro

ISBN 9798402791947 (paperback)

First paperback edition June 2022

Book cover design by Kostis Pavlou

Interior Design / Formatting by Indie Publishing Group

Edited by Jericho Writers

For my sister and mother.

CONTENTS

I	IMMOLATION	1
II	RESURRECTION	77
III	TRANSFORMATION	233
IV	CULMINATION	331
V	ZENITH	381

🎧 At publication, a playlist with all the music tracks referenced in this novel is available on Spotify.

I

IMMOLATION

1

Goodbye Johan

Amsterdam, Sep 2019

All of us are so fixated on that one big thing that will, at long last, change our lives and deliver us Freedom (with a capital 'F'). In reality, there's no Big Bang, rather a sequence of smaller events, one cascading into the other, which will ultimately set us free. Break that chain, anywhere, and your dreams will be derailed (for a long time) or shattered forever.

"No, Johan, you've been much more than just a catalyst in my life. You're one of four main keys to unlocking my life, my liberation." My breath stammered and tears continued to stream down my cheeks. "And yet here we are bidding each other farewell!"

For the last time, I stepped out of Johan's medical practice, located on the outskirts of Amsterdam's historical center. The moment the front door closed behind me, I felt my body give in to nausea and emotional exhaustion. Feeling wobbly, I reclined against the red-brick wall. *Stop it, Zoë! Cut the crying, already!* I looked down – a trickle of teardrops spattered on the gravel next to my shoes. *Damn it! On top of everything, there goes my bloody makeup too! My mascara and eye shadow are probably all messed up now.*

This wasn't how it was supposed to end between us. Johan had always admired the strength and resilience of my character and yet, on this occasion, the very last time I would see him, I completely abandoned this so-called *strength of character.*

When Johan buzzed the front door open to let the next patient in, I knew that was my cue to get going and ASAP. Hurriedly, I crossed the small plaza and entered Stuyvesant Singel, a handsome street brimming with hip and trendy shops. Some fifty meters down the street and a few meters past Lanterna Rossa, a cozy little cinema in Art-Deco style, I stopped to admire an optician's shop display window. *Snazzy!* The fashionista in me couldn't help but admire the array of designer sunglasses – from the Pradas to the Guccis to the Diors. They were arranged like a galaxy of stars and planets, suspended in midair in front of a screen of vertical mirror panels. As my attention moved from the sunglasses to the mirrors, I was transfixed by a quadruple reflection of myself. A tall, lanky, vamp-ish looking woman with chestnut-brown hair, hazel-green eyes, chiseled high cheekbones and a wide mouth stared back at me. In her gaze, I couldn't help but notice a hint of deep-rooted hurt and sadness, which try as she might, she couldn't completely conceal. I closed my eyes and tore myself away from my reflections. Pulling out a pair of Tom Ford shades from my red shoulder bag, I slipped them on and turned into a small alley, which would take me away from this congested tourist hotspot and to the raw and edgy environment of Engelenbogen.

Emotionally drained and feeling somewhat messed up, I decided to forgo public transport and walk the one and half kilometers to Amsterdam Central Station. I reckoned I could use a brisk walk alone to clear my mind and reflect on my state of affairs.

Engelenbogen, which literally means 'Angels' Arches' in Dutch, is a relatively quiet street, running adjacent to an old railway viaduct which extends all the way to a wide canal just before the Dutch capital's central station. The arches under the viaduct, which were once used for storage of railway maintenance equipment, have been tastefully transformed into minimalist, smart-looking galleries. I wandered past the eclectic and quirky mix of artisanal shops and studios, offering anything from eco-friendly soaps to kinky, Gothic-style leather corsets.

Between my mental reflections, of what had transpired in the past two hours and flashbacks of the last five years, I admired the delicate gold-colored artefacts which decorated the orange brick walls between the arches. They resembled something like antique shingles from the lost golden age of the Dutch Republic (yes, Holland was once a republic before reverting to being a monarchy). Little things like that make me happy, I mused to myself, and I could use some 'happy' right now.

As I wandered further alongside the arches, I reminisced over some funny and not-so-funny incidents that I had encountered in this very street across the years. Like the time when a group of young men in a banged-up navy-blue VW Golf honked the car klaxon and shouted at me, "Hey you, porn star, come here!" And when I didn't oblige their wishes, their shouts quickly morphed to, "Hey you, fucking whore, come back! Who do you think you are? Angelina Jolie! Don't walk away like that!" Or the time that creepy loverboy[1] (at least that's what I think he was) on a silver-colored scooter verbally harassed me, insisting I give him my name and phone number. *Are you kidding me?* Of course, I didn't. On the other hand, there were also some fond, happy memories like the time I walked past a group of college students who were unloading boxes from a rental truck. One of them ran after me and offered me a red rose. That was really sweet and touching, and if I'm honest with myself, the only time in my life I had experienced a spontaneous act of quasi-romance (if I may call it that). Looking back, I should have stopped and chatted with that handsome young man, instead of rejecting the rose and hastily walking away.

Once I had arrived at Amsterdam Central, I decided to stop at Dunkin' Donuts and treat myself to a flat-white coffee (French vanilla flavored, of course) and a Nutella-filled doughnut. Fuck it! I really need to indulge my

---

1 Loverboy: in Holland and in the Dutch language this refers to a charming young man who seduces young women and after a short 'grooming' period manipulates them into the sex trade.

sweet cravings right now. Honestly, to hell with my waist-line! At least until the weekend is over.

At platform 14A, I boarded the high-speed train to Rotterdam and settled in a window seat somewhere halfway down the furthest train wagon, i.e., the one right behind the locomotive engine. After gorging the Nutella dough-nut and clinically licking my sticky fingers clean, I washed it all down with the flat white. Feeling a little chirpier, I opened my smartphone to check for new messages. There was nothing urgent or interesting, so I clicked WhatsApp away and opened the OneDrive app.

For close to a decade now, I've kept a digital journal, which I've christened 'Jules'. Jules has faithfully recorded a broad array of things for me like my thoughts, conversa-tions, notes, events, experiences, memories, poems, to-do lists, letters, recipes, lyrics, and even PowerPoint presen-tations. Basically, anything I deemed worthy of recording and perhaps, one day, to read again. Initially I had saved the journal entries on my laptop. Today, all my journals are stored digitally in the cloud, which I can easily access 24/7 via the OneDrive app.

I scrolled down my journal entries: hundreds upon hundreds of them. Luckily, those which I had felt to be important or valuable, I appended with a $ symbol (hey, Jules, we all have our quirks!). For some entries I added an extra symbol – to be more specific, it's the headphone symbol 🎧 . Being a fervent (no, more than fervent – I would say fanatical) music listener, very little in life moves, inspires, and soothes me like music does. Losing myself in tunes, beats, grooves, and rhythms has been an escape, a safety valve and an antidote to the shit that life has a habit of constantly throwing at me. My M.O. is to read a journal entry and then listen. Read then Listen. I'm envious of those who can do both simultaneously, but I don't have this talent.

Jules, I honestly wish you could listen to the music which I've paired with some of my journal entries – you know, so that you can really understand me. Sometimes it's not the whole song that resonates with me, but one segment of it or even just a few words.

The train broadcasting system crackled and whirred to life: "Ladies and gentlemen, due to technical issues on the high-speed track between Schiphol Airport and Hoofd-dorp, we regret to inform you the departure of this train has been delayed indefinitely. We advise you to check the NS[2] app for the latest information and alternative travel options to Rotterdam."

The passengers, who were already in the train, shook their heads, cursed out loud and then poured out of the train wagons like streams of scarabs. I, on the other hand, was in no hurry today, so I decided to hunker down in my seat and scan my journal entries. I put my creamy white Bose headphones on and scrolled to the first journal entry in the second half of 2014 which ended with the $ symbol and pressed *Play.*

---

2 NS = Nederlandse Spoorwegen, *Dutch Railways*

2

Are You Mr. Bean?

Journal entry # 607$
Megalaar Logistics, company HQ,
Amsterdam, Sep 2014
🎧 Emeli Sandé – Clown

"**M**aher, could you step into my office for a second?" My manager, a veteran of this colossal logistics company (we're talking air, land, and sea freight on a global scale), held the door to his office open as he ushered me in. Closing the door behind me, he jerked his head to the left to indicate that I should sit down. I never felt comfortable in one-on-one encounters with my manager. Somehow, they always managed to make me feel uneasy and nervous, as if an industrial-sized mega-powerful spotlight was switched on and directed squarely at me the moment I was seated in the designated chair.

"What can I do for you, Daan?" I held his gaze.

"Tell me, Maher, are you Mr. Bean?"

"Huh! What do you mean?" I was confused. A little bitter as well.

"Did you look at yourself in the mirror, before you left home this morning?" Daan snickered.

"I'm not following you! Daan, what on earth are you talking about?"

"Well, there's some white shaving foam hanging from your left ear." He made no effort to suppress the sly smirk on his long face.

I felt my face flush and body temperature shoot up a couple of degrees. I desperately wanted to unbutton the top button of my dress shirt and loosen my tie, or better still, to throw it away. The chocolate-brown Cavalli business suit, which I was showing off at work for the first time, felt at least two sizes too small. *This can't possibly be true; it's a Machiavellian tactic which Daan is employing to unsettle me. That's how he is. Crafty!*

Looking away from Daan, I extended my left hand upward toward my left ear. Feeling the fizzy light foam between my thumb and index finger, I closed my eyes in utter embarrassment and disbelief. Really, there was nothing I could say to redeem myself, so I decided to play it as cool as I possibly could.

"Thank you, Daan, for pointing this out. I have a meeting in five minutes. I should be going."

"One minute, Maher. I have something else to say to

you." He paused a little too long for maximum psychological impact. I hated his mind-fuck games. "Maher, what's wrong with you?"

Now I was really starting to feel uncomfortable.

He continued, "Are you okay? You look very pale and tired."

"I didn't sleep well last night. Problems with my girl-friend. Nothing serious," I parried, hoping to dodge further interrogation about this point.

"Well, to be honest with you, I'm concerned about you, professionally speaking." He paused again for effect. "You used to be one of the star players in my team; *the* go-to proj-ect manager for those high-profile, high-challenge initiatives spanning across multiple divisions in our company."

"I used to be?" I fired back. Funny, even to my ears, it sounded more like rhetoric than a question.

"Did I take a gamble in assigning you as Project Leader of Priority M? You know I stuck my neck out for you."

That's bullshit. Don't fuck with me, Daan, this early in the morning.

"No, Daan. I was assigned as project manager of Priority M on merit. No one did me any favors. Megalaar needed a bridge-builder, someone who could give a broad team cohe-sion and a shared sense of purpose. Management needed an Alsatian, not a pit bull, and I fit the bill." I looked down at my wristwatch and feigned impatience. "Daan, we have a one-on-one meeting scheduled between us this Thursday. Let's talk then." I jumped out of my seat and before he could say another word, I bolted out of his office. I didn't bother to close the door, knowing this irked him.

In my hurry to put some distance between me and him, I

collided with Jena, Daan's secretary (or management assistant – the company's preferred term).

"Hi, Maher," Jena greeted me. "Are you okay?"

"I'm fine," I replied, trying to keep any semblance of cool I had left. I did notice a little twinkle in her eyes.

I liked Jena. She was one of the very few non-judgmental and totally down-to-earth persons working in the company's headquarters. "Thank you for asking, Jena, but I have to run!" I lied – my next meeting wasn't due for at least half an hour.

I hurried back to my desk. I picked up my bag, all the while conscious of my colleagues' eyes ogling me. Genuine concern in their eyes? Maybe. But now, all I can think of is to disappear somewhere beyond those eyes. I dismissed their inquisitive glances and scampered, like Charlie Chaplin being chased by a New York City cop. 14, 15, 16, I reached the central hallway. 17, 18, took the staircase next to the lifts. 19, 20, 21, 22, I scurried down the stairs, taking two steps at a time, I made it to the sixth floor. 29, 30, 31, from the landing of the sixth floor I made a straight dash to the invalid's restroom. Thank goodness! It's not occupied. My first bit of fucking luck today. I opened the door, stepped in and slammed it shut behind me.

I closed my eyes and clenched my fists and jaws so tight that every sinew and muscle in my face tensed to bursting point. Trembling from the pressure, I looked up and wanted to let out a roar of exasperation and agony. The well, where those feelings emanated from, runs very deep. The words "*Fuck me!*" echoed and bounced back and forth a million times in this stupid head of mine. Unclenching my fists, I leaned forward, planting my hands either side of the washbasin. Panting like a wounded animal, I took stock of my image in the mirror. What looked back at me was awful: a haggard, hungry-looking face, bloodshot and tired, hazel-green eyes, shaggy chestnut-brown hair, a little too unkempt, and a medium complexion that appeared too white and pale for someone of Mediterranean extraction. *Maher, you little shit, how could you do this to me! Don't you get it yet? In this corporate environment, image and perception is everything, and you just fucked up. BIG TIME!*

I dropped my head down and shook it repeatedly in disbelief as it dawned on me that the damage was even worse than I had first realized. I must have looked a right fool this morning as I made my way from my home in Utrecht to the company's headquarters in Amsterdam. All those people I came across in the street, at the station and after that in the train. *Fuck!* This morning, I even crossed paths with our division's Vice President in the corridor. "Good morning!" I saluted him, a little too eagerly as he walked past me. He looked at me and smiled without saying a word. Now I know why that freaking hypocrite smiled back. Far from acknowledging my existence, in any positive way, he was amusing himself at my expense. Honestly, if I had a choice, I would erase myself from existence right here and now. The more I thought about my day so far, the more depressed and mentally drained I felt.

I'd had enough. I opened my bag and pulled out a large bottle of codeine cough syrup. Pouring a quarter of the bottle's thick caramel-brown liquid straight into my mouth, I swallowed very slowly. Feeling the opiate's initial sweet burning sting in my throat, followed by the welcome warmth radiating throughout my chest, I managed to relax a little.

3

Jena Shares
Her Thoughts

Journal entry # 609$
Megalaar Logistics, company HQ,
Amsterdam, Sep 2014

"Can I join you?"
I looked up from my stale Gouda cheese and ham sandwich and saw Jena standing a few meters from me with a mug of steaming hot coffee in her hand.

"Please," I gestured with my hand toward the empty stool.

Okay, here it comes… 1,2,3.

"Are you okay, Maher? You look pale!"

I rolled my eyes and wanted desperately to scream out loud that this freaking world should just give me a break and stop throwing this annoying question/statement combo at me. She noticed my negative body language and was about to withdraw when I intervened. "I'm sorry, Jena. I didn't mean to be rude but you're like the eighth person to say this to me today, and the day is still young."

"Well, I'm not just anybody," she scolded me. "We've known each other for almost five years, and you *know* that I'm coming from a good place when I ask about you."

I glanced at her and felt a spark of warmth inside me. I even managed a smile. She was right. She's truly a candid and warm-hearted person, as opposed to many of the *corporate animals* at this company's headquarters, who are hyper-driven by inflated egos, astronomical ambitions and single-minded agendas to further their careers at any cost, including the careers and livelihood of others. I had no doubt whatsoever that her concern for me was genuine. I sighed. "I've been suffering from hernia-like symptoms, only medical science hasn't been able to pinpoint the cause. Usually with a hernia, it's either a bulging disc in your spine or a pinched nerve between the discs. In my case, it's neither."

"So, what are you going to do next?"

"Oh, probably what I've always done!"

"And what's that?"

"'Keep calm and carry on moving' is my moto in life." I was being smug but sincere. "I mean to say, I just keep moving on and try to mentally block the pain. It should pass away after a while."

"Hmm, that doesn't sound healthy to me." There was more concern in her eyes now than there was before.

"Well, it's worked for me so far. Don't worry! I'm also considering Japanese acupuncture, so I'm not relying solely on the *pain-blockage-by-stubborn-brain-power* technique."

"Yeah, Maher. You should take your health more seriously."

"How about you, Jena? How are you doing? And your son, David?"

Jena and I had something in common. Both our parents had escaped from their homelands in search of safety and security for their respective families: hers from the Maluku Islands, an archipelago which belongs to Indonesia; in my case, my parents fled from Lebanon.

With her jet-black hair, dark Indochine eyes, olive complexion and Rosario Dawson looks, she stood out in an office environment full of blondes.

"David, he's good. He's getting help at school to cope with his dyslexia. It's not easy for him to see all his classmates move on while he struggles to keep up. But he's a tough cookie."

"And you, Jena? How about you?"

She smiled. "As a single mother, I've got to juggle a million things from work to David to all the other stuff. But I manage. I'm pretty content with things."

"Are you happy here in Holland?" I was curious.

She looked somewhat puzzled. "Yes. It's my home. Aren't you?"

"I can't honestly say that I am. I've always had a love/hate relationship with Holland. Don't misunderstand me, I'm massively grateful for all the benefits this country has provided me over the years, but somehow, I just haven't been able to make it my *home*. I've been thinking more and more about emigrating. Maybe to Brazil or Canada. Does that sound crazy to you?"

"No, not at all." She paused a little. "Sometimes I just think that what we are really trying to escape from is ourselves."

"Okay, Jena. Let's not get too philosophical, please!"

She blushed. "How about work? How's that going?"

"Good. I'm good at what I do. I mean project management. I'm good at giving the project team a sense of structure, clarity and direction. With me, every team member knows exactly what is expected of him or her. No politics. No personal agendas. No hierarchy. No bullshit."

Jena nodded her head in agreement. "Yes, I've heard a lot of good things about you."

"Really?"

"Definitely! Your colleagues do appreciate you, you know?"

"Oh, I'm not so sure about that." I shook my head. "Despite all my hard work, it's like I'm becoming a bit more invisible with the passing of every day. I feel that I'm not appreciated or taken seriously, especially by higher management. Do you know that feeling when you're talking to someone but they're mind and attention is elsewhere?"

"That's not true, Maher!" Her voice was serious. "Anyway, you shouldn't put too much emphasis on what others think. The only validation that ultimately matters is your own."

"Hmm, I don't agree with you on this, Jena," I cut in. "We are not hermits. In a modern society, it's all about the dynamic between individuals and groups. This dynamic is driven by the continuous judgement and perception of each other. You're only as good as your last film, book, speech, project, whatever."

"Now who's being dogmatic?!" She winked at me.

It was my turn to blush. "Touché. Sorry."

"No need to say sorry. I can see you're a pretty driven person. Just don't forget to take care of your health. And also, to smile from time to time."

I stopped myself from rolling my eyes again. "Oh my God! Look at the time, Jena. It's been nice talking to you. I mean it. But now I really need to get going to my next meeting."

Later that day, Jena sent me an email:

Hi Maher,

I really enjoyed our little talk today. Let's repeat sometime soon. I wanted to share this link with you. Please take a look:

https://youtu.be/L0MK7qz13bU

With affection,

Jena

I clicked on the URL in her email. It was an animated video clip on YouTube. After 12 seconds (of the four-minute video clip) had elapsed, I clicked it away. *This is childish,* I thought to myself, and I deleted Jena's email.

4

Breaking Up
with Emilia

Journal entry # 622$
Utrecht, Oct 2014
🎧 Kylie Minogue – Slow
George Michael – Cowboys and Angels

7 0's and 80's sports cars, European travel (I have my own travel blog), gourmet hamburgers, West Country Cheddar, Italian coffee, Rioja wines, Formula 1, Argentine Tango (both dance and music), architecture (particularly Bauhaus and Art Deco) and kinky sex. Emilia and I had so

many interests in common and we truly loved each other, so why is our relationship falling apart?

Like many couples, we met at a private party at a mutual acquaintance's home. I wasn't really looking that evening, but she found me. I admit that when our eyes connected across the room, there was instant sexual tension between us. Later that winter evening, as our limbs seductively intertwined while we danced to the silky voice of Kylie Minogue singing *Slow*, she reached up to my lips and bit them. As she clasped my lower lip between her teeth, I ran my fingers through her hair all the way to the back of her head and pulled hard. At this, she closed her eyes and let out a sensual sigh.

On our very first date, we made love. Several times. To spice things up she brought some cuffs and a mini flogger with her.

"Don't get excited," she smirked. "Those are not for you!" After a short pause to gauge my reaction, she continued in a very matter-of-fact tone of voice. "Will you use them on me?" she asked, as if this was the most natural thing in the world to ask for. I hesitated initially then decided to oblige her wishes.

After that came the horsewhip, single-tail whip, bullwhip, leather floggers, cat-o-nine-tails, canes, spanking tawses, nipple clamps, ropes, electric wand, candlewax, menthol cooling gel, and ice cubes. She instructed me in their use and coached me until I had become proficient. Whatever physical pain she made me administer her, it just wasn't enough. She took it all greedily in and demanded more, more, more. Her lust and hunger for physical pain was insatiable, but I had my limits. That frustrated her as she accused me of not being a true Dom, short for Dominant, which I had never claimed to be, and more to the point, I didn't see myself like that.

Much later she would confide in me that for a very long time, she had sought a man who could 'break' her. Jules, in BDSM that required a play-partner that was able to take her to the very limit of what she could take (pain-wise) until she 'subbed out' into subspace, which is somewhere where one floats when you are between consciousness and passing out. For her, 'subspace' was the ultimate bliss. She had only experienced it once before and to the man who could take her there again, she swore to give herself completely – body, heart, and soul. She had desperately hoped I would be this man. However, in her plan there was one huge flaw: no matter how hard she tried to cajole and manipulate me, I rejected her burning desires to be this so-called dominant man.

The previous summer, I had sought to rekindle the romance in our dwindling relationship and as a birthday gift for her, I had arranged for a road trip to the Adriatic coast of Croatia and northern Italy. We would take turns driving my white 1978 Lotus Esprit S1 sports car, similar to the one Roger Moore drove as James Bond in *The Spy Who Loved Me*. We would drive five to six hours a day, preferably on winding provincial roads and retire at the end of the day in small boutique-style hotels.

The first leg of our road trip had taken us from Utrecht to a small Bavarian village on the outskirts of Munich. That night, we had high-octane sex. We tore each other's clothes off and sank into a frenzy of animalistic and wild lovemaking. Hour after hour we went at it at such a breakneck speed as if our lives depended on it, until we both ran out of fumes, peaked, and expired together, simultaneously.

The next morning both our bodies were covered with bite and scratch marks, and, Jules, to say that we were famished to the core is an utter understatement. In fact, we were so hungry, the other guests of the boutique hotel (mostly well-to-do pensioners) watched in bewilderment, disapproval, and disdain as we demolished half the food at the breakfast buffet.

'

Emilia turned the ignition keys and the Lotus roared back to life. She revved the engine a few times, turned her head in my direction and winked at me.

I shook my head. "You're such a petrol-head, you show-off," I scoffed at her. Mischievously, she winked a second time with her mouth wide open, shifted the gear to one and set us screeching in vengeance on our way to Salzburg, the second leg of our road trip.

Fuck! Emilia, you're so sexy! I couldn't help but ogle her from the passenger seat. With her slender body, beautifully bronzed skin, dark-blond hair and icy blue eyes, she oozed sex appeal. Loads of it. Her athletic frame was only slightly smaller than mine and standing at 1.79 meters she was a mere two cm shorter than me. Many a time, we would exchange leather jackets. To her chagrin, I was particularly fond of wearing her vintage black and green Ducati leather motorbike jacket.

Emilia was an expert at driving cars and motorbikes. She loved fast cars. She referred to her driving skills as a craft. In mountainous terrain, she minimized the use of brakes, preferring to slow down by shifting gears up and down as needed, and she never made the engine complain or cry out in agony. Not once. Always revving and shifting gears exactly at the limit the car enjoyed. For a sports car built in 1978 that was no small feat.

From Salzburg, we continued to Ljubljana, Zagreb, Zadar, Prizna, Rijeka, Pula, Trieste, Millstatt, Nuremberg, Aachen and back to Utrecht. On every leg of our journey, we had enjoyed the driving (or craft as she kept reminding me), the food, the wine, the historical sights (we were both fond of citadels and castles; something about them appealed to our kinky natures), the landscape, the seascape, the rich culture of each country (from Germanic to Balkan to Italian), and the crazy nights of cocktails, dancing and sex.

On the fifth day of our road trip, we made a spur of the moment change to our plans. From the Croatian capital, Zagreb, we decided to head to the medieval port town of Zadar, on the Dalmatian coast. It was a tip from an amiable couple we met in the lobby of our hotel in Zagreb. It would provide the mystery element to our otherwise meticulously planned trip.

Having arrived in Zadar, we parked the Lotus outside the old town's walls and continued our journey on foot. Once past the ancient fortifications, in an instant I felt a mystical connection with this place. The old town of Zadar, which is located on a peninsula, spoke to me in an enigmatic foreign tongue. Strange, though I did not know a word of Serbo-Croat, I was able to follow it. We marched deeper and deeper through canyon-like, narrow alleys and small hidden plazas surrounded by a mix of Roman,

Byzantine and Venetian buildings. I guess Emilia, like me, was feeling romantic as she took my hand and interlocked fingers. The previous night she had seemed quite agitated with me, so this came as a pleasant surprise. Hand in hand, we wound our way through the old town toward the vanilla-white marble promenade on the northern tip of the peninsula. It was quite late in the afternoon when I heard what sounded to my ears like the haunting, melancholic calls of whales. *Really? Whales in the Adriatic? No.* It turned out to be *Morske Orgulje* or the Sea Organ. A series of water channels connected to organ pipes under the white marble steps that cascaded from the promenade into the sea. As water flowed into the channels, the organ pipes played a random, hypnotic tune. The more I listened, the more mesmerized I was with this place. This was no fluke, I felt. Coming to Zadar was meant to be.

"I'm going for a dip; will you join me?" Emilia inquired, as she started undressing. She had her Adidas black bikini under her clothes.

"No, I'm going to sit on the marble steps and let the gentle waves of the Adriatic and the Sea Organ claim me. I pray they take me somewhere very far away."

"Suit yourself." Emilia frowned but decided not to push it. Step by step, she descended into the Adriatic until all that was left of her was her head bobbing happily on the water's surface.

I waved at her as she took off like a torpedo toward the shores of the island in the distance. Taking in the trance-inducing, mellifluous sounds of *Morske Orgulje*, I asked the sea: *Tell me, what sad secrets do you keep deep inside you? Tell me and I'll share with you mine.*

Emilia's wet lips on my mouth startled me out of my reverie. A little hot and disorientated, I opened my eyes. She stood above me with hands akimbo and limbs dripping with seawater.

"Hey, Maher. Wakey, wakey! Were you asleep all this time?" She smiled down at me. "So, what story did the sea tell you, after all? Care to include me in your secrets?"

"No," I shook my head lazily. "That's between the Adriatic and me. I made a solemn oath not to tell." Not wanting to dwell on this point any longer, I quickly changed the subject. "C'mon, darling. Let me buy you a delicious seafood dinner. Alfresco and a cold bottle of Maraština, to wash it all down."

'''

Next day, on the winding, mountainous coastal road alongside the Istrian Peninsula on our way to Trieste, Emilia asked, "Are you trying to send me a subliminal message?" I had played George Michael's *Cowboys and Angels* for the umpteenth time on the car stereo.

"Sublimin-what? What on earth are you talking about?" I reacted, confused.

"It's 'subliminal'. Are you trying to indirectly send me a message? Through the lyrics of this song?"

"Huh? Of course not."

"So why are you playing this particular song over and over again?"

"Duh! Because I like his music. Is that a good enough reason for you?" I snapped back.

"But why?"

"Other than the fact that he's one of the greatest singer-songwriters of our times, I identify intrinsically with him."

"How so?"

"Well, he's a tortured soul, just like me."

"Tortured soul," she repeated (more to herself) and after that fell silent for a long time.

A few hours later, as we made our way across the Slovenian-Italian border, she asked, "How come?"

"How come what?" I shot back. I wasn't on the same page as her.

"How come you think of yourself as a tortured soul?"

I paused for a while. "Please, Emilia. Not now! Ask me this question again when we get back home, and I promise to give you and answer."

Once we had arrived in Trieste, we drove in circles around the historical city center overlooking the Adriatic Sea. It took us a while to find a parking garage where we could safely leave the Lotus. Once parked, we made our way directly to Antico Caffè San Marco.

Trieste is a true Mecca for coffee aficionados. More than any other city in Italy, Trieste is inseparably linked to European coffee culture and the global coffee trade. It is a major coffee port and hub, where green coffee beans are brought in from as far away as Ethiopia, Columbia, Jamaica, and Java (just to mention a few). And it is in Trieste, where a substantial chunk of the coffee-bean mountain is processed, roasted and ground into the coffee blends you and I love. Of course, here in Trieste, pride of place goes to *Illy* – the world-famous coffee brand. With all this heritage, it is no wonder that the Triestines drink twice as much coffee than the rest of Italy.

Antico Caffè San Marco is a literary café boasting a baroque and Art Nouveau interior, books galore and, of course, the world famous Triestine coffee. We were in illustrious settings here. The likes of James Joyce and Franz Kafka had beaten a path to this very spot so many decades before us.

Our mouths were by now salivating as we inhaled the wafts of roasted coffee beans and delicious Austro-Hungarian pastries. At a small table in the corner, Emilia and I talked literature and politics as befitting the place but in her naughty eyes I could read only one thing: *kinky sex tonight*.

"That can wait until after supper this evening, milady," I exclaimed out loud.

She burst out in uncontrollable laughter; blushing, she blew away half of the cappuccino froth from her cup. "You owe me another cappuccino!" She was all smiles.

I love seeing you happy, my darling.

An article in *The Wall Street Journal* had once christened Trieste as 'Italy's Most Beautifully Haunting City'. How very true – both Emilia and I were demonically possessed by her. If Trieste was an actress, to me she would be Julie Frances Christie, who played Lara opposite Omar Sharif in *Doctor Zhivago*. She is a classy, elegant and sexy lady. The graceful and silent type. She will happily flirt with many suitors but would remain forever faithful to her one and only lover. That cannot be said of her more illustrious, promiscuous, and extroverted sister, Venice.

The next few days, we spent the time like starry-eyed teenage lovers as we explored Trieste on foot and by scooter.

From her piazzas to her Vienna-style grand cafés and the cobblestone alleyways which zigzagged up the hills that surround the city from three sides. Neither of us wanted to leave our alluring, melancholic Trieste. Deep inside, we both knew she could very well be the last drop of glue in our crumbling relationship. But leave her we did.

I let Emilia drive the final leg of our road trip from Aachen to Utrecht. During those concluding hours on the road, an eerie silence fell between us. All one could hear was the whir of the engine and the chirping of the gears as they coupled and decoupled up and down. The silence was only broken when Emilia finally pulled the car into the parking spot in the garage underneath my apartment building.

She turned off the car ignition, and the Lotus fell silent. All teary eyed, Emilia turned in her seat to face me.

"So why?" she asked.

"Why what?" A feeling of ominous déjà-vu fell upon us.

"Why are you a tortured soul, Maher?" My eyes welled up with tears.

"Because, Emilia, I'm utterly lost. I don't know who I am anymore."

5

Lebanese Mezze

Journal entry # 634$
Leiden, Oct 2014
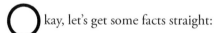 Fairuz – Le Beirut

O kay, let's get some facts straight:

1. Mezze is to the Lebanese what tapas is to the Spanish.

2. Jules, if anybody tells you that mezze is Syrian, Turkish, Greek, Palestinian or Israeli, they're Lying (with a capital 'L') because mezze is originally from Lebanon.

When it comes to mezze, my mother is unequalled. So,

what selection of mouth-watering and finger-licking mezze has she cooked for us today?

- Tabbouleh – salad made of finely chopped parsley, tomatoes, mint, onion, bulgur, and seasoned with olive oil, lemon juice and sea salt

- Baba Ganouch – roasted aubergine, yoghurt and tahini blend

- Humus – chickpea, garlic and tahini blend

- Kibbeh – sautéed pine nuts and spicy minced meat in a crunchy fried exterior

- Fatayer – miniature triangular pies stuffed with spinach

- Warak Enab – grape leaves stuffed with a mixture of minced meat and rice; seasoned in spices

- Kufta – lamb or beef meatballs, filled with onion, parsley, breadcrumbs and spices; barbecued on skewers

- Fattoush – salad with crispy lettuce, fried bread and veggies

- Labneh – tangy yoghurt cheese, served with olive oil and za'atar

- Manakesh – flat bread topped with za'atar, sesame seeds and olive oil

- Rakakat – spring rolls stuffed with a mixture of tangy white cheese, parsley and toasted sesame seeds

- Kanafeh – cheese, sugar and butter pastry smothered in orange-blossom syrup; served as a desert

Fifteen small, earthenware plates of mezze on the table with a bottle of Primitivo wine (from Puglia) to complement it all. *Et voila!* The perfect weekend family dinner, you would think! So, dear Jules, what's wrong with this picture? Well, for goodness' sake, we're a Mediterranean family – there should be boisterous laughter, loud chatter, verve, gusto and jokes galore being thrown back and forth. My mother should be alternating between lovingly feeding my father with her hands one minute and chiding him the other. We (their three children) should be animatedly exchanging tidbits of information (or misinformation) we'd picked up lately on social media. In short, the great, big, fat, happy *familia Mediterránea* dinner. Except it wasn't. The five adults sitting around the rectangular table were more akin to church mice. Quietly, almost solemnly, nibbling on their food with hardly a word spoken between them, as if they had just returned from a funeral. Huh! How come? Jules, I hear you ask.

Well, the answer is pretty simple. It's all due to the family's very own capital HIM – my father, the uber patriarch, the man seated at the head of the table. Mr. Bashar Shibli is a larger-than-life character who has the notorious ability to suck the life energy out of anything. Like a celestial black hole, his presence is at once ominous and overbearing.

As far as my father is concerned, life (our lives) revolves in its entirety around him. He's the center, the sun in the Shibli solar system and we are mere planets. No, I correct myself: we are mere asteroids (barren celestial rocks) revolving around HIM. We are the accessories, which he needs to boast to the outside world: *Look how great I am with my beautiful wife and three children, all of them outstanding graduates of higher education and with four masters and a doctorate degree between them.* Except this was no Lebanese version of the Ingalls[3] family. The Shibli family, residing in Leiden, Holland, is a completely and irreversibly dysfunctional entity.

Only three subjects have ever been discussed around this dining table:

1. My father's extraordinary life achievements (totally exaggerated, of course) and the enormous personal sacrifice he's made for us. *Are you kidding me!?*

2. Politics and current affairs of Lebanon and the wider Levant region, including Syria, Israel, Palestine and Jordan. *Newsflash! Baba, we don't live in the Middle East.*

3. Grandchildren, or more to the point, when were we going to grant him those? *Sigh.*

In his heyday, my father was a top bureaucrat at the Ministry of Justice (of Lebanon) with a reputation for being charming, authoritarian, obstinate and incorruptible, almost to a fault. He was being groomed by his superiors in the ministry to take over the reigns as minister until an altercation with a local but powerful warlord-cum-politician had completely derailed not only his political ambitions but his entire life.

The notorious politician in question had discretely approached my father for a favor – let's call it a personal favor for which my father would be rewarded handsomely, i.e., a large bribe (something along the lines of a secret

---

3 Ingalls family, as made popular by the 70's TV series *Little House on the Prairie.*

Swiss bank account with a big fat six-figure sum in hard currency). Not only did my father reject the overtures to facilitate this favor, he boasted in an interview to *An Nahar*[4] about how he had rebutted this powerful politician and shamed him publicly. This would later turn into a national scandal.

Thereafter came the reprisals, initially in the form of anonymous phone calls threatening to kidnap one of his children if he did not leave the country. Later, envelopes containing a powder (allegedly Ricin) were sent to his office at the ministry. These threatening phone calls and letters made little to no impression on my father. The crunch moment arrived when he narrowly and miraculously survived a booby-trapped car bomb. Only then did it dawn on him that he had to leave Lebanon ASAP.

With the help of some friends and sympathetic associates, he had arranged for safe passage for himself and his family to Holland, where he sought political asylum. That's already twenty-one years ago. Then, I was only thirteen and my brother and sister respectively, twelve and three years old.

In all the years since we had arrived in Holland, my father never allowed us to settle down, put down roots and call Holland our new home. He kept us psychologically in a state of perpetual flux. Every year he claimed that at year's end or even within a few months, we would be back in Lebanon where we belonged. However, when it came to his children, all did not go according to his expressed plans and wishes. There came a point when we, the two sons, wised up and decided to pursue our lives indepen-

---

4 An Nahar – a leading Arabic-language newspaper published in Lebanon

dent of our father. This included us giving up the Lebanese citizenship and becoming naturalized Dutch citizens. Of course, we did all this behind his back. Later, when he found out, he went ballistic – how dare we take such a decision without his consent and approval? He accused us of treachery, of betraying father and country. We let him huff and puff to his heart's content, all the while keeping on our determined path to disentangle our lives, as much as possible, from his. Finally, our plans culminated in both my brother and I abandoning ship. As college students, we had arranged for a government loan, which facilitated our departure from the family home. He had lost his grip on his sons' lives. However, unfortunately, this did not apply to my sister, ten years my junior. She remained, for all intents and purposes, a captive at the family home and a victim to his increasingly erratic and authoritarian whims.

The silence around the table was finally broken by my father.

"Nadine, pass me the labneh," he mumbled, extending his hands toward my sister. My mother rolled her eyes and stared at him, objection and contempt all too apparent in her eyes, but my father ignored her. I read her thoughts because I too was thinking along the same lines. As far as the children are concerned, the word 'please' simply does not exist in my father's vocabulary. To that, I would add the words 'thanks' and 'sorry'.

My father then turned to Zachariah, my brother, and with a mouth half full of labneh and bread he asked, "So, Zachariah, what do I tell my dear friend in Norway? Are you going to visit them to see his daughter, Dinah?" To this my brother muttered something unintelligible.

"What?" my father cut in. "I couldn't hear your answer. Speak up!" He began cranking up the pressure.

How typical of this fucking manipulating bastard.

My brother was already in a serious relationship with a Dutch woman whom my father completely disapproved of, not only because she was of a different culture but more importantly because she wasn't able to bear him a grandchild. The fact that she was literally the best thing that had ever happened to my brother, had as far as my father was concerned, no merit whatsoever. My brother's girlfriend had almost single-handedly helped my brother recover from a very serious depression. Zachariah finally mustered up the courage to reply.

"It's not a good time, I mean at work, for me to take some time off, even if it's just a few days," he said.

"So, what on earth do you propose I tell my friend in Norway?" my father continued, with his signature psychological intimidation.

"I don't know," my brother snapped. "Perhaps in a week or two things will quieten down at the office, and we'll see then." That's Zachariah Shibli for you. He never had the courage to tell my father to back off. So true to his soft, non-assertive nature, he simply kicked the can a few yards down the road. Inevitably, my father finally aimed his proverbial guns as me.

"And you, Maher. What's up with you?"

"Emilia and I are good," I lied. "Thank you for asking."

"Boys, I'm truly disappointed in you!" he exploded. "Am I supposed to just sit back and see my branch of the Shibli family die?" Irritation and exasperation were written in every furrow on his forehead. My mother finally broke her silence.

"It's all in God's hands, Bashar. When God wills it, it will happen."

My father looked at her with pure disdain.

"Woman, when are you finally going to marry off your children? Isn't that supposed to be your role?"

"No, Bashar. That's not how things work anymore. Besides, as long they are healthy and happy, I'm happy for them."

I was pleasantly surprised; it's not often that my mother stands up to him. *Thank you, Mama.* I silently mouthed the words to her.

Frustrated, my father left the table as we continued to eat. For the first time this evening, we felt something that might faintly qualify as lightness.

"Nadine, get me my medication and a glass of water," my father's voice boomed as he called out to my sister from the living room. He switched on the TV and set the channel to LBCI[5]. News about a car-bomb explosion in downtown Beirut reverberated throughout the house. My father further cranked up the volume, just in case the neighbors couldn't hear.

I helped my mother with the washing up. When we were finally alone in the kitchen, she turned to me. "Sweetheart, I noticed that you hardly ate anything today. I can also see that you've lost a lot of weight in the last few weeks. I'm worried about you."

I looked into her amber-honey eyes. "No, Mama.

----

5 LBCI: Lebanese Broadcasting Corporation International

Please do not worry. It's just the stress at work. I will be okay. I promise." She replied silently with a sad smile.

I love you, Mama, with all my heart! My mother is truly a beautiful person, both inside and out. If only she hadn't met my narcissistic father and fallen for him. With her stunning looks and lovely character, she deserved so much better than this cruel card life has dealt her, especially since we left Lebanon.

Physically, my mother could be mistaken for a more attractive but way less visible sister of Chiara Mastroianni, the French-Italian actress. As a young woman in Lebanon, she was highly sought after as a would-be wife. Literally dozens of eligible bachelors from Lebanon's high society tried to court her. She rebuffed them all, falling for the charms of the rising government bureaucrat (i.e., my father), who turned out to be the rottenest apple in the barrel.

I took my mother's hands in mine and gently kissed her forehead. "I love you, Mama," I whispered in her ears. "There's no better mother in this world." I felt her body quiver in my arms as she sobbed quietly on my shoulders.

"And your mezze remains unequalled. Just like Nigella, you're a rock-star cook, Mama. Truly." She looked up at me with her sad puppy eyes and kissed my chest. She hugged me and held me tightly for a very long time.

6

The
Racket Downstairs

Journal entry # 640$
Leiden, Oct 2014
🎧 Aaron Carpenter – Proud

This morning I felt extremely conflicted about going to see my parents for the traditional family Sunday dinner. Even by his flagrant standards, my father has been rather verbally aggressive toward us lately although my mother, brother and sister usually absorb with a high degree of patience and docility whatever anger and vile language he throws at them, just letting him be without reacting. Jules, that depiction doesn't apply to me. When he pushes hard, I push back, equally hard. Couple this with my father's winner-takes-all mentality and we have a combustible mixture that could possibly lead to a violent conflagration, today or next week. Sometime soon. With my energy level so low lately, I just couldn't stomach another fight with him. In the end, I did decide to go, if only to see my mother and sister.

On my way to my parents' home in Leiden, I picked up Zachariah, who lived just two blocks away from my apartment in Utrecht. Be that as it may, we hardly saw each other except during the weekly pilgrimage to our parents' home. Our relationship was more cordial than warm. He did respect me a lot though, I being the elder brother. In Lebanese culture (and the wider Arabic world), being the eldest son carries considerable weight. Fathers are commonly addressed as father of <son's name>, or in the Arabic language 'Abu' followed by <son's name>. So, my father was usually addressed as 'Abu Maher' by friends, acquaintances, and colleagues.

Dinner was the usual solemn procession. Well, at least he didn't bring up the three subjects. What a relief! Once we had finished eating, clearing the table, and putting the dishes and cutlery in the dishwasher, my sister and I retreated to her bedroom upstairs.

Unlike the lukewarm relationship with my brother, Nadine and I were very close. I loved her to bits. In my view, she was not only the beauty but also the brains of the three Shibli siblings. Not only did she have two master's degrees (in Law and Zoology) from the prestigious University of Leiden, but she was also physically a very attractive young woman. With her milky bronze complexion, long lustrous black hair and almond-shaped dark eyes, heads would turn when she walked by. Think of a younger and more exotic version of Sandra Bullock.

Nadine and I loved talking books, music, and films. We could easily lose ourselves to this bewitching trinity for hours on end. However, today we didn't talk much. Nadine's mood was subdued. Something was wrong – I could feel it in my bones. Matching our blue mood, she slotted George Michael's *Listen Without Prejudice* into the Philips CD player. Slowly she walked back to her bed and planted herself right next to me.

"Maher, I need to tell you something." Her words were heavy.

"What? Are you alright?" I looked at her with anticipation and a little dread.

"No, no, I'm fine. It's about Mum." At the mention of Mama, I was no longer half-reclining on her bed but as straight as a pole.

"What? Tell me. What's wrong with Mama?" My heart started palpitating.

"Please, you need to understand that I'm sharing this with you in confidence. Mum made me promise her not to tell you and Zachariah."

"Nadine, please, just tell me! What's wrong with Mama?" I was by now on tenterhooks and couldn't take any more suspense.

"Mum's health is failing. Last week she had some tests done at the hospital. The results are not good. One of her kidneys has failed completely and the other is working at 80%. The doctor has given her some pills to stabilize the kidney that's still functioning."

"Fuck me!" I jumped to my feet and ran my fingers through my hair in agitation. "Why didn't she tell me and Zachariah about this? Maybe we can help."

"Calm down, Maher." Nadine was now looking anxiously at me. "She's getting all the medical help she needs. She made me promise her not to say a word to you. She's adamant; she doesn't want a fuss about this," she continued. "Please sit down, Maher. There's more I need to share with you." I slumped back onto my sister's bed. By now, I was ashen faced.

"The doctors have also noticed some anomalies with Mum's heart. The final test results are not in yet. However, the doctor suspects that one or more valves in her heart are leaking. The doctor cautioned that open-heart surgery needs to be considered, as an option of last resort, if the diagnosis is severe heart leakage."

"No, no, no, not Mama. This can't be happening to her. She's still so young." My eyes glistened as light refracted through the teardrops in my eyes. My entire body convulsed in agony and emotional distress. Feeling my pain, Nadine put her hand around my shoulders. "She will pull through this, Maher." She tried her best to console me. "We've got to believe this."

"I feel like running down to her and holding her in my arms right now," I said, shaking my head in disbelief, "but I will respect her wishes for now. There's no way one can keep something like this bottled up inside for long. I will call her in a few days' time to let her know that I know. I'm sorry, Nadine, but not all promises are meant to be kept, especially with something as life-threatening as this."

Minutes ticked away and nausea gripped me. I felt so

disorientated that for a moment or two I lost consciousness. When I opened my eyes, I wasn't entirely sure where I was until I heard Nadine's voice calling at me.

"Maher, Maher. Are you okay? I think you passed out for a few seconds or so."

"I will be alright. Just give me a sec." As I started to register my surroundings more clearly, I picked up the haunting notes of George Michael singing *Mothers Pride*. *How freaking fucking appropriate!*

"I need to go downstairs for a second. Will you be okay?" Nadine asked. I nodded in reply.

She came back with two mugs of hot chocolate.

"Here, this will make you feel better. It's Blooker's Dutch Cacao – the best in the world." I took the mug from her hand but could only muster up a meek smile as a thank you. She reclaimed her spot on the bed beside me. We sipped our hot cacao milk in silence, both of us lost in contemplation.

Some time had passed when I asked, "Nadine, can you read me one of your poems, please?" She turned and looked somewhat quizzically at me.

"What, you mean right now?"

"Yes, please. I've always loved your poems for their blues, raw emotion and authenticity. They've always spoken to the deepest part of me, and what better time than now."

She put her mug down on the bedside table and walked to a black lacquered chest with Chinese motifs in the corner of her bedroom. After rummaging through the contents of the chest for a minute, she pulled out an old leather notebook.

To the pitter-patter of raindrops on the window pane,

Nadine recited a selection of her poems. They transported me to the sad and lost world of a young woman; a magical butterfly, which as a caterpillar was once upon a time captured by humans and entrapped in a glass jar. A glass jar which has been her home and perennial prison ever since.

Nadine's raw and captivating words came to an abrupt halt when we heard a loud thud and shouting downstairs. We looked at each other. I rushed toward the commotion to see what was happening.

My fears that my father would once again show aggressive behavior toward one of us was now playing out in real time, right beneath our feet. In the living room, he let loose another torrent of expletives at my brother. Zachariah, hunched in a chair with his head drooping, just took one verbal punch after the other, without any repost or reaction. Incensed by the injustice of the unfolding situation, I took a few steps toward them. As I did this, I heard my mother call after me, "Maher, please, don't."

For goodness' sake, Mama. Would you please stop kowtowing to him. He's not your master.

"You have no right to call Zachariah's girlfriend a whore!" My voice was loud, crisp and clear. My father suddenly became aware of my presence. With a face that suggested more amusement than irritation, he pushed his head slightly back and narrowed his eyes.

"What do you want, Maher?" he said, half-laughing at my audacity.

"What I want, sir, is for you to stop calling Zachariah's girlfriend a whore." I paused for my words to sink in. "Those are not the manners and high standards of behavior that you taught us." At this last statement, his face turned red then crimson then purple. His lips began to quiver.

"Get the fuck out of my house, you son of a bitch!" he barked at me. "I don't want to see your face in this house again. Ever." For a frightening moment, I thought he was going to charge at me like a raging bull, but thank heavens he remained rooted to his spot. Otherwise, things could have turned very ugly.

"I'm leaving. Zachariah, I will be waiting in my car, if you want to come as well," I said to my brother.

Raw with anger and charged with emotions on the purple-red end of the spectrum, I marched like a rebellious soldier to the front door, trying all the time to avoid eye contact with my mother. As I stepped outside the house, I had to dig deep and muster up all the discipline and restraint in me not to smash the windshield of my father's shiny black Mercedes, parked in the driveway.

7

Raw Poetry N° 1

Journal entry # 641$
Leiden, Oct 2014

Till Never *by my sister, Nadine Shibli*

I cannot imagine and dare not feel
Anything
Do not speak because I'm scared to reveal
Everything

The disintegration of a family
Viral

Slowly but irreversibly
Final

We grew older together
Too old
Nothing left to give each other
All sold

For an insincere measure of peace
Tranquillized
Holding in rage fighting for release
Intensified

Pain comfortably awaits our notice
In time
Locked in the reality of this
In rhyme

As poetry flows away
Forever
Becomes just one more day
Till never

8

4:11 A.M. / Eyes Wide Shut

Journal entry # 649$
Utrecht, Nov 2014
🎧 ZAYN – Insomnia

I t's 4:11 a.m.
My eyes are shut,
but I am not asleep.
Wide awake
In bed
With eyes wide shut.
Completely shut.

Desperately hoping,
Pleading to the heavens
Praying that somehow,
From sheer exhaustion,
I will fall asleep.
What folly! Typical me, so naïve.
It isn't working.
Try as I might,
Thanks to this bloody insomnia
I simply can't fall asleep.

I decided to open my eyes to check the time. How many more hours till I need to get out of bed and prepare for the working day ahead? I picked up the smartphone from the bedside table and stared at the digits on the screen. The time was 4:11 a.m. Yet another night was about to expire without a second's sleep. It's been like this for the past six months.

What is happening to me? Perhaps, more importantly, why? My entire life seems to be in a vicious circle, quickly spiraling downward. My relationship with Emilia is over. My mother's future is uncertain. My work performance has deteriorated to the point I can't bluff my way out of a bad situation anymore. My health is failing to the point I'm finding it hard to function normally. Tasks which were once simple to carry out, are by the day, getting tougher and tougher to execute. So, Jules, if somebody today were to ask me how I felt? If I were to be genuine and honest with them (and myself), I would provide them with the following list of ailments:

- Exhausted, both mentally and physically

- Depressed, sad and miserable
- Heavy, lacking energy and motivation
- Angry, mainly with myself
- Frustrated, with all aspects of my life
- Exasperated with just being alive
- Disconnected, from myself and environment, i.e., people
- Empty and void
- Physically hurting from medically unexplained lower-back pains and hernia-like symptoms

To sum it all up, I'm no longer a human being. I am but a shell that is nominally functioning like a human being. A shell that will probably altogether collapse soon. I give it another five to six months. Tops! With regards to the 'why' part of this question, i.e., why is this happening to me? I dare not go there! It's my deepest secret. A secret I've buried so deep inside me, that at times I myself had forgotten about it (or had hoped to forget about it). A secret, which I've carefully hidden and suppressed all my life. No. I dare not open this Pandora's box.

9

Pizza Mutilation

Journal entry # 651$
Utrecht, Nov 2014
🎧 M83 – Go!

took the sizzling hot pizza *tonno* out of the combi microwave oven and put it on the kitchen counter to cool down
for a few minutes. With a handful of green olives and rucola
on top, that would be my dinner for today and tomorrow.

I had around five minutes to kill. I reopened the oven
door and felt a blast of hot air in my face. Inside the oven,
it was still glowing hot. I rolled up my shirt sleeves, expos-
ing the lower part of my arms. Today, it's going to be my

left arm. I bit my lips hard and extended my arm inside the oven chamber. In my mind, I started the count-down: *5, 4, 3, 2, 1, now! Do it, you fucking bastard!* I turned my arms, clenched my hand in a tight fist and pressed the lower part of my arm (just above the wrist) firmly against the edge of the metal casing. AAAARGHH! My eyes swelled up with tears. After a few seconds elapsed, I snatched my arm back. Doubling like a wounded animal, I buried my arm in my chest.

Jules, you know that I eat a lot of pizzas and always wear long sleeves. Now you know why.

10

Blackout

Journal entry # 658$
Company HQ, Amsterdam, Dec 2014
🎧 Phantogram – Black Out Days

In the meeting room, I scanned the faces of my colleagues around the large rectangular table. They represented several divisions of our company. Besides myself, there were twenty-one participants attending today's project meeting, including Jena, my unit's management assistant. Of the twenty-one colleagues, I would classify four as allies, thirteen as neutral and four as foes. Of the foes, Kurt was especially nasty. He is a high-flying Strategic Product Manager and management high-potential asshole from the Marketing department (which nowadays goes by the fanciful label of the Customer Excellence department). Kurt was not only my colleague, he was my nemesis within the company. Ever since the project started, around eleven months ago, he's been actively plotting and scheming to have me replaced as project leader, preferably by himself. My day of reckoning with him will come sooner or later. Of that, I'm sure.

As project leader/manager, my prime objective is to deliver the project's main goal within the given constraints of money, time and most importantly, people. Most of my colleagues are fine, decent, hardworking professionals, but you're not always dealt a good hand.

The key to a successful and productive meeting is first and foremost preparation. As project manager, do that thoroughly and barring an act of God, the meeting should go smoothly and be fruitful. It is paramount that at the conclusion of the meeting, the majority of participants feel satisfied with the points discussed and the progress made. As for the project manager, you're only as good as your last project meeting. So, I take every single such meeting very seriously and prepare thoroughly.

For today's meeting, the agenda consisted of five topics and we had one and half hours to cover them. As we covered each topic, I would translate the discussion into action points and assign those to the colleagues around the table.

We had covered three topics adequately, when I called for a five-minute coffee break. On the dot, five minutes later, my colleagues streamed back into the meeting room and took their places at the table. I reconnected my laptop to the TV screen mounted on the wall at one end of the room.

"Okay, let's resume the meeting," I announced, as all eyes turned toward me and the PowerPoint slide on the TV screen.

"Over the next twenty-five minutes we will focus on the IT side of the implementation, and I would like to give the floor to—" *Damn it! What's his name again?* I blacked out, for what felt like an uncomfortable eternity. As hard as I tried to focus, I couldn't recall anything related to the meeting. Everything went blank, including the names of my colleagues. I tried to cover up my blunder with some generic blah-blah that came to mind.

"The IT challenges facing us in the next few weeks are pretty complex and to help us break down this complexity into laymen's terms, I would like to—" Again, my mind went blank. I felt my body temperature rise. A heavy film of perspiration, which was buffeting my forehead, started dripping. By now, I was aware of the embarrassing fact that my colleagues were whispering amongst themselves and making faces. Kurt especially was enjoying my painful predicament. The whole situation was starting to feel like a fiasco. My first public disaster as a professional.

Suddenly, my smartphone started ringing. I retrieved it from the inside pocket of my jacket and stared at the name on the screen: Jena. Jena, who was seated diagonally opposite, was ringing me. I looked at her, but she pretended to be taking notes.

"Sorry, this is urgent. I need to take this call. Excuse me." I put a hand on the colleague's shoulder who was seated directly to my left.

"Mike, could you kindly take over from me while I take

the call?" He nodded. I trusted Mike; he was an ally. As I walked out of the meeting room, I heard Kurt scoff, "Maher, saved by the bell, are we?" This set off a loud brouhaha of male and female laughter. Thirteen neutral colleagues and four foes. *Damn it!* All this is at my expense.

I closed the meeting room door behind me and wished the ground would open up and swallow me forever. I was mortified by this humiliation but I knew I had to go back in, if only to stop Kurt from claiming victory. After five long minutes, I returned. Mercifully, the meeting concluded without any more blackouts.

My colleagues streamed out of the room, except for Jena, who remained seated at her place. Once everyone had left and we were alone, she looked at me with sorrowful eyes. "Maher, you blacked out during the meeting. Not once, but twice. Am I right?" The question hung heavy in the air between us. I couldn't look her straight in the eyes. With my head hanging down, I mumbled my apologies.

"Thank you, Jena, for getting me out of a very tight spot. What you did with that phone-call decoy was pure genius. If you hadn't intervened, I would have been crucified! I owe you a bucketful of gratitude." I dared to make eye contact with her again.

"You don't owe me an apology or anything like that." Jena held my gaze. "Maher, what you owe is yourself some medical help. For goodness' sake, get it quickly."

I couldn't help but notice Jena's eyes glistening with a film of tears. *If this is what I think it is, Jena, please don't. I'm not worth it. You deserve someone a hundred thousand times better than me. I'm a mess of a human being with a secret deep inside me you won't like.*

11

Ode to Laura Jane Grace

Journal entry # 662$
Utrecht, Jan 2015
🎧 Against Me! – True Trans Soul Rebel

At dawn on this cold and misty Sunday, I was thunderstruck by a deeply touching and emotional interview which I heard on the radio. The interview was with Laura Jane Grace, singer/songwriter and frontwoman of the punk-rock band Against Me! Laura spoke viscerally and candidly about the pain, struggle and lack of support she had experienced while transitioning from male to female, from

Thomas James Gabel to Laura Jane Grace. In her voice, you could hear and feel the deep-rooted sadness of this courageous transgender woman, who had battled the mind-boggling odds stacked up against her, while so many around her, left, right and center, abandoned her. No wonder her band is called Against Me!

All her life, Laura had resisted, rebelled and fought for the basic human right to be herself. Something 99.9% of humanity not only takes totally for granted but is hardly, if ever, confronted with, i.e., being born with a mismatch between mind and body. In Laura's case, her mind is female while her body is male.

Something about her story touched me so deeply and profoundly that right after the radio interview had finished, I jumped out of bed, picked up a pen and started writing a poem about Laura and her struggle. I decided to give the poem the title, 'Ode to Laura Jane Grace'. As I wrote it, I felt possessed by something primal deep inside me. Remarkably, this was the first time in seven years anything poetic had come out of me. I had long since assumed that that well of inspiration and imagination was forever dry. In the days when I still wrote poems, it normally took me anything up to an hour to write a first draft; this time I was finished within a few minutes.

A few hours later, when I reread 'Ode to Laura Jane Grace' back to myself, I felt emotionally supercharged and seized by something powerful, obscure and as of yet, unexplainable.

12

Tipping-Point

Journal entry # 663$
Utrecht, Jan 2015
🎧 Sylvain Chauveau – Pour Les Oiseaux

For a while now I've been agonizing about the poem 'Ode to Laura Jane Grace' which I wrote last week. For a whole week, I've had this nagging feeling that there was something fundamentally wrong with it. So, today I picked up the notebook in which I had madly scribbled down the poem and read it out loud. When I finished the recitation to myself, it hit me. It hit me like a sledgehammer. I felt perplexed. My eyes became watery, my vision blurred, and my heart constricted inside my body. I knew what was wrong with the poem, but I was petrified with Fear (with a capital 'F') to acknowledge the truth: that I had used Laura Jane Grace as a camouflage, a decoy, because the poem was not about her. No, Jules. The poem was about me.

I was once again in the potent grip of the same innate power that a week ago had possessed me to write the poem; this time it was forcing me to correct the poem by stripping away the mask. When I finished making the essential changes, my hands were shaking, and silent tears came running down my cheeks. I wanted to run away, to escape, to hide. I ran to the front door. How do I escape from myself?! I turned around and ran to my bedroom and stood trembling in front of the mirror. I shouted at my reflection.

"SAY IT! SAY IT! SAY IT!"

"No. No, no, I can't!" Quadrillion voices inside my head replied. Once more, I felt a dreadful panic, and I wanted to run away but I couldn't. My feet were rooted to the ground. I knew right then and there that the *coup de grace* moment, which I had been avoiding all my life, had finally arrived.

I looked deep into my eyes and said out loud, "Maher, you ARE fucking transgender! This is it. The truth is: you are a trans woman!" The pressure continued to build inside me until I let out a hair-raising scream:

"I am a WOMAN!" That visceral female voice, which I had never managed to extinguish, reverberated like a thousand thunderous echoes inside my head. That exact moment, the earth shook beneath me. I was shattered. I was a pane of glass, splintering into a million pieces. I fell down to my knees and with my head buried in my hands, I started crying like I've never cried before. The grief, sadness and agony of a lifetime poured out of me like torrential rain; all the while, my body went into a sequence of rolling convulsions. The wailing and sobbing were unmistakable – they were not of a man but of a woman. A woman who for the first time in her life was seeing the light of day.

For the next three days, I found myself in an emotional whirlwind. I felt nauseated and dazed. I'd entered a twilight zone, where I would go from one panic attack to another.

The mudslide of questions came at the tail end of the proverbial torrential rain of emotions: Am I going mad? When I become a woman, will everybody ridicule and laugh at me? Worse still, will they verbally and physically abuse me? Will I be safe? Will I lose the people I love? My parents, my family, my friends? Will I lose my job, my income? Will I lose my home? Is there anything, at all, which will remain the same?

At the heart of this perfect storm of fear and anxiety, which had now completely engulfed me, there was a tiny spot of tranquil serenity. The serenity of my self-acceptance as a trans woman. I knew very well that there was no future for me as a 'man'; I had truly reached the end of that line, for the simple fact that my mind, heart and soul would never find peace in a male body. Moving forward, I can't see any other way to my salvation and the chance to live an authentic life, other than to physically transition into what I truly am, and always have been – a woman. Her name, *my* name, is Zoë.

13

Tipping-Point Poem

Journal entry # 664$
Utrecht, Jan 2015

A Trans-Existential Crossing

by Zoë Shibli
('tipping-point' poem – conceived on 18th January 2015; however,
finalized on 25th January 2015)

Identity disturbed
Identity shaken to the core
A female voice screaming inside me,
so primal, so powerful, it won't let go.

Two choices: sink or swim
Enormous waves crashing within me
while I start to swim toward that far-away shore.
I realize I'm on a new voyage
to the other side
But I have no roadmap, no masterplan
The compass gives no clarity
No consolation

~

False peace shattered forever
Taboo breached
The fractured dam is finally broken
The male straitjacket torn
and cast away.
I'm terrified!
I fear my fate, this destiny
Who am I?
What am I?
I'm really hurting
I'm really distressed.
Will I be alone on this journey to womanhood?
For the rest of my life?
No companion, no friend, no ally.
Abandoned by all
Will anybody really care?
Help me make the transition?
I hear the cynic inside my head say:
"Get real! They won't listen, won't care!
Support will be token/lip service, at best,
And they'll find your decomposing body in a
remote motel."

Stand and struggle alone: Against Me! Me Against
the world!
Will I breakdown?
NO!
I'm a fighter, an Amazona, unbreakable!
Can I turn back?
NO!
Is there *überhaupt* a choice?
NO!
Will my world come tumbling down?
NO!
Am I destined to oblivion?
NO!
How many times do I have to say *fucking* NO!?

I *will* rise from the ashes
Phoenix reborn
Transition from Maher to Zoë
A beautiful trans woman
A brave new world
A miracle, a dream
Free at last
to be my true self:
A woman
Alive
To live a *real* life
before I die.

14

Nomenclature

Journal entry # 674$
Utrecht, Jan 2015

In the days that followed the radio interview with Laura Jane Grace, my interest peaked in all things transgender. To help myself understand this subject better, I looked up the definition of a few words, which she had used during the interview, like 'transsexual', 'trans woman' and 'gender dysphoria'.

Since my recent cataclysmic experience and having finally recognized myself as being transgender, I find myself in totally unchartered territory. Jules, that terrifies me. How on earth do I even go about transitioning from male to female? I needed to educate myself ASAP and start working on a plan to make that existential crossing to the other side of the gender divide.

I had no illusions that this journey was going to be very long, difficult, tough, exhausting, expensive and, yes, dangerous. That's six adjectives, dear Jules, and I'm being frugal! Furthermore, there's no guarantee that I'll even make it to the other side, and success is at best relative. From the limited research I had done so far, I could only conclude that on an individual level, there was no bigger change a human being could undergo. Transitioning would turn my life upside down and inside out. It would impact every single dimension of my existence, whether it be physical, emotional, psychological, social, occupational, relational, financial, or legal. Nothing in my life would remain unimpacted and unaltered. On the relational level, it would jolt every single relationship I had, with my family, friends, acquaintances and colleagues. One thing was for sure, I was going to lose some of them along the way.

With all the staggering consequences on the horizon, for myself and my loved ones, is it really worth it? Lately, I've asked myself that question over and over a million times. Is it REALLY, REALLY worth the galactic sacrifice? My answer every single time, believe it or not, Jules, is YES. Definitely yes! It is not a choice. I have to do this.

If somewhere down the line, a medical expert was to say to me, *Listen, Zoë, there's only a five percent chance you will survive this journey. Do you still want to go ahead with this?* My answer would be an unequivocal *Yes!* I would rather live another two months as a woman than another twenty years as a man. Sounds dramatic, but 100% true.

Okay, so back to my research, what have I learned?

This is my take on the basics:

- transgender: a person born with a mismatch between their biology and gender identity

- transgender woman or simply trans woman: a woman born trapped in a male body

- transsexual: a trans woman who will go (or has gone) all the way, medically speaking. This includes SRS (Sex Reassignment Surgery), i.e., sex-change operation

- Gender Dysphoria: the neuro-biological condition which causes a (severe) conflict between oneself and the gender assigned at birth. If you're (diagnosed as being) transgender then you have gender dysphoria.

So, what are the characteristics of gender dysphoria? Here's a (summarized) list:

- Having extreme discomfort with the gender you were assigned at birth

- Having extreme discomfort with one's primary and secondary sex attributes

- Having a strong desire to be rid of one's primary and secondary sex attributes. So, if you're a trans woman, the list of physical male attributes you want to (desperately) get rid of are, amongst others: male genitals, facial and body hair, all the male characteristics of your face (including the Adam's apple), male voice, muscle volume, etc.

- Having a strong desire for primary and secondary characteristics of the other sex. Again, if you're a trans woman, this means desperately wanting to have: a vagina, breasts, a bigger bum, smaller waist, softer skin, etc. Basically, all the physical attributes that society, in general, associates with being a woman.

- All of the above 'disturbances' should cause clinically significant distress and impairment in social, occupational or other important areas of functioning.

Yep! I've got all of the above! Now that I've shaken off the pretense of being a man and accepted my status as transgender, I am finally able to recognize all of the above-mentioned in myself. In other words, I'm suffering from gender dysphoria.

Goodness me! That list is mind-boggling! And that's just the medical/physical side of things. Where, in Heaven's name, and how, do I start healing?

15

The Specter &
the Spectator

Journal entry # 677$
Utrecht, Feb 2015
🎧 Rachel Rabin – Raise the Dead

Let's put the medical talk to one side for a moment. Jules, do you know what it means when a trans woman tells you she feels trapped in a male body? Well, let me elaborate on that.

I know what it feels like to wake up sad, very sad, and with tears in my eyes every morning. I know what it's like to go through the day feeling shit – I mean seriously shit. I know what it's like to feel disgust, total disgust, even revulsion at the sight of my male body in the mirror; so much so that I regularly hurl insults at myself, and every time I want to physically hurt myself. And I do.

I know what it feels like to be hopeless and depressed; when you no longer believe in life; when you've come close, very close to concluding that you're not meant for the land of the living. I know what it feels like to be eternally lost. When running away is not a solution because the only thing you truly want to escape from is yourself. I know what it feels like when my head is on the verge of implosion, not for an hour or a day but always.

I know what it feels like to be in perpetual panic mode, like having just realized you've lost your cell phone, wallet or house keys, and then press continuous repeat. I know what it's like to feel extreme tension all the time, like a wire strung to its maximum and, at any moment now, it is about to snap. I know what it feels like to be frightened, even terrified that someone wants to kill me for just being me. I know how deeply wounded I feel when someone addresses me as 'sir' or 'mister' – *fuck it! Can't they see my female essence?* I know how I feel when I can't make any relationship work, because I'm supposed to pretend to be a man to the woman I love. I know what it feels like to be consumed by jealousy every time I see a cis woman[6], in my age category, walk past me at the train station, in the supermarket, or in the street. *I don't want her. I want to be her!*

I know what it feels like to be a mere shadow and an observer in my own fucking life – the specter and spectator.

---

6 Cis woman or cisgender woman: a woman born with a body that matches her gender identity

I know what it feels like when, day after day, you're just surviving – instead of living. I know what it feels like when you are nothing more than a hollow shell. I know what it feels like to go to bed every night with tears in eyes wide shut. This, Jules, is the horrible feeling of gender dysphoria, and it's killing me.

16

Whacky? When?

Journal entry # 678$
Utrecht, Feb 2015

Jules, it's not all gloom and doom. You know me – I can be pretty goofy when I'm happy.

Fuck, I really can't remember the last time I felt that way. Damn it. This journal entry was meant as an antidote to the previous one, not to emphasize it. Okay, I'll be blunt: all that's standing between me and death is my never-give-up mentality. Is it an inexhaustible well, though?

17

So, What Happens Next?

Journal entry # 679$
Utrecht, Mar 2015
🎧 Cailin Russo – Phoenix

"Good morning, Verstegen Real Estates. How can we help you?"

"Hello, you're speaking with Maher Shibli. I would like your help in selling my apartment in Utrecht."

The last few weeks I've gone through a period of deep introspection. Though the doubts and the fears about the road ahead remain ever-present, ominously so, a number of existential truths have become as clear as daylight to me:

- I needed to stop this charade of pretending to be a man. I would never live an authentic life with my mind constantly warring with my body. I needed to be at one with my body, and the only way to achieve this is to physically transition from male to female.

- The deep feelings of unhappiness and distress about being trapped in a male body were never ever going to go away. It is not a 'phase' which will one day pass away. To the contrary, the gender dysphoria is getting worse – more intense and more difficult to cope with, with the passing of every day.

- This agony and misery, which dominate my life, if it remains untreated will lead to my total self-destruction. I'm already on a dangerously accelerating downward spiral to death.

- To have peace with myself, I needed to start listening earnestly to my female essence and stop suppressing her or running away from her, from me.

- It is okay to be transgender – being transgender is not a crime. I knew I was going to have to work very hard to banish my inner demons of self-hate and internalized transphobia. I'm under no illusion it will take a gargantuan effort to reverse decades of external brainwashing and conditioning that poisoned my mind into believing anything LGBTQ is wrong. Basically, I'm going to have to reprogram myself to love myself and the diversity of the human race.

Way before my tipping point, I knew deep down that acknowledging my identity as a transgender woman was a matter of 'when' and not 'if'. Figuratively speaking, it's like the metaphorical train in the distance (from a Spaghetti Western movie), chugging its way toward you. You just know one day that train is going to hit you.

Feeling I was about to embark on the most significant chapter of my life, I made two decisions: 1) to sell my apartment in Utrecht and relocate to a new city, where hopefully I can transition anonymously. 2) to start feminizing my body. I was well aware of the fact that for the serious stuff like hormones and surgery I would have to rely on the medical system. However, there are a few things within my control and current financial means like permanently removing all facial and body hair. Laser and electrolysis seem to be the most likely options for this purpose.

On Google, I searched for Funda.nl, the most widely used real estate search engine in the Netherlands. Okay, what type of new home am I looking for, Jules? After selecting the price range, to filter down the list of results, I ticked four of the checkboxes and chose the following criteria:

- Type of housing: apartment
- Location: on waterway
- Parking: underground garage
- Region/Province: Zuid Holland

The search engine returned eleven listings, most of them located in the port city of Rotterdam. I had a very good feeling about the first option on the list.

P.S. I love the song which I've paired with this journal

entry. I know zilch about League of Legends; on its own this song captures, for me, the transgender zeitgeist. When listening to this track, I crank up the volume to the max. Sorry, neighbors!

II

RESURRECTION

1

Dinner with the Ex

Journal entry # 682$
Schiphol Airport, Apr 2015
🎧 Pet Shop Boys – The Way It Used to Be

Two days ago, I received an unexpected call from Emilia. On the phone, she sounded happy. I would even go as far as to say that she was excited to speak to me. After our separation, we hadn't seen each other for several months, so we decided to have dinner together this evening after work. I invited her to have some gourmet hamburgers and Belgian fries at the Runway Café at the Schiphol Airport Sheraton. It was a cosmopolitan and tastefully decorated place, which we both knew well and felt comfortable in.

I intentionally arrived half an hour early and claimed a table in a very quiet corner. With the spotlights dimmed and Miles Davis' *'Round About Midnight* record playing in the background, one could be forgiven for thinking this place had something romantic about it. However, when I suggested we meet here, romance was the furthest thing from my mind.

I wasn't sure how I was going to approach this evening's rendezvous with Emilia. On the one hand, a part of me desperately ached for her. On the other hand, I had already made quasi-peace with the fact that our separation was more or less final and that there would be no going back on that. Furthermore, I had also resolved to come out to her as transgender and to let her know that I intended to move forward with transitioning. She would be the first person that I would come out to. Jules, to say this made me very nervous is the understatement of the month.

I rubbed my sticky palms and kept looking down at my Zeppelin wristwatch. Another ten minutes till our appointment. When I looked up, there she was. Radiant, sexy, Emilia. We stared at each other for a little too long. In her eyes, I saw equal measures of apprehension and excitement as if this was a first date. I didn't want to admit it, but I felt the same way. As I started pushing my chair back to stand up and greet her, she hastily took two steps forward, leaned in and kissed me on the mouth. This I wasn't expecting, but before I could make up my mind whether to kiss her back, she withdrew and took the seat opposite me.

"You're looking good, Emilia. Happy to see you! How have you been?"

"I'm good," she replied. "You're looking good too."

"Don't. Please don't, Emilia. Not now! Let's not lie to each other. I know that I look like shit. Only this morning, a colleague at the office asked me point blank if I'm dying."

"That's ridiculous. Of course, you're not dying. The brute directness of the Dutch. I apologize on behalf of my compatriots. Who do they think they are!? No respect for one's privacy, whatsoever."

"Stop! Emilia. I appreciate what you're doing here. Don't blame it on the Dutch. The truth is, if I don't seek medical help, it might not be long before I kick the bucket." Emilia fell silent. Shock and concern clouded her eyes.

"What? Why? What do you mean, Maher?" she asked.

"It's not what you're thinking, probably. And I will make it through. I hope." I hesitated for a few seconds, wondering how to go about telling her. "Please, before I elaborate on my situation, let's order some hamburgers and Heineken beers. Also, I'm longing to hear how you are doing?"

Emilia hesitated to move the focus from me to her, but finally succumbed to my persuasion. She gave me a run-down of her life after our separation. She had found a new job as a saleswoman at a nationally acclaimed motorbike dealer in Amsterdam.

"Way to go, Emilia!" I saluted her with my beer bottle. "That's super news. Except I'm not so sure about the sales-woman part. You're probably going to spend as much time in the workshop with the mechanics as you are with potential customers." I flashed a foxy smile at her. In response, she stuck the tip of her tongue out at me.

"What do you know about it, Maher?"

"Oh, a lot actually. Petrol-head!" In return, I stuck my tongue out back at her.

After the scrumptious hamburgers, I ordered us some Karamel Sutra Ben & Jerry's ice-cream with the café's signature warm chocolate-fondant cake.

"Maher, the suspense is killing me. You always do this to me. Tell me what's going on with you?"

"You mean you don't want to hear about my new apartment?"

"What new apartment? Did you sell our, uh…? I mean, your apartment in Utrecht?"

"Yes, and I bought a new one in Rotterdam. It's great actually. It has a panoramic view of the port with ships and boats galore, sailing by on the River Maas. It's industrial and edgy, very Bauhaus; I think you'd like it. You should come visit me soon. I'll get the keys in early June."

"Congratulations! But how come suddenly all this change?"

"Talking about change, this is nothing. It's just the tip of the iceberg."

"So, then please tell, before the suspense kills me." Exasperation became the dominant tone in her voice.

"Emilia, I'm transgender." *There! I've said it.*

Emilia's mouth gaped wide open as she returned the spoon with a piece of the molten chocolate cake back to the bowl. After a deafening pause, she reacted in a soft, almost whisper-like voice. "Transgender. Maher, are you sure about this?"

"Yes," I affirmed. "Are you surprised? Or shocked?" Again, Emilia fell quiet before she finally answered my question.

"No. Actually now that I think more about it, it's starting to make sense. You were never a typical male. Your androgynous looks and long wavy hair are, after all, what drew me to you physically. Look at you! With some makeup and a dress, half of the people in this café would probably think you're just another woman. Lose another kilo or two and you'll probably fit in my clothes." She fell silent again. I could almost see the cogwheels of thought revolving in her head.

"And the other half? You said one half would think I'm a woman. What about the other half? How would they see me?"

"As a transvestite. A cross-dresser, probably."

"Ouch! I was afraid you were going to say that." I cringed in my seat. "Fuck! I can't bare the humiliation of being perceived as such."

"Sorry! I didn't mean to be so direct."

"No need to apologize." I made a mental note to investigate ways to deal with this problem until the hormones kick in. Hopefully, the hormones will be the solution long term.

"And?" I asked.

"And what?" Emilia put on a puzzled face.

"C'mon, Emilia. I know you too well. You want to ask about her."

"So, Pantera! That viscous bitch you unleashed on me, she's the real deal. Isn't she?" Her voice was agitated and loud enough to catch the attention of the diners at the tables nearby.

"Stop, Emilia! I'm shutting this subject down. After all this time, I didn't expect her to ruffle your feathers this much," I snapped back. With Emilia, I've learned being curt and firm is the best gambit whenever she becomes emotional about Pantera.

"I'm sorry, Maher. You're right. That was uncalled for. So, what are you going to do next?" she asked.

"I'm going to transition from male to female."

"You mean you're going to have a sex-change operation?"

"Please lower your voice. Or perhaps you'd like to announce it on the airport broadcasting system? And yes, if you want to put it bluntly like that, I want to have the operation."

"Sorry! I didn't mean to raise my voice. Again."

"You're forgiven. Again." I smiled.

"What are you willing to lose for this, Maher?"

"I don't quite follow you. What do you mean by lose?"

"This is high-stakes poker. It could cost you dearly. Have you thought about the consequences?" I nodded.

"Yes, I understand the question now. I'm willing to lose everything, my life even."

"Are you absolutely sure about this, Maher?"

"Yes! Every atom in my body tells me that I must do this. This is my destiny from the day I was born, and I'm going to see it through. Come what may."

"Where does that leave me?" Her eyes shifted to the side to avoid contact with mine.

"Excuse me?"

"Maher, I'm not lesbian."

"Huh." I didn't see this curveball coming. "I don't know what you're talking about. We are separated after all." *Does Emilia want us to get back together?* Stillness enveloped us; we both decided not to push the subject any further.

After I had settled the bill, it was an awkward walk with Emilia to the subterranean railway station, located right under the airport terminal.

Palpable unease gnawed on my already frail nerves. We waited at the platform for our respective trains that would take us to different destinations. We stood side by side but avoided eye contact like two shy strangers on a blind date.

Her train arrived first. She turned to me and swiftly kissed me. It was a soft, wet kiss on the mouth. Taking a few steps backward, she pulled out a little package from her handbag.

"A little gift for you," she said. I reached out to take it and our fingers touched clumsily. We both blushed. Emilia stepped into the Intercity train to Amsterdam. Just as the doors were about to close, she called out enthusiastically, "Hey, what about your name? What's your new name?" The train doors closed before I could reply. *It's Zoë. My new name is Zoë.*

As the train pulled away from the platform, a sharp painful stab in my stomach told me that that was probably the last time I would ever see her. My darling Emilia. My throat constricted and my vision blurred. I wanted to cry. Shout out at the top of my voice. *Fuck it, Emilia. Darling, how could you do this to me? Utterly abandon me when I need you most. Can't we be friends? … No, Zoë! Stop, Zoë! Don't you do it! Don't you dare cry for her!*

Emilia's parting gift was a deck of tarot cards. Once or

twice during late night conversations about the paranormal, I must have mentioned that I was curious about tarot.

I read somewhere that tarot, astrology, and numerology are inextricably intertwined. Jules, my interest in this might surprise you. However in tumultuous times anything goes. Perhaps the tarot is, as some claim, a tool to help one connect with their subconscious, with their inner space, and beyond that, the cosmos. After all, to quote the famous astronomer, Carl Sagan: *we are all made of stardust. And to the stars one day we will all return.*

2

Pantera

Journal entry # 683$
Utrecht, Apr 2015
🎧 of Verona – Dark in My Imagination
Kovacs – Night of the Nights

It was the summer of 2013. Emilia had been incessantly nagging me for weeks about my inability to truly *dominate* her and ultimately take her to her much-coveted *subspace*. I finally gave in.

"If that's really what you want from me, there might be a way," I yielded after some considerable hesitation. "I can't do edge play[7] as Maher, but perhaps Pantera can."

7 In BDSM, edge play is to bring the submissive 'close to' or 'on' the edge of what he/she can tolerate in terms of pain

"Pantera? Who's that?" Emilia exclaimed. "I'm not interested in being dominated by a woman."

"She's a different kind of woman. Pantera is my female alter ego." Upon hearing this, Emilia's ears transformed into finely tuned antennae.

For a while now, with the gender identity conflict raging furiously inside me (which much later I would understand to be gender dysphoria), I started developing Pantera, first in my head and later in the real world, as my female alter ego. Pantera would be my safety valve, which I would utilize whenever the pressure inside me to become a woman reached fever-pitch levels. Not releasing this pressure in one way or another, I knew would be fatal.

Through Pantera, I was for the first time in my life indirectly in touch with my female essence. As Pantera, I felt more at ease with myself. I was more grounded, authentic and daring.

As is usually the case with me, when I commit myself to something, I go all the way. That applied to Pantera too. From the outset, I had decided that Pantera would become a classy *femme fatale*.

By watching hours and hours of makeup tutorials on YouTube and subsequently experimenting extensively, I became better than anyone I know, both privately and at work, at applying makeup.

When it came to clothes, I decided to go for a few expensive pieces. Less is more, and Pantera, she's definitely not timid or apprehensive in expressing her sexuality through her clothes. Her shoes were all high heeled. Her boots were all thigh-highs. As for her statement piece – it was a leather corset, which she'd wear externally, of course. Female power, all the way.

"Hmmm! You have an alter ego." Emilia looked me straight in the eyes. "I didn't know that."

"Yes," I said, holding her gaze. "How do you feel about that?"

"Intrigued. Fascinated. Honestly, this excites me!"

"Emilia, a word of caution – I've never done SM as Pantera before. I don't know how that will turn out. One thing I'm certain of, though, is that she's not Maher. By that, I mean she's way more intense and could possibly take you to places you might not want to go to or even like."

"Well, there's only one way to find out, isn't there?" Emilia had a cheeky smirk on her face.

"Emilia, I don't want to sound cliché, but when it comes to Pantera, it could very well be a case of *be careful what you wish for.*"

"You worry too much, Maher." Emilia clicked her tongue. "Bring her on, and she'd better take me to the edge. Either way, I'm confident I can handle her."

"Okay then. Tonight, you have a date with Mistress Pantera."

"Mistress?"

"Yes. Pantera is a Dominatrix."

"That's audacious. Now I'm truly aroused by this revelation, Maher."

"At seven o'clock this evening, you will leave the apartment," I instructed her. "At exactly nine o'clock you will ring the bell on the intercom three times. Two rings in quick succession then count to four and ring the bell a third time. Is that clear?"

"Yes, Mistress." Emilia grinned and couldn't stop herself from blurting out a gruff laugh.

You laugh at me now but wait till you meet Pantera.

At seven, Emilia left the apartment and straight away, I began my preparations for the Night of Nights:

1. Shave face and body immaculately. Not a single facial hair to be seen, either on my face or neck. Not even minutely visible.

2. Cleanse face thoroughly and liberally moisturize.

3. Apply makeup:

    - Givenchy magic kajal for the eyes' waterline,

    - Bobbi Brown eye shadow for the smoky eyes look,

    - Chanel eyeliner for the cat's eyes effect,

    - Yves Saint Laurent Red Paradox liquid lipstick for the lips,

    - Christian Dior Forever for the foundation,

    - Shiseido for the plum-colored blush,

    - Sensai for the translucent fixing powder, and finally,

    - Smashbox for the mascara.

After applying the makeup, I went back to the bedroom and pulled out a black RIMOWA suitcase from under the bed. Simultaneously rotating the left- and right-hand dials, I smiled when the locking mechanism finally produced that satisfying click. From the suitcase, I took out:

1. A long, black silk Qipao dress by Shanghai Tang.

This oriental Chinese dress is sleeveless and has very high slits on the sides.

2. A pair of Wolford Fatal pantyhose.

3. A pair of stretch leather Balenciaga thigh-high boots. These had ten-centimeter stiletto heels

4. A pair of buttery soft black leather Lanvin opera gloves.

5. A jet-black bob-style wig.

When I finished putting everything on, Pantera had completely and comprehensively manifested herself. There was no trace of Maher left. None.

'

Pantera checked herself minutely in the long mirror. Once satisfied, she walked to the drawer cabinet and from the lowest drawer took out a bottle of YSL Opium *eau de perfum.* One squirt of perfume behind each earlobe, *et voila!* Pantera was ready for the kill.

Emilia rang the door intercom at four past nine. Pantera picked up her favorite horse whip and checked herself one final time in the mirror. Satisfied, she made her way slowly to the front door and opened it.

"You are four minutes late. I instructed you to arrive at nine o'clock sharp." Emilia stood in the doorway with her mouth agape. "Are you going to come in?" Pantera continued. "Or do you want me to drag you in by the ear?"

"Oh my God, Maher, you look fucking A-M-A-Z-I-N-G. Fierce! 100% like a professional Dominatrix."

"Shut up, you imbecile. I'm not Maher. Don't ever

confuse the two of us again." Blushing, Emilia corrected herself.

"Sorry, Pantera."

"Take a few steps forward and stand still in the middle of the corridor. I want to inspect you." Emilia did as instructed, while Pantera locked the door behind her. With her horsewhip in her gloved hands, Pantera slowly circled around Emilia a couple of times.

"Don't look at me! Keep your eyes to the floor at all times unless I instruct you otherwise." Her cruel, fiery eyes fixated on Emilia. "Now bend down and take off your shoes." Emilia followed the instructions and took her shoes off. As she was about to stand up again, she heard the hiss of Pantera's whip followed by a sharp sting on the side of her right hip.

"Ouch. That hurt," Emilia shrieked.

"Did I give you permission to stand up?"

"No, Pantera. You didn't."

"I'm Mistress Pantera to you, you little shit! Now get down on your knees." Emilia got down on her knees while defiantly locking eyes with Pantera.

"Emilia, you think you are my equal, don't you?" As ever her sassy self, Emilia continued maintaining eye contact.

"I warned you once. I'm warning you again – you confuse me with Maher at your peril. Keep antagonizing me and your punishment will be extreme." With lightning speed, Pantera grabbed Emilia by the hair and pulled back hard until Emilia conceded and closed her eyes shut.

"You do not look at me, unless I give you permission to. Do you understand?"

"Yes, Mistress." Pantera's horsewhip hissed through the air again and this time struck Emilia on the upper left arm.

"From now on, Emilia, you will strictly adhere to three basic rules:

You will always address me as Mistress.

You may not talk unless I've given you permission.

You only do what I tell you. Is that clear?"

"Yes, Mistress."

"Now go to the bedroom and wait for me there." Pantera walked to the kitchen. There she poured herself a glass of Rioja red wine and lit a cigarette before she rejoined Emilia in the bedroom.

"Drop your trousers to the floor, you little fuck!"

"Yes, Mistress."

"Now put your hands behind your back and keep your eyes lowered." Pantera fastened a pair of steel cuffs around Emilia's wrists and turned her sub's body around to face her. This time Emilia kept her eyes lowered.

"Good," whispered Pantera sensually in Emilia's left ear. Drawing a deep breath on her cigarette, she blew the smoke in Emilia's face. Emilia choked and coughed a few times.

"Does that smoke bother you, Emilia?"

"No, Mistress."

"Good! Because if it did – it wouldn't make a difference. Before we commence with your training, do you consent to BDSM with me, Emilia?"

"Yes, Mistress. I do."

"Tell me what the three safe words are."

"'Orange' for slow down, 'Red' for stop and 'Green' for continue, Mistress."

"Those safe words are vital for your safety. Never hesitate to use them, if needed. 'Red' means we stop the session for good, and I release you."

"Yes, Mistress," Emilia nodded.

"As your *Domina*, I lead and control the narrative, but you moderate it with the safe words. Does that make sense to you?"

"Yes, it does, Mistress."

Pantera sat on the bed and lay the horsewhip to one side. From a green leather bag, she pulled out what looked like a hard leather strap.

"Now, Emilia, I want you to bend down and lie across my knees. I'm going to give you a spanking with my leather tawse." Emilia followed the instructions and laid herself across Pantera's knees with her bare bottom hanging on one side.

"One, two, three," Pantera started counting. The tawse made a dull thud as it slapped Emilia buttocks hard. The pain shot up Emilia's spine and she arched her back sharply. Pantera grabbed Emilia's hair again and pulled it carefully backward until Emilia's neck tensed.

"Emilia, can you still breathe normally?"

"Yes, Mistress."

Pantera continued with the spanking until Emilia's bum turned a dark purple hue.

"Rest assured, Emilia, I never allow the skin to break or bleed. Just a few more." The last three spankings were very hard. Emilia's eyes welled up with tears from the pain.

"That's enough spanking. Did you like that?"

"I prefer it faster and less intense, Mistress."

"I know. But it's not about your pleasure anymore.

It's about mine." Pantera clicked open the handcuffs and freed Emilia's hands. She allowed Emilia to remain lying across her knees until her sub regained sensation in her arms. While they both waited, Pantera sensually caressed the stretch marks on Emilia's bottom.

"Can you feel your arms now?"

"Yes, Mistress."

"Stand up, Emilia, and take off all your clothes." While Emilia took off her clothes, Pantera pulled out a snake-tail whip from the bag.

"Now, stand facing that wall with your back toward me. I want to see your legs apart at shoulder width and ten fingers on the wall. Do it now!" Pantera's whip sizzled through the air and cracked a hair's breadth away from Emilia's body. In the next hour, Pantera took Emilia on a dizzying journey through pleasure and pain. Finally, she ordered Emilia to lie on the bed, spreadeagled and face up. With some hemp rope she tied Emilia's legs and hands to the four bed posts. Pantera took off her silk Qipao dress but kept her thigh boots on. She stepped onto the bed, stood astride Emilia's body and looked down at her sub's face.

"Look at me, Emilia. I'm going to terminate the session. I don't think you can take any more."

"Don't you dare stop now!" Emilia's eyes were on fire. "I'm so sorry, Mistress. Green. Green. Please, I beg you, continue."

After another hour, or was it two? – honestly, Jules, I do not recall – it was all over. Pantera straddled Emilia's body and lifted Emilia's head gently upward with her left hand.

"Emilia, I want you to count to ten." Emilia looked

dazed. She tried to move her lips but could only manage a muddled slur of unintelligible numbers.

"Stop counting, Emilia. Congratulations! You made it. Welcome to subspace."

After intense SM play, I knew it was absolutely crucial to provide Emilia with equally elaborate aftercare. Aftercare is the exact opposite of SM. One basically pampers the sub with all the care, love and comfort required until the sub *makes it back to earth*. I wrapped Emilia in a woolly bathrobe and held her tightly and lovingly in my arms for a very long time until she regained her sense of orientation. When I was satisfied that it would be safe to leave her alone for a few minutes, I laid her head gently on the pillow.

"Darling, I'm going to the kitchen to get you something to eat and drink. We need to build up your energy level and rehydrate your body. Will you be okay?" Emilia nodded in response.

I came back to the bedroom with a long glass of water, a mug of hot cocoa and a small plate of salted caramel bonbons, Emilia's favorite. I put on some comforting classical piano music and slowly fed Emilia the cocoa and bonbons. Thereafter, I helped her drink the water slowly.

"Baby, before you fall asleep, I'm going to take you to the bathroom to wash your body and hair. You sweated a lot tonight. I want you to sleep clean. I put her arm around my neck and lifted her body.

"You are so strong, Mistress."

"Baby, it's just me now, Maher. Pantera's gone."

"Gone? Why? Where?" Emilia sounded genuinely saddened by this news.

"Shhhh. Don't worry about Pantera."

In the bathroom, I laid Emilia gently in a tub of warm water and for the next half hour I washed every inch of her body with a sponge and gentle soap. Finally, I dried her up with a fluffy wool towel and tucked her into bed."

"Sweet dreams, darling," I whispered and kissed her forehead.

It was already past four o'clock in the morning, and I was exhausted to the bones. However, *no rest for the wicked.* I still needed to remove Pantera's makeup and have a hot, steamy shower, before I too could lay my head down for a good night's sleep.

'

When I woke up, I found Emilia's side of the bed empty. Panicking, I looked frantically around and found her sitting on the floor, huddled in the corner. I jumped out of bed and ran to her. She was sobbing.

"Hey, baby. What's wrong?

"Don't touch me!" she barked back.

Confused, I stood up and took a step back. "Whatever, Emilia. Have it your way."

Emilia stood up and started throwing a tantrum, shouting and hitting me repeatedly until I became irate. *Enough is enough!* I wasn't going to take this childish behavior from her anymore, so I grabbed her wrists and pinned her hands against the wall above her head.

"Stop it, Emilia!" She looked at me with eyes expressing both lust and revulsion. She tried to kiss me, but I moved my head away from her. With a final shake, I released her hands. With her hands free, she shoved me to one side and ran to the bathroom where she locked herself for the next half an hour. Still very much exhausted from last night's ordeal, I went back to bed.

"I'm sorry, Maher. Baby, I don't want to lose you!" Emilia slid back in bed and spooned my body, pressing her breasts against my back. Wrapping her right hand around me, she kissed the nape of my neck and licked it like a kitten a few times. "I love you, Maher. But I hate Pantera." At this, my body tensed, and I felt a burning anger swell up deep inside me. I shook Emilia's hand off me.

"Fuck off, Emilia! I don't need this confusing, bullshit attitude from you. I'm going to sleep on the couch!"

During a simple breakfast of Earl Grey tea and Danish rolls, we sat at the dining table in silence across from one another. Two angry and pissed-off souls. I was the first to speak.

"Would you care to explain your tantrum?" Emilia's only reaction was to shrug her shoulders. "Look at me, Emilia, when I'm talking to you."

"I can't. I see *her* when I look at you."

"I don't get it. Pantera fulfilled your dreams and took you to *subspace*. You should be worshipping at her feet, not detesting her."

"I admit that she did take me to subspace, and it was paradise. She's better at SM than you will ever be, Maher. But Pantera is a sadistic bitch, and I can't stand her. I'm so confused because as much as I love you, Maher, I loathe her. And you and she are one and the same person."

"Let me tell you why I think you hate Pantera so

much," I said, incensed. "You hate her because she's flipped the dynamic between us. Because of her, you're no longer in control. With Maher, you were essentially in charge. Isn't that what they call *topping from below*?" Emilia shrugged her shoulders one more time, so I continued. "Pantera was having none of your shit. She took control of things right away. She's the true dominant. She'd essentially reversed the dynamic between us and that has shaken you to the core. Hasn't it?"

At last Emilia eyes dilated and her nostrils flared up. "You and your stupid power dynamic theories, Maher! Answers are not always complex, you know. Are you really that blind? Can't you see it?"

"See what?" I was taken aback by her ferocity.

"When I agreed to be dominated by Pantera, I assumed it was role play, meaning a man playing the role of a woman. But that's not what it turned out to be – Pantera is actually a woman! I viscerally felt it – her female energy. And I categorically refuse to be sexually dominated by a woman." I was gobsmacked and didn't know how to respond to this.

¡'

That *Night of Nights* ushered in two fundamental changes. First, our relationship shifted to a love/hate bond. BDSM was replaced by wild, angry sex, which resembled something like a cockamamie catfight. Sex with a lot of biting, scratching and hair pulling while we fucked each other. On more than one occasion, I heard Emilia call out Pantera's name repeatedly when she was in the throes of an orgasm. However, the next morning when I confronted her with it, she would vehemently deny it. Secondly, the events of that notorious night caused the first substantial and irreparable tear in the male straitjacket in which I'd been confined and constricted all my life.

Looking back at that fateful summer night, paradoxically Emilia got one half of the equation right but was way off the mark on the second. She was spot on about my essence being female but was utterly wrong about Pantera. The truth is I'm not Pantera. I'm jaded but kind-hearted Zoë. Pantera was, is and always will be my dark side. She is my alter ego.

One of the ironies of my life is that I had created Pantera to manage, contain and ultimately subdue my female essence. However, in reality, she turned the tables on me. Pantera was not only responsible for the undoing of my relationship with Emilia, but more ominously, she instigated the unravelling of Maher and became the harbinger of Zoë's liberation. *Hail Pantera!*

3

Zoë Ventures Out

Journal entry # 687$
Utrecht, Apr 2015

Today, marked Zoë's baptism by fire. For the first time, I've ventured outside the comfort of my home in female clothing and makeup.

Since I was going to move to Rotterdam in two months' time, I thought why not go do some window shopping there? Furthermore, I wanted to minimize the risk of running into someone I know here, in Utrecht.

With regards to fashion, I'm leaving the sexy dresses

and stiletto shoes to Pantera. For Zoë, I had decided to adopt a rock-chic style with a touch of classical elegance.

Today, I put on a pair of skinny jeans, a maroon-red buttoned shirt, retro-style black leather boots with block heels and, for that touch of Parisienne, a forest-green silk scarf. Since time immemorial, I've had a soft spot for women who wore scarfs, the type you see airline steward-esses wearing. On a more practical note, it's an elegant way to cover my Adam's apple. Unfortunately, that's not the only part of my body, which needed to be concealed. Those ugly bits down under, i.e., the male genitalia, had to be pushed all the way back and tucked in firmly. I wore sturdy shapewear panty-slips to keep them effectively hidden way.

One other important area to be addressed are, of course, the breasts, or in my case, the lack thereof. For the time being, I had no alternative to a bra stuffed with makeup sponges, which I'd picked up at the HEMA[8].

The makeup was softer than Pantera's. So, no smoky and cats' eyes look. I also tried to soften my jawline with the aid of some shading but am not entirely satisfied that that did the trick. As for my hair, I chose to go with a slicked-back hairstyle. Fortunately, my hair is thick and has already grown to shoulder length. Thank heavens, that on both my father's and mother's side, we do not have *alopecia androgenetica* or male-pattern baldness.

To finish it all off I put on some minimalistic Calvin Klein silver jewelry and a few squirts of YSL Manifesto *eau de parfum* on my wrists. *Zoë, it's time. It's now or never.*

The moment I set foot outside my apartment, I felt extremely self-conscious, as if the sky had parted and God's

---

8 HEMA is a Dutch variety chain store

own spotlight was aimed with laser-like precision at me. Inside my head, a thunderous voice proclaimed: *Who goes there? Is it a man or a woman? Human or alien?*

My heart began to beat faster, and my breathing became shallower. 15, 16, 17, 18. Heavens, I need to keep my nervousness in check, otherwise I won't make it to the front door of the building let alone to Rotterdam. In response, I heard the voice in my head snort: *What front door? Sister, you're taking the utilities exit to the side alleyway.*

Once outside the apartment block, I found myself hugging the facades of buildings, as if that provided some shadow and stealth, as I made my way to the central station. Once at the station, I hastily boarded the first train departing to Rotterdam, which mercifully was already at the platform.

Phew! I was relieved that the first segment of my journey went without mishap or coming across someone who knew me. Seated in the train, I kept nervously glancing around to see if anyone was checking me out. So far so good. I looked down at my wristwatch. *When is this damn train going to make a move?*

A mother and her child settled in the seats opposite me. The mother seemed too preoccupied with her smartphone to notice me. However, her little brat, who couldn't have been more than five years old had his eyes transfixed on me from the get-go. A few minutes had passed, and his eyes were starting to burn a hole in me. I could see that he was trying to figure me out. Before he had the chance to raise the alarm and seek his mother's assistance in clarifying the conundrum, I quickly picked up my shoulder bag and made a dash for the next coupe. I found two adjacent seats which were empty, and I settled in the one next to the window. As the coach filled up with fellow passengers, I couldn't help but notice that all the seats had been occupied except for the vacant seat beside me. *Were people avoiding it because of me?*

Finally, the conductor blew his whistle and the train started pulling away from the station. A minute or so from our departure, it suddenly struck me that using my personal Dutch Railways pass (with Maher's photo) could prove to be very embarrassing when the conductor started doing the customary rounds of checking tickets. In my mind, I could already picture it: *Miss or is it mister? Is that your train pass? It says Mr. M. Shibli. Is that you?* Of course, with his voice raised for maximum effect, the other passengers would start to take notice. *You fool, Zoë. Why didn't you purchase an anonymous paper ticket from the vending machine?*

For the second time, I left my seat and made my way to the lavatory. Even though I abhor train lavatories (the funky smell alone could knock you unconscious), I locked myself in and decided that no matter what, I wasn't going to open the door until we arrived in Rotterdam Central Station. Luckily, that dreaded knock on the lavatory door did not materialize. When the conductor announced the next stop would be Rotterdam on the train's broadcasting system, I closed my eyes in relief and thanked my lucky stars (the lavatory smells not withstanding). 40, 41, 42, 43. The train doors flung open, and I sprang in one leap onto the platform like a frightened gazelle.

At Rotterdam Central, I was tempted to abandon my expeditious mission and take the first train back to Utrecht. *Okay, Zoë, you need to calm your nerves first. Just go to Star-*

bucks, get yourself a flat white and a blueberry muffin, find an inconspicuous seat, hopefully in a corner somewhere at the back of the café, and take a breather.

At Starbucks, I stood in line to place my order. In the queue, there were two customers before me: the first, an elderly man and the second, a young woman. When the young woman reached her turn to order, she was addressed as 'miss'. I wondered how they were going to address me. The question started rotating round and round in my head like a buzzing satellite. When I reached the top of the line, the assistant turned to me.

"What can I get you?" asked the assistant. No 'miss' for me. That irked me.

"A flat white and a blueberry muffin, please."

"Under what name will that be?" Again no 'miss'.

"It's Zoë." I paid and walked to the end of the counter for my order to be filled.

"I have a flat white for Zoë," a second assistant called out.

"That's me!" I raised my finger.

"Here you go, miss. Sugar, sweetener and other con-diments are at the opposite counter." *OMG, she called me 'miss'.* I had to stop myself from grabbing her by the shirt and giving her the biggest hug of her entire life. I sufficed with "Thank you very much." I took my coffee, picked up two Canderel sticks from the condiments' table and made my way to the back. Once seated, I exhaled deeply. Thank you, Heaven! I sorely needed that morale boost.

Half an hour passed before I had regained sufficient confidence to continue with my mission. I picked up my shoulder bag and headed for the train station's main hall.

Wow! What a beautifully designed building, I thought to myself. From a design perspective, it was truly a masterpiece of modern architecture. I wished I could take it all in without that knot of nervousness lodged in the pit of my stomach. I tried to give myself a pep talk: *Oh, Zoë. Don't worry, that day will come. Surely.*

From the station, I made it on foot to Rotterdam's famous *Lijnbaan* shopping quarter. On my way, I noticed that I walked as close as possible, without being noticed, to other pedestrians. As Maher, I would never do that. As Zoë, I was trying my best to blend in, which is code for being as 'invisible' as possible. I especially gravitated toward taller shoppers as they would offer maximum coverage.

After two hours had passed with the pretense of window shopping, I was relieved that no one had *clocked me,* called me out or tried to shame me. I was ready to call it a day and go home. Although I was famished, I didn't have the stomach to put myself to the gender test again while ordering a snack.

Back at Rotterdam Central Station, I purchased a one-way ticket to Utrecht from the vending machine. The return journey to my apartment proved a little less nerve-racking. Though welcome, this was little relief.

The moment I set foot in my apartment, I felt an unbelievably heavy load fall from my shoulders. I was thoroughly exhausted but glad to be safely home once more. In the living room, I slumped on the couch and laughed out loud. *Zoë, you passed your first test.* What am I feeling, right now? Vulnerable. Alone. Scared. Determined to push on.

With the adrenaline in my body subsiding, I remembered that I was starving. I needed to make myself something quick and simple. I put together a tuna salad sandwich.

With my stomach finally satisfied, the project manager in me knew that it was time to evaluate the mission. The plusses and minuses of my first time out in public as Zoë.

Negatives:

- Extreme nervousness.
- Tendency to seek cover and the shadows.
- Children are *treacherous*. They can and will out you.
- I'm way too sensitive about what others think of me.

Positives:

- Being addressed as 'miss' – a first ever.
- No one addressed me as 'mister' (yet).
- No double-takes (yet).
- No trouble walking for lengthy periods of time in high heels, albeit block heels.

Result: a pass

Score: 6 out of 10 (encouragement factored in)

Next steps and Actions:

- Repeat soon. You need to build up your confidence.
- Work on your posture.
- Start developing a thick skin and do it fast. Jules, I confess that's going to be a mighty challenge. I won't mind being called out for being transgender. Unfortunately, that's not what people do – when they call a transgender woman out, they *clock*

her as a 'man'. When that happens, I'm sure it's going to feel like being stabbed by a dagger. Mere words cannot adequately portray the disgrace and humiliation of being misgendered.

<u>Conclusion:</u> It's going to be an incredibly rocky few years ahead before I make it to the other side. I heard the cynic's guffaw in my head: if, at all, you make it to the other side.

4

Codeine Crazy

Journal entry # 690$
Utrecht, May 2015
🎧 Martin Davich – Danger Ahead

K nowing you have cancer does not cure it. Likewise, with gender dysphoria. My condition has only intensified and worsened since my 'tipping-point' experience, earlier in the year. The pain, distress and depression are becoming more debilitating by the day. Without an effective medical treatment, what alternative is there but to try to sedate and dampen my pain? Others turn to alcohol or hardcore drugs. I've sought solace in codeine which, once ingested, the body metabolizes into morphine. Recently, I've started upping the doses and mixing it with alcohol. Other times, I take it in as *Lean* or *Purple Drank*[9]. I'm not stupid. Of course, I'm worried that this could go horribly wrong. Heaven, please forgive me!

---

9 A recreational drug beverage, originating in Houston, Texas, prepared by mixing prescription cough syrup with a soda, usually Sprite, and hard candies.

5

Rotterdam, Aangenaam[10]!

Journal entry # 697$
Rotterdam, Jun 2015
🎧 The Beautiful South – Rotterdam (or Anywhere)

Although I've been living in Rotterdam for a week, I've had little time to explore my new home city (yes, Jules, it does feel like home). It's been pretty hectic – working all day and night on renovating and getting my new apartment, on the outskirts of the city center, ready.

Feelings aside, only time will tell if I have made the

---

10 Aangenaam: 'my pleasure/nice to meet you' in Dutch.

right choice in relocating to Rotterdam – to start my process of physically transitioning from male to female. It's a city I scarcely know, but in theory appealed to me because of its cosmopolitan vibe, cultural diversity, maritime character and raw industrial edginess. Also, I wanted to be close to water. None of my friends and acquaintances live in Rotterdam. Essentially, I'm alone here, but that doesn't intimidate me. On the contrary, standing on the threshold of the most significant chapter of my life, it feels invigorating to start from scratch.

When it comes to Dutch cities, Rotterdam is an anomaly. Whereas most towns and cities in Holland are elegantly and classically blended, Rotterdam feels like it's been chopped up, mixed up and put back together, resembling a patchwork, or more accurately a mishmash, where old historical buildings cheerfully clash with hypermodern skyscrapers on the same street. Musically, I would say, Rotterdam is a jazz concert while other Dutch cities are classical symphonies. I wanted to understand why Rotterdam is the way it is.

On this breezy, overcast day, I set out early in the morning to explore parts of the city. I started my trek on foot along Rotterdam's *Brandgrens*[11] (Jules, that's Fire Periphery in Dutch), which delineates the area of the city destroyed by the Nazis during World War II. The line, which cuts through the heart of the city, is physically marked by hundreds of red-colored LED spotlights integrated in the city sidewalks. I followed the 'red circles' to Plein 1940.

Plein 1940 is a somber, gray, barren square, which is located behind the Maritime Museum. When I arrived

---

11 https://www.brandgrens.nl/en/home

there, there was hardly a soul to be seen, except for a few kids busy skateboarding. I walked toward the imposing abstract bronze sculpture in the center of the square called *De Verwoeste Stad* (that translates as the Destroyed City).

The sculpture depicts a disfigured human being with arms raised in horror toward the sky. The head of the figure is thrown back as if wailing in agony and grief. A big gaping hole in its chest and abdomen symbolizes the absence of its heart.

I can identify with the message and emotion this sculpture portrays. With some trepidation, I approached the base of the sculpture and touched it. I couldn't help but ask it a question: "Dear, tell me w*hat happened here?*"

Tuesday, May 14, 1940

It was a bright spring afternoon when the sky suddenly thundered and darkened as a squadron of 90 Heinkel He 111 bombers of the Third Reich's Luftwaffe descended in wave after wave on Rotterdam's historical center. At precisely 13:27, the carpet-bombing started. In less than a quarter of an hour, large swathes of the city center were reduced to rubble. The ensuing smoldering inferno raged for days and obliterated to ashes any structures that had initially survived the blitzkrieg. The result: 30,000 homes, shops and offices destroyed. 900 people killed and 80,000 people made homeless.

Hmm, so Rotterdam is a tortured soul, as well, albeit on a scale and magnitude infinitely beyond me and my comprehension.

Later that day, I did some online research about the

sculpture at the plaza, behind the Maritime Museum. From Wikipedia, I learned that *De Verwoeste Stad* was designed by Ossip Zadkine, a Russian-born French sculptor. He was inspired to create the sculpture shortly after the Second World War when his train passed through the ruined center of Rotterdam, while travelling from Paris to visit a friend in Holland. Ironically, the square base is made of Labrador granite blocks from Norway, which were originally intended for a statue of Adolf Hitler in Berlin.

From the sculpture of *De Verwoeste Stad*, I made my way along the Leuvehaven to the Erasmus Bridge, one of Rotterdam's most beautiful modern landmarks.

Rotterdammers affectionately refer to the Erasmus Bridge as *De Zwaan* (The Swan) because of its graceful white lines and elegant geometric beauty.

Today, I feel haggard, disjointed, hollow and ailing somewhat like *De Verwoeste Stad*. Someday, one day in the future, I hope I will be more like *De Zwaan*.

Jules, did you know that Rotterdam's motto is *'Sterker door Stryd'*, i.e., 'Stronger through Struggle'? Likewise, I feel my journey is a struggle to be my true self and like Rotterdam, I must believe that this struggle will only make me stronger.

Next week I have my first appointment with a psychologist specializing in gender dysphoria.

6

Social Non-Circle

Journal entry # 699$
Rotterdam, Jun 2015

Since my separation from Emilia, my social circle has dwindled remarkably. Most of my acquaintances were, first and foremost, Emilia's friends. It was quite clear to me that they did not intend to maintain contact with me anymore, now Emilia and I were no longer a couple. Today, I count my friends and acquaintances on the fingers of one hand. I find this quite depressing that, excluding my family, this is all the social network I have in the world. Yet, as an introvert, it doesn't necessarily surprise me. Growing up, as a child and later as a teenager, I've often found that I had more affinity with characters from books, novels, and films than my fellow real-life peers.

In my tiny social circle, I had two BFFs: Willem and Ashok. These two men couldn't have been more different. Willem was a Hollander, born and bred, with blond hair, blue eyes and built like a bear. We've been friends since 2009 after meeting on the equestrian scene. Back then, we were both very fond of horses and horse-back riding. A few years ago, we had a horseback riding vacation together in Cuba. That was one of the few truly happy times in my life, when I was able to disconnect from my issues. We rode through picturesque Spanish colonial towns, tobacco plantations and picture postcard beaches. All this beauty with not a single McDonald's or Starbucks in sight. Pure bliss. *Cuba! Autentica!* Before my relocation to Rotterdam, Willem and I met regularly at *bruin cafés*, which are traditional Dutch pubs, in Utrecht, where he still lives. Willem is not much of a talker, but a great listener. I love him as a friend; he is as solid and reliable as a rock.

As for Ashok, he is what Dutch society calls *Nieuwe Nederlander*, or a new Dutch citizen. He's a mix of both Hindoestan[12] and Creole heritage. In the early 1990s, his parents immigrated to Holland from Suriname, a former Dutch colony in South America. Tall, athletic, with a dark complexion and frizzy hair, he is handsome and has that Latino swagger about him, although in all honesty he doesn't have a drop of Latino blood in his veins. I've known Ashok since my college years and in many ways, he's the

12 Hindoestan: an ethnic group in Suriname, whose forefathers were immigrants from the Indian sub-continent

closest thing to a soulmate I have. We could engage in conversation for hours and hours on just about any subject under the sun from politics to religion, society to sport, history to science. He does have somewhat of a South American temper and a streak of machismo.

I valued both men's friendships tremendously and hoped with all my heart that that would remain intact, after I come out to them. I pray to Heaven that both are okay with me transitioning. Jules, in all honesty, I'm terrified they'll push me away. That's why I've procrastinated in letting them know about Zoë. As of yet, both of them have no knowledge of what I've gone through since the beginning of this year. To them, I'm just Maher, one of the lads.

This evening, I had dinner plans with Willem. He was keen to see my new apartment in Rotterdam and catch up on 'good times'. Luck would have it that Willem was quite fond of hanging out in Rotterdam. In his previous profession as a physiotherapist, he once owned a practice in Kralingen, one of the more upscale neighborhoods of the city.

Willem arrived at my home exactly on time. That's Dutch punctuality for you! None of the Mediterranean bullshit of arriving an hour late. 19:30 is 19:30, period. End of discussion.

Willem approved of my apartment and complimented me on the location. According to him, the stunning vista of the port from the eleventh floor, by itself, more than justified the price I had paid for it.

For dinner, we had decided to go to Witte de With-straat, one of Rotterdam's hippest and trendiest streets, for a tasty bite and hanging out. Foodwise, we opted for Bazar, a boutique hotel-cum-Mediterranean fusion restaurant. It was packed full inside, so we settled for a table for two outside on the sidewalk. The weather this evening was warm and balmy, so we actually preferred this option (to sitting indoors). I ordered their signature Couscous Fish and an El Tunisi soup, a hearty Tunisian fish soup with saffron, salmon and fruits de mer. Willem went for the *Meeghoe*, a skewer of grilled prawns in curry sauce. All complemented with a few bottles of *Wieckse Witte* (the best 'white beer' from the southern province of Limburg).

Willem gave me an update of the latest developments in his life. He had wanted to work for a charity in Africa, Asia or Latin America for some years now. What particularly interested him was helping poor farmers, who had been impacted by soil erosion or desertification. He dreamt of making dry, arid lands bloom again with green vegetation and sufficient produce for the farmers. This would allow them to earn a decent income to support their families and send their kids to school. Having approached two dozen charitable organizations, including Oxfam, he finally landed a job to lead a large ecological project in the state of Rajasthan, in India. The project would last a minimum of twelve months and he was due to depart in August.

"That's only two months from now!" I exclaimed, very much surprised. "God, Willem, I don't see you for three weeks and you pull this rabbit out of the hat!"

"I know. Shit happens!" He was all smiles.

"Congratulations! Here's to the success of your project in India." In my mind, this news was something of a mixed bag. On the one hand, I was ecstatic for Willem. This had been his dream for a long time now. On the other hand, for me, this couldn't have come at a worse time. Being one of my dearest and closest friends, I was counting on his support when I came out as transgender. That's assuming he didn't dump me altogether. The 64,000-dollar question constantly pitched at the back of my mind. Which of my friends and acquaintances will I retain on my imminent journey to womanhood, and who is going to abandon me? *Oh, Willem. I desperately don't want to lose your friendship. You are so dear to me.* We clicked beer bottles.

"*Proost*, Willem! I wish you much success in the coming months."

"Hey, what about you, Maher? What have you been up to lately? I see you've grown your hair. Very feminine!" He chuckled. "People might start thinking you're gay."

I was itching to spill the beans about everything. About being transgender. About my ordeal since January this year. About Zoë. About my ironclad desire (and decision) to transition. About my recent visit to a transgender support group and the information they shared with me. About my upcoming appointment with a gender psychologist.

"I'm okay, Willem. I'm focusing on getting settled in Rotterdam. Perhaps making a few more friends here." I chickened out. We clicked beer bottles again.

"Here's to Rotterdam," he said.

"To Roffa.[13]"

---

13 Roffa means 'cool' in Surinamese-Dutch dialect. It is also street slang for Rotterdam

7

Hello Johan

Journal entry # 700$
Amsterdam, Jun 2015

D r. Johan de Zeelander, gender psychologist based in
Amsterdam, was highly rated and therefore recommended by a number of trans women, whom I had spoken
to recently while attending a transgender support group
meeting. Crucially, Johan was previously part of the *Genderploeg*, a medical unit made up of psychologists, endocrinologists, surgeons, and researchers with one mission – to
diagnose and treat patients with gender dysphoria. This unit
is officially part of Westeneinde Ziekenhuis, a university

hospital in Amsterdam. The other tip, which I had picked up during the support group meeting, was not to contact the *Genderploeg* directly. A much more effective route to get on their program is through a referral by a medical expert.

Although Johan now runs an independent practice, he's maintained and cultivated his close ties to the *Genderploeg* and that's for a very good reason. In Holland, it's the *Genderploeg* that has the exclusive right to: 1) officially diagnose a patient as having gender dysphoria, 2) authorize and prescribe the use of hormones, and 3) authorize and carry out SRS (Sex Reassignment Surgery).

On the phone, Johan cautioned me that the first face-to-face appointment would be an intake or interview to determine whether he would take me on as a patient. Jules, talk about piling on the pressure to nail this appointment. That said, the initial vibe, which I got from him on the phone, was that he was skeptical.

'

Johan ushered me into a smart-looking office on the first floor of a handsome early twentieth century red-brick building, in Berlage[14] style. I was expecting to meet a shaggy, intellectual looking man, in his late fifties or early sixties, possibly with a beard and bespectacled. That's not what Johan turned out to be. I estimated that he's in his late forties. With turquoise-blue eyes, small nose, and curly brown hair. Actually, I find him quite attractive. I mean Michael Keaton-esque kind of attractive. He wore a navy-blue V-neck pullover, a pair of Levi jeans and white Nike

---

14 Hendrik Petrus *Berlage* (21 February 1856 – 12 August 1934) was a prominent Dutch architect

trainers. He had this casual air about him, which was at once both reassuring and disarming.

I took my place on a creamy white leather sofa while he sat opposite me on a black leather Barcelona chair, the type designed by the famous Bauhaus architect/designer Mies van der Rohe.

"Welcome, Zoë. It's Zoë, isn't it?" he fired the first interview salvo.

"Yes, but officially I'm still Maher."

"Maher," he repeated. "Where's that name from?"

"It's Arabic. I'm originally from Lebanon."

"How long have you been here, Zoë?"

"For approximately eighteen years. I was thirteen when I arrived in Holland with my parents."

"Your parents still live in Holland?"

"Yes, in Leiden." I noticed Johan's eyes narrow a little.

"Are you already presenting as a woman, full time?" he asked.

"No, not full time. At work, I still present as Maher, as a 'man'. In my private life, I try to present as much as possible as Zoë. What you see before you now."

"Have you already come out as transgender to family and friends?"

"Only to my ex-girlfriend."

"Alright, Zoë. What can I do for you?"

I gave him a summarized account of who I am and what had transpired in the past few months, augmented with some facts from my past. All the while, Johan listened with close attention, while his eyes were locked on me like sidewinders. Poker faced and no smile, not even a hint, I had the distinct perception that he wanted me to feel intimidated. However,

I forced myself to maintain, as much as possible, eye contact with him, until his eyes were no longer unsettling me. When I finished talking, he remained silent for a long time. *Tick-tock. Tick-Tock.* I was getting nervous. *What's going on in that head of yours? I desperately want to know. Did I explain myself well? I thought I did reasonably well, but now I'm not so sure anymore. Did I say too much, too little, or the wrong things?*

"You're certainly 'passable', Zoë." Johan finally broke his silence.

"I'm sorry, I don't understand what you mean by 'passable'?" My heart sank a little. *Is he trying to dismiss me?*

"That's a term, which is widely used in the transgender community, to describe a trans person who can physically pass as the gender they identify with. In your case, a woman." He paused a few seconds. "Alright, Zoë, I will take you on as a patient."

Phew! Thank goodness! I was clearly relieved, and he saw it.

Johan went on to explain that he was not in a position to prescribe feminizing hormones as this was something, in practice, only the *Genderploeg* was authorized to do, as per the medical regulations of this country. He described his role as that of a 'coach', who would guide me step-by-step through the process or program, which could take years to complete if the *Genderploeg* subsequently diagnosed me as having gender dysphoria.

"Zoë, two things: 1) I'm going to need a referral letter from your family doctor, and 2) for our next appointment, I'm going to give you a very big homework assignment. I want you to write your 'Life CV'."

"Sorry, what's a Life CV?" I inquired, but I was mostly irritated. I hate homework.

"See it as an essay about your life, from your birth till the present day. Include in it all the details you think are relevant to your condition. Email it to me within two weeks. I will schedule our next appointment three weeks from now."

"Okay," I said, reluctantly. "How long should this essay be?"

"That's up to you. Some patients write two A4 pages, others twenty. And Zoë, I'm going to need you to be very transparent with me about every aspect of your life and personality. I need that to be able to make a definitive evaluation and diagnosis of your case."

For someone who has led a very secretive life, that was a big ask.

"Of course, Johan. I will be an open book," I assured him. I wasn't being entirely sincere.

8

Psycho Tactics

Journal entry # 701$
Rotterdam, Jun 2015

In the West, if you're transgender, coming out is merely the starting block for a very long process to recognition. Basically, it's the medical authorities that will ultimately decide whether you're eligible to transition (from male to female or vice versa) and give legal access to the necessary healthcare, both in terms of medication and surgery. By implication, and there's no two ways about it; it's the medical authorities that effectively decide your status as transgender, because let's be honest, what's the point of coming out as transgender if you are stuck in your current body and are unable to transition.

Through my online research and the conversations which I've had with a wide spectrum of trans women, I get the distinct impression that some trans women try their best to second guess the medical experts. In other words, instead of relating their facts *fatto per fatto*, they tell the experts what they think will help them gain access to medication. Jules, I'm pretty sure that the vast majority of trans women don't do this out of malice but out of the strong belief that doing so will expedite the decision-making process by the medical experts and therefore their access to feminizing hormones and anti-androgens.

After my first appointment with Johan, I did a lot of soul-searching about what information I will share with him and hopefully later with the *Genderploeg*. I will give him (and them) insight into almost every aspect of my existence, i.e., my life, my history and character. Three things I will exclude from the (sharing) list. I will keep to myself my codeine addiction, BDSM and Pantera. Transgender people, like everybody else, are also entitled to some privacy.

9

Child at the School Playground

Journal entry # 703$
Amsterdam, Jul 2015
🎧 Duran Duran – Come Undone

"I'm pleased with the input and level of detail you've provided in your *Life CV* assignment, Zoë." Johan expressed his satisfaction as he laid a hard copy of my twelve-page document on the table in front of him. "Today, I want to go through this document starting first with your early life."

"Before we dive into that, Johan, there's something I need to say to you," I interrupted him.

"What's that?" Johan straightened his glasses while looking directly into my eyes.

"I do want you to realize that the contents of my *Life CV*, which I've shared with you, provide a great deal of very private and personal insights into my transgender life story. I hope you understand that opening up is a very painful and difficult process for me. We are, after all, dealing here with my deepest secrets; secrets which, for a very long time, I've been ashamed of; secrets which I've kept carefully hidden all my life. Basically, you're asking me to bare my soul – I have and I will continue to, knowing that this is an important part of my quest to transition to womanhood." There was a slight tremor in in my voice as I looked at Johan's poker face. I had hoped to read a little sign of sympathy in his eyes and face. If it was there, I couldn't see it.

Heavens, Johan, I hope you will show me some empathy and emotion in the weeks and months to come, while I open up more and more of myself to you.

"I am, and have been for a very long time, a tortured soul," I continued. "Since my childhood, I've always been conscious of my *female essence*, of being different from the boys and of wanting to be a girl and later a woman. However, until quite recently, this feeling has been inextricably coupled with extreme fear and deep shame, so much so that I couldn't even bring myself to acknowledge that deep down I am female."

"I see." Johan nodded his head a few times, took off his glasses and started rubbing the lenses with an orange-colored cloth.

"Zoë, I want to start with your earliest memory of

yourself not being a boy?" He put his glasses back on and with his right hand, gestured that I should continue.

"From the time I was a child of around four or five years, I sensed that I was different from the other boys. I couldn't help but feel that I was more like a girl. I remember as a child I would regularly sneak into my parents' bedroom when it was empty. There was a beautiful, baroque-style white dressing table with a large oval mirror on top. This dressing table had floral leaf carvings accented in gold lacquer. In front of the table there was a matching stool with a cushioned top covered in pink satin, where my mother sat for many hours getting ready for those famous Beirut all-night regales. Dozens of my mother's perfumes bottles, lipsticks and a jewelry box adorned the top of the dressing table. I recall that I, too, would sit on that stool for hours on end and try on my mother's earrings and jewelry, putting on her lipstick and spraying her perfume on my neck and wrists, mimicking what she did. When I was finished, I would put on her purple fedora hat and compliment myself on being a very pretty girl. One day, my mother caught me in this 'act'. I recall her fury at me. She started yelling at me, shook me repeatedly, and shouted again and again, "Heaven, why did you do this to me?" Then she embraced me in her arms and burst into tears. I didn't really understand why she was so angry with me. I felt confused, ashamed, and sad that I made my mother cry so much. So, for years, I avoided my mother's stuff until one day when my parents were visiting my grandparents' home in the mountains of the *Mont Liban* region, I sneaked into their bedroom. I couldn't stop myself from putting on one of my mother's dresses, her lipstick and jewelry. I recall feeling very happy to be a girl again."

"Zoë, why do you think your mother burst into tears when she saw you like that?"

"I never actually asked her about that. Everything about me being girl-like, even at that age, my parents wanted erased. It seemed like it was taboo, even more than taboo. You just don't talk about it and hope one day it will go away."

"Tell me more about Ruzanna, Zoë. Who was she and what did she mean to you?"

"Ruzanna was a blond, blue-eyed Armenian girl, who was one year older than me. I adored her. I wanted to be with her, act like her, play like her, talk like her, laugh like her. I genuinely felt like I was her younger sister. Her mother was a senior teacher at the small Christian Maronite elementary school we went to in East Beirut. When I heard the ring of the bell at the start of each break, I remember I would dash out with great excitement into the playground looking for Ruzanna. She and I were inseparable and played with the other girls, day in, day out. When I was with her and the other girls, I felt happy. I felt close to who I really am. It was a time full of female laughter and energy until one day Ruzanna's mother shouted at the girls to go inside. I remember that, as my friends were doing as they were told, Ruzanna's mother grabbed me aggressively by the arm and held me back. She looked down at me with the same blue eyes as Ruzanna's, except hers were cold and cruel. "Maher, stop this silliness!" she said with a sarcastic smirk on her face. "Stop acting like Ruzanna! You are not a girl! You are a boy!" Then she burst out laughing. That moment I felt the ground shake underneath me. I had been ridiculed and laughed at by Ruzanna's mother. Feelings of embarrassment, anger and humiliation consumed me. Next day, Ruzanna told me that we couldn't play together anymore, that from now on I should play with the boys. Only.

As an act of rebellion, a day or two after my humiliation, I wore a pair of colorful hairclips shaped like butterflies in my hair. They were a gift from Ruzanna. When the teacher told me to take them off, I refused. The fact that the boys and girls in the classroom all laughed and mocked me only made me more obstinate and I kept them on. Finally, the teacher sent me home early – punishment for being disobedient. Evidently, the school had informed my parents, because when I arrived at our apartment, my father and mother were waiting for me. With one hand, my father grabbed me by my hair and lifted me off the ground. With the other hand he clubbed my head really hard, again and again… 19, 20, 21 (this is something I do – when I'm hurting more than usual, I start counting). When my father finally released me, bruised, and battered I crawled like a mortally wounded animal into a corner and cried for hours. Nobody came to comfort me, not even my mother. The following day my parents had my hair shaved off. Can you imagine? A six-year-old kid pulverized, clobbered half unconscious and whose hair is shaved off as if I was a criminal. Why? What for?

"My father's beating triggered something violent and irreconcilable inside me. I realized for the first time that my feelings of wanting to be a girl, like Ruzanna, were 'sinful' and 'very wrong'. From that moment on I was consumed by self-loathing and disgust. At school, from a distance, I kept watching Ruzanna and the other girls. I was jealous and angry. They get to be themselves, whilst I get to be… nobody. It hurt me to my core that I wasn't like her. In time, I succumbed to the wishes of others and surrendered to the fear inside me and around me. Society basically forced me to be something I'm not. A lesser human being. After that, I recall becoming timid, shy, quiet and withdrawn. I became a loner. The female laughter inside me was extinguished. I thought forever.

"In the next few years, the message of 'Toughen up, boy!', 'Be a strong man like your father', was incessantly drummed into me. I didn't want to disappoint my parents or make them angry. To the contrary, I wanted them to love me and be proud of me.

From a very young age, for reasons of self-preservation and self-protection, instinctively I knew that I had to bury my female essence very, very deep inside me. What followed were long years of inner conflict, turmoil, guilt and extreme denial."

By the time I finished reciting those painful memories from my early years, I was clearly shaken. My hands were trembling.

"Please, Johan, don't ask me any more questions. I'm feeling extremely raw right now." I knew one more question from him and I would break down in tears.

"That's alright. That's enough for today, Zoë. We'll continue in two weeks' time." For the first time since I met Johan, I noticed a twinkle of a tear in his eyes.

10

Jeunesse Terrible

Journal entry # 704$
Amsterdam, Jul 2015
🎧 Eminem – Beautiful Pain

I waited for Johan in his practice's consultation room while he made me a cup of tea. I liked this about him – he always asked me before we got into the serious stuff if I would like a coffee or tea. Once I let him know my choice, he would prepare it for me in a small pantry, located just outside, in the corridor.

Johan came back with a tray with a teapot and two cups.

"Here we are," he smiled. "Pickwick's rooibos honey tea for two." He laid the tray on the white coffee table between us.

"Let me take it from here," I offered as I picked up the teapot and poured it into the cups. "Do you take sugar?"

"No, thanks." He shook his head. "How are you doing, Zoë?"

"I'll be honest with you, I'm on the edge. Barely holding things together."

"Hmm. How long can you go on like this?"

"You're the expert. I was hoping you could tell me."

"Zoë, I need you to answer my question."

"As long as there's hope, light at the end of the tunnel, I'll survive."

"And what is that *light at the end of the tunnel?*"

"A full transition, including hormones and sex-change operation," I answered unequivocally, while holding his gaze.

"And what if that is blocked by the *Genderploeg?*"

"Then I'm damned." I paused for a few seconds. "I'll save some money and go to Thailand for the operation. The hormones I'll get online."

"Zoë, what would you do if all the doors were closed to you, including Thailand?"

"I think we both know the answer to that. There's only one viable way out of this dark tunnel. Today, I see a glimmer of light very, very far away. If this light goes out permanently, I won't last long in the pitch darkness. I won't have to take my own life, if that's what you're trying to clarify; gender dysphoria will take care of that for me." Johan put his cup back on the table, all the while fixing his eyes on me.

"Zoë, there's always hope. You have to believe that. And

I'm here to help you get to the light at the end of that tunnel. Okay?"

"Okay," I agreed. What else was I supposed to say to him? That in reality I'm a plastic cup away from overdosing on Lean/Purple drank.

"Let's move on to the next part of your Life CV – your youth. Briefly, before we do that, there's one part about your childhood I would like you to clarify. In your Life CV, you talk about wanting to be Catwoman. What did you mean by that?"

"I meant it in the context of games and role play in the school playground. Growing up, like most children and teenagers, I loved watching cartoons. However, while my male peers liked playing male superheroes like Batman and Superman, I secretly wanted to be Catwoman. She was, for me, the embodiment of the uber-feminine. It hurt me in the pit of my stomach that during role play, girls could pretend to be Catwoman, while I couldn't because I was a so-called 'boy', and that somehow it was wrong for me to want to be Catwoman."

"Moving on. How would you describe your youth?" Johan inquired.

"I'm sorry to be vulgar, but I would describe my youth as being S-H-I-T. It was mostly distress and pain."

"Can you expand on that?"

"At the onset of puberty, I recall becoming more and more alarmed and distressed at what was happening to my body. All that hair sprouting out of my body, my arms, my legs, my face... *oh no, please not my face*. I was so fond of my smooth skin, and it was all disappearing right in front of my eyes. It was sickening! I mean excruciatingly painful to see. And to add insult to injury, my voice started to break. Until the age of fourteen, I had a girl's voice. Whenever I would answer the phone (an old-fashioned landline phone), back in the eighties and nineties at my parent's home, the caller (if it was a stranger) would always address me as a girl. Secretly, I loved being perceived as a girl, but it came with a sense of embarrassment. I mostly obliged the caller and just pretended that I was a girl and never told them that I was actually the 'son' of Mr. and Mrs. Shibli. When I handed the phone receiver to my father or mother, they would look baffled and confused at me, when the caller would say something to the effect of *you have a very nice daughter*.

I really hated the physical changes I was going through. By that I mean the masculinization of my body. I couldn't help but notice that the girls continued to have smooth skin, but their bodies were becoming curvier and their bosoms fuller. I was green with envy. Many times, to the point that I became so emotionally distressed, I was physically sick.

The only conciliation I had was that my physique didn't change. While the boys around me were becoming bulkier and more muscular, by the day, I remained thin and slender. Furthermore, I was conscious of the fact that I had an atypical male body. For example, I had larger bosoms compared to the boys. Also, I had long, loose wrists, which none of the boys I knew had.

At school, I was pestered for some of my more obvious effeminate characteristics, such as my high-pitched laugh and feminine hand gestures. The most humiliating experience in this regard happened when I was around 11 years old. The Physical Education teacher at my elementary school always made us take a shower naked after each cross-country run. I felt uncomfortable about my body, so I always waited until all the boys had finished showering before I stepped into the open showering area. However, on one occasion, the P.E. teacher physically manhandled me into the showering area while it was full. It didn't take long for the boys to notice my larger bosoms. They started pointing at me and laughing out loud. *Look, Maher, has little tits, just like the girls!* After this incident, I recall feeling so humiliated and embarrassed that I pretended to be sick so that I could skip school for the rest of the week. Always suffering in silence and too proud to share my hurt with anyone."

"What about sports, Zoë?" Johan asked.

"I didn't like group sports or rough contact sports like football and rugby. I did all I could not to participate, and if I did, I was more or less side-lined by the boys. I couldn't blame them. I was quite shit at it. On top of that, I was an outsider; I didn't belong. Later, in my twenties, I did pick up épée fencing. That's something I became very good at. My slender body with thin long arms and legs lent itself well to it. It was also a way for me to channel my hurt and anger, in a controlled way, at the human race."

"What do you mean by that?" Johan interjected.

"I mean the human race has been cruel, very cruel to us queer people, who are born different, who do not fit neatly into the male or female categories."

"Zoë, things are changing for the better. But it does take a while for things to change, so you have to be patient."

Given the life expectancy of many transgender people, a while is unfortunately too long.

11

Pater Furore

Journal entry # 706$
Amsterdam, Aug 2015
🎧 Circle of Dust – Onenemy

" **M**y father Hates (with a capital 'H') transgenders and what they represent, probably more than any-thing else in the world. I would even go so far as to say that his loathing for transgenders surpasses the hate he feels for the Lebanese politician who orchestrated the destruction of his career, political ambitions, dreams and subsequent exile from Lebanon."

"That's your perception, Zoë, and not necessarily the reality of how your father views transgenders," Johan intervened.

"No, Johan, that's not a perception. It is an observed fact."

"Would you care to elaborate?"

"I believe it was late 2003, a few days before Christmas, my parents, brother, sister and I were watching LBCI, a Lebanese satellite channel, at my parents' home in Leiden. At the end of the late-night news reel, the presenter announced that in a few minutes, they would be broadcasting an interview in full with the Arab world's first person to undergo a sex-change operation. Those specific words 'sex-change operation' made all of us take notice and our eyes locked like heat-seeking missiles onto the TV screen, as if the presenter had just announced the confirmed landing of the first alien on earth.

When the interview started, the camera zoomed in on a gorgeous looking woman, who looked, with her long chocolate-brown hair, blue eyes and Mediterranean complexion, every bit the supermodel. Totally not what we were expecting, i.e., an awkward man in women's clothes. I do not recall her name, so let's call her Léonie. Although the interview was definitely set up to make a mockery out of her, Léonie refused to be rattled and spoke eloquently and touchingly about her life's ordeal as a transgender woman. She spoke about her escape from Lebanon to Europe, where she had to sell her body to survive and later on to pay for the surgery as part of her physical transition. Years later, she migrated to the United States, where she finally found some semblance of happiness. She married an

American businessman, who recognizes her as the beautiful woman she is, inside and out.

The male interviewer was uncharacteristically rude and obnoxious toward her. He asked her questions he definitely would not have asked had she not been trans. Questions about her genitalia and sex with a man, all the while implying that she was not a woman but some kind of deranged homosexual man pretending to be a woman. She kept her cool and composure and answered all the questions in a calm but noticeably sad voice. By the end of the interview, it was evident that she had gained the moral high ground. She seemed an honest, authentic and deeply caring human being. If the TV channel's objective was to roast her, not only did they fail miserably, but it also totally backfired.

The moment the interview concluded, my father leapt out of his chair, took a few steps toward the TV set and started shouting one expletive after another at the TV. He was furious at the satellite channel for giving this 'snake' (that's the term he used to refer to Léonie) air-time to poison the minds of innocent Lebanese and Arab viewers. He shouted that she deserved to be lynched or shot by firing squad for the shame, disgust and dishonor she had inflicted on her family and country. My father's torrent of hatred went on for at least the next ten minutes. Finally, my mother stepped in to calm him down."

"What did that outburst do to you, Zoë?"

"I remember feeling very sad for Léonie and sickened by my father's reaction. Léonie seemed to me like a gentle and tender woman, who had suffered a lot. She definitely did not deserve this outpouring of hate and vitriol on and off the screen."

"Is that all you felt?" continued Johan.

"Do you mean, did it touch me personally? Of course, it did."

"And your father's anger?"

"Yes, it confirmed to me once more that I had to do everything in my power to suppress and extinguish that voice inside me, which told me every day of my life that I'm a woman. At that stage in my life, I didn't consider what Léonie had achieved as something I could ever contemplate doing myself, let alone replicate. I wasn't that brave, and the consequences were mind-boggling."

"What do you think your parents' views are today with regards to transgender people?"

"To put it into perspective for you: as far as my parents are concerned, being gay is strictly taboo. As for being transgender, that's way beyond taboo. It's sacrilege. It is with deep pain and sorrow that I'd have to admit that my parents (and the society they belong to, which is not here in Holland) are deeply transphobic and aggressively intolerant of anything outside the heterosexual male/female binary. Indeed, transgenders are considered sexual deviants and degenerates. They are the lowest of the low. The work of the devil. For a 'son' to be transgender is a great 'curse' on any Lebanese family and an excruciatingly painful 'embarrassment' for them. It sickens me to say this: probably in their eyes, honor killing is considered a legitimate course of action if their child is transgender."

Johan considered carefully what I had just divulged to him. "Have you already thought about how you're going to come out to your parents? That step in your process is not far away."

"No, I haven't, but thinking about it now terrifies the hell out of me."

"Terrifies you? And yet you will continue on this path?"

"There's nothing in this world that can stop me. Johan, there is no going back."

"Not even your parents' wrath?"

"No. Absolutely nothing."

"Are you willing to lose your parents, Zoe?"

I closed my eyes. *This is too painful.* Deep down, I knew the answer but I didn't want to say it out loud.

12

Johan's Diagnosis

Journal entry # 709$
Amsterdam, Sep 2015

Johan informed me today of his provisional medical assessment based on his evaluation of my condition in the past three months. His diagnosis is that I am suffering from gender dysphoria in combination with a mild paranoia. In other words, I'm a slightly strung-up transgender woman. Thank Heaven, he's categorically eliminated all other psychological conditions such as schizophrenia, bi-polar disorder, borderline personality disorder, chronic severe depression, etc.

Although, as far as he's concerned, this diagnosis is definitive, he's obliged to say that it's 'provisional', given the fact that it's ultimately the *Genderploeg* at Westeneinde Hospital, which will make the final and definitive decision, based on their own diagnosis. With this in mind, he's instructed me to contact the hospital and make an appointment for an intake consultation with the *Genderploeg*.

Secondly, he advised me to start preparing, under his guidance, for coming out as transgender to my siblings, friends, acquaintances, colleagues and, of course, my parents. There is no one-size-fits-all coming-out formula. Therefore, for each target group, we'll need to define a separate plan.

My own thoughts: finally, some progress. Buckle-up, kid, and fasten your seat belt. Life's about to get much more turbulent.

13

Coming-
Out Strategies

Journal entry # 712$
Amsterdam, Oct 2015

J ohan and I have agreed that it's necessary to have three separate coming-out strategies, designed for each of the following groups:

- First strategy is aimed at my siblings, friends and acquaintances.

- Second strategy is aimed at my parents.

- Third strategy is aimed at my colleagues, at work.

The first strategy, which Johan calls the *baseline* strategy, is made up of the following steps:

1. Make an appointment with the sibling, friend or acquaintance, preferably separately (i.e., one at a time) and do it in the privacy and safety of your own home. Tell them that it's something highly personal and very important.

2. For this appointment, you will present yourself (for the last time to them) as Maher. Remember, they are completely in the dark about you being transgender and that you're a trans woman called Zoë. Presenting as Zoë right away will be too much information for them to process in one go and will distract them from the message you will need to communicate lucidly, in detail.

3. Provide them with as much background information as you deem suitable. It's important to mention that you've been seeing a medical expert, a gender psychologist, for a while now and that he's diagnosed you as having gender dysphoria.

4. Explain gender dysphoria to them in layman's terms. It's a medical condition, which means that the person is born with a mismatch between their mind and body. In your case, the mind is female, the body is male.

5. Explain that you've already been diagnosed as transgender by a qualified gender psychologist and that the next step is to seek medical expertise and

care from the *Genderploeg* at Westeneinde Hospital in Amsterdam.

6. After spilling the beans, give them time and space to absorb and digest the information. You should welcome any questions they may have.

7. Be prepared for any kind of reaction, ranging from solidarity, acceptance and support at one end of the spectrum and shock, disbelief and even anger and revulsion at the other end. Do not show any anger or irritation if their reaction isn't to your liking. Stay calm. Be patient and understanding.

8. Inform them that you trust them to keep this information confidential and to respect your need to tell others in person.

9. Inform them about your new name and let them know that this is the last time they will see you as Maher. Next time they'll see you as Zoë, i.e., a woman in women's clothes and (if you want) makeup.

10. Let them know that from now on you want them to address you by your new name and to use female pronouns (she, her, herself) when talking to you and about you.

11. After coming out, wish yourself good luck; you're going to need it. Keep in mind that some friends, acquaintances and even siblings may not be comfortable (right away) with you being transgender and need time to process and accept this information. Some of them might never be

comfortable with this and will eventually disappear altogether out of your life. It's a price many trans women regrettably have to pay for their coming out.

As for coming out to my parents, this could prove to be an ugly, very nasty and probably explosive experience. So, I should prepare for the worst and expect the unexpected. Johan recommended the following steps:

1. Write them a letter (preferably in their mother tongue: Arabic or French) explaining everything pertaining to you being diagnosed as transgender, including that the whole process will be under the strict guidance, monitoring and control of medical experts like Johan and later on the *Genderploeg*.

2. Have your sister and/or brother give them this letter.

3. After your parents have read the letter, set up an appointment with them on neutral ground, like a hotel or a café. Make sure to go with an ally; hopefully, that will be both of your siblings.

4. Apply steps 2 to 11 of the base-line coming-out strategy with one important caveat. During the appointment with your parents, be prepared to leave the venue ASAP should your father become verbally or physically violent.

5. Do not expect them to be supportive. On the contrary, you should prepare for a deluge of shock, disbelief, anger and extreme disgust.

As with regards to coming out at work, that's still in progress. We will only execute that plan after the *Gender-*

ploeg has made their diagnosis, assuming their diagnosis is congruent with Johan's assessment. According to Johan, in this fucking world (he didn't actually use the F-word), nothing is a given.

14

Nadine, May I Introduce You To..

Journal entry # 712$
Rotterdam, Oct 2015
🎧 Pretenders – I'll Stand by You

If there's one person in the whole world, whom I desperately do not want to lose, that's Nadine, my sister. I woke up bathed in sweat this morning, thinking that's exactly what's going to happen in a few hours when I come out to her.

If I was a set of six strings on a classical guitar, five of the strings have already snapped. Jules, today the tension in my body has reached critical levels, by that I mean heart-failure-inducing levels. When Nadine called this morning to let me know that she would be an hour late, a part of me wanted to cancel, to postpone the event till another day, when I'm calmer and more collected. *When's that going to be?* the cynical voice inside my head asked, with justification. True. That's not a good idea. No, I just needed to keep to Johan's script and I should be fine. *What was step 6 again?* I think I checked my consultation notes a dozen times already. *Couldn't I have done this on the phone?* No, not a good idea; Johan strongly advised against that option. *Stop this relentless doubting and questioning, Zoë, or you're going to give me a heart attack.*

‚'

When Nadine finally arrived, I threw my arms around her and embraced her with all my strength. This could very well be the last time I can do this. Streams of tears started pouring down my cheeks. Nadine felt my body quivering.

"What's wrong, Maher?"

"Nothing. Please come in. Can I get you a coffee or a tea?"

"Forget the damn tea. Maher, tell me what's wrong?"

"There's something very personal and important that I have to share with you today."

"I know, that's what you said on the phone. I'm here for you, my dear brother."

"Nadine, do you have any idea what it is that I want to share with you?"

"Yes, I think so."

"What is it that you're thinking?" I asked.

"I think you want to come out to me." She took me by surprise.

"Come out as what?"

"As gay."

"You're right about the first part. I did ask you to come because I wanted to come out to you. However, you're wrong about the second part." I paused for a few seconds. "Nadine, I'm not gay, I'm transgender." Nadine put her cup down on the coffee table.

"Transgender?" I sensed her astonishment and confusion. I could see that there were a hundred questions starting to formulate in her mind.

"Yes, Nadine. I'm transgender."

"As in a woman trapped in a man's body transgender?"

"Yes, I'm a trans woman."

"Sweet Mary in Heaven, Maher. I don't know what to say?"

"Don't say anything, yet. Just hear me out, please?" That sounded very much like a plea, because that's exactly what it was: a plea for understanding from a desperate soul.

"Of course, Maher. Take your time. I can see this is not easy for you."

"Nadine, I've been living with this secret since I was a child in Lebanon. Due to extreme fear and because I thought it was something bad and wrong inside me, I kept it carefully hidden all my life. But I can't anymore. If I don't do anything about it, it's going to kill me. Not in ten years' time, not in a year but much sooner than that. To save myself, I have to do this. I've already sought medical help."

"Medical help?"

"Yes, I've been seeing a gender psychologist, a very good

one. I've already carried out his instruction and contacted the *Genderploeg* at Westeneinde Hospital in Amsterdam." I could see Nadine's eyes swell up. She started crying.

"I'm sorry, Nadine. It was never my intention to hurt you, but I can't go on like this anymore." Nadine walked up to me, threw her arms around me and gave me a big hug.

"Please do not say 'sorry'. There's nothing to be sorry about. I'm just so sad that you've had to live with all this pain and guilt all your life." We cried together for what felt like an eternity.

"Hey, Nadine. I would like to share something else special with you?"

"What is it?"

"It's my tipping-point poem. The poem that finally released me from my cage." As I read it out loud to her, I could see her get very emotional.

"That's a beautiful poem, but very, very sad."

"Nadine, I want you to know that it's only my body that's going to change. I will still be me." I went on to explain to her the process that lay ahead of me, based on the information Johan had shared with me. When I finished, she hugged me again.

"I've always wanted a sister. All this time, I had her without knowing." Nadine was still crying.

"Thank you, Nadine. You don't know how terrified I was of losing you."

"Lose me? Never! I love you dearly, Maher."

"I love you too." I smiled. Anticipation was written all over my face.

"Why are you smiling like that?"

"Do you want to know my new name? As a woman, I can't be called Maher."

"Wow, you have a new name? Yes, of course, tell me."

"Zoë. It's Zoë. With an umlaut. You know, two dots on top of the letter 'e'." Nadine smiled.

"Zoë. I love it." She paused. "But wouldn't you want a Lebanese-Arabic name?"

"We are as much European as we are Lebanese. Zoë felt right, right from the moment I accepted that I'm a trans woman. I'm thinking about 'Amel' as a second name, like Mama's. That's Arabic for 'hope'. The hope that Mama and Baba will accept me, someday."

"Both names suit you."

"By the way, Nadine?"

"Yes, Zoë," she smiled, her eyes teasing me. I, too, had to get used to being called that.

"The next time you see me, I won't be wearing men's clothes anymore. I will be presenting as a woman. Also, I'll be wearing some makeup. Just like you are now. Like many women do."

Nadine smiled. "I can't wait to see Zoë."

"There's something else I need to tell you."

"You mean there's more?"

"There's always more. I'm getting hungry. Shall we start cooking?"

We prepared an Indonesian *rendang* beef stew with *Pandan* rice and green beans. To go with it, I opened a bottle of California Zinfandel wine.

"So, who are you going to tell next?" Nadine asked while we ate.

"Zachariah next," I said, "then Willem and Ashok."

I paused and looked at her to gauge her reaction. "Then Mama and Baba." Nadine frowned.

"Mama and Baba? That's going to be nasty."

"Yeah, that's gonna be really ugly."

"Have you thought about how you're going to do that?" Nadine's question hung heavy in the air.

"Johan, my gender psychologist, he's advised me to write them a letter explaining everything. After they've read the letter, to see them in person. Somewhere neutral with other people in the vicinity like a hotel lobby or a café. And hope they don't erupt in my face, spewing anger all over me." I could read the alarm and concern in Nadine's eyes.

"Anyways, let's worry about that another day." I desperately wanted to cherish this moment of fleeting happiness. I raised my glass of red wine.

"To sisters!" I toasted us.

"To the Shibli sisters!" she replied.

15

Dancing with Ziggy

Journal entry # 715$
Rotterdam, Oct 2015
🎧 Korn – Word Up!
Nek – Sei solo tu

I'm alarmed at how little social interaction I have at the weekends these days. If this trend continues unabated, the office will soon be the only environment where I'm partaking in some kind of social interaction. Spending the entire weekend alone without a single contact is scary – even for a closet introvert like me. Jules, I was determined (more like desperate) that that wasn't going to happen to me this weekend.

By word of mouth (both off- and online), the message

had spread that there was going to be an 'underground' Queer rave in Rotterdam, not very far from where I lived. From a safety perspective, I would have preferred to go there with a group. But, hey I was fed up waiting for someone to invite me. Furthermore, if the circumstances so dictate, this girl isn't afraid of going it alone.

Although this was going to be my first party as Zoë, I wasn't going to let fear or modesty tone me down. I made use of a few of Pantera's clothes and accessories like her shiny, black faux-leather leggings and long leather gloves. Finishing it all off with a pair of black suede Rapisardi over-the-knee boots, with high heels, of course, and a red beret, I was ready to rock the night.

While pondering whether or not I should order a taxi, Google Maps indicated that the party venue was a twenty-minute walk, give or take, from my apartment. I decided to chance it and walk the distance, even though it was dark and chilly outside.

When travelling on foot, Johan advised me to always stick to the main roads. Yes, there would be a much higher chance of prying eyes on me, but if anything was to go wrong, it's simply much safer to be at a place where there are more people. Being the obstinate type, I ignored his advice, and decided to do what I usually did, meaning take the quieter and more tranquil side streets.

While walking down a long, leafy residential street lined with large oak and chestnut trees, I noticed a red BMW approaching. Its front windows were completely wound down and the car audio system blared some kind of rap music in *creole* Portuguese. The BMW pulled into a parking space just a few meters diagonally opposite to where I was. Two men, whom I guessed to be Antilleans or Cabo Verdeans, stepped out. It didn't take long for them to notice me. Probably I was on their radar all along, and that's why they stopped.

"Hola *guapa*," the short, stocky one called out at me. "Can I ask you something?" I broke eye contact with them and hastily picked up my pace, trying to put as much distance between me and them. When *shortie* noticed that I was hastily moving away from him, he became verbally aggressive.

"Hey you, puta. I just want to talk to you. You whore, you *peniswasser*." At this point, the other man intervened and calmed him down. Thank Heaven for that, for there was hardly another soul on the street who could have come to my aid should anything ugly have happened. *How dumb can I be for ignoring Johan's advice? Better still, Zoë, take a cab next time, you fool!*

Frankly speaking, Jules, I was more terrified than offended. That they had taken me for a prostitute was in some perverse way a compliment; it did please me that they thought I was an attractive woman. Nonetheless, I was terrified they would discover that I'm not a typical woman and that that revelation would rapidly translate into lethal physical violence. Two big men like them could reduce me to a pulp at the drop of a hat. At this realization, I found myself nervously scurrying like a terrified cat until I made it, huffing and puffing, to the derelict school building. Although the rave was already in full swing, first, I had to calm myself down. Flush and somewhat out of breath, my heart was still beating at a super elevated rate and adrenaline was rushing throughout my body. I retreated out of sight and took a minute or two to compose myself before anyone took notice. Hey, I still wanted to look cool for the party.

It's ironic that as Maher, I'd never once felt in danger in such circumstances, i.e., while strolling in the dark in the streets of a Dutch city. And yet as Zoë, I felt danger on my very first evening walk out. *Was I dressed a little too edgy, maybe too sexy, too risqué?* Although I was rattled by what had happened (or could have happened), I was determined not to let it subdue my mood. By Jove, I was determined to have a good time tonight.

Once inside the old school building, I joined a group of trans women with whom I was casually acquainted. I had met some of them previously at a support group meeting. We were in a large hall, which was semi-partitioned into two equal parts, with a raised podium at one end of the hall. On the podium, a DJ was pumping out the decibels, mostly euro-pop and remixes of classic disco tracks, from electronic equipment with fancy names like Yamaha, Roland and Technics. On the walls, random scenes from Tony Scott's 80's cult-movie *The Hunger* were being projected. Why this film? Jules, I'm not sure, but the most probable reason that comes to mind is David Bowie. Perhaps the rave organizers wanted some of Bowie's cool factor to rub off on their show. Also, David is very much an icon of the queer community. We simply adore him.

We formed a cluster of ten trans women socializing together not far from the DJ's podium. I couldn't help but notice a group of men close by who were ogling us. Their incessant fixation on us was disconcerting. *What on earth did they want?* Furthermore, they seemed a little out of place – they were older and didn't have that quirkiness that one sees in LGBTQ folk, especially at a party. They looked too straight. When I pointed them out to one of my fellow trans women, she immediately understood what I was on about.

"These types of men, yeah, you'll always find them hanging somewhere around us at a party," she said.

"What type of men do you mean?" I inquired.

"Usually, straight men who are into trans women. They see us as some kind of fetish. That's our lot in life – most men want to smash our brains out and some want to fuck us."

"Huh! A fetish?"

"Yes, they get a sexual kick from being with a trans. Better watch out for them. If you're not careful, before you know what hit you, one of them will get between your legs and in your knickers. Stick with us and you'll be okay."

I snorted out a nervous laugh. *That's preposterous! What on earth is the world coming to?* On the other hand, it wasn't really that surprising – was it? I mean, the trans women in this group were mostly tall, slender, long-haired, androgynous and, in their own peculiar way, attractive too. And dare I say it, exotic, like sexy towering Amazonas. Physically, they defied any straightforward categorization as male or female. They were something 'in between' and exhibited both male and female physical characteristics – a colorful platoon of Ziggy Stardusts.

"You're new at this, aren't you?" she asked.

"You mean partying? Yes, my first time out partying *en femme*[15]."

---

15 en femme: dressed in women's clothes

"No, I meant you've only recently started transitioning?"

"Yes, how can you tell?"

"I can see that you're not on hormones yet. Have you started seeing the *Genderploeg* at Westeneinde Hospital yet?"

"I'm waiting for them to call me back for an intake appointment."

"That could take a while. They have a backlog of three to four months. If you want to get on hormones, let me know. I might be able to help."

"You're Silvia, right?" I recognized her from the support group meeting. "How about you? How far are you?"

"I've already completed the first phase at Westeneinde. The *Genderpleog* has already given me the green-light to start taking hormones. I will start soon."

"Silvia, I think you'll look great once the hormones kick in. You already look very feminine."

"Thanks! You too. Something tells me both men and women will be falling head over heels for you once you've completed your transition."

"You're being very generous," I blushed, "but thank you for the compliment, all the same."

"Would you like a drink?" Silvia pointed with her right hand toward the exit.

"Yeah. Could kill a whisky-cola! If they have it here."

"Whisky-cola. Nah! Probably not." Silvia shook her head as we broke off from the group and headed out.

Once in the corridor, we turned into the first room to our right. It turned out to be a sizeable kitchen with pale-green walls and a gigantic rectangular wooden table in the middle. The surface of the table was littered with

Heineken long necks and Absolut vodka bottles, as well as a dozen cartons of Coolbest orange juice. Compared to the main hall, this place felt tranquil. There were less than half a dozen people hanging around.

"So, ladies, what will it be?" The barista called out at us. Silvia opted for a beer. I went for a vodka-orange. Armed with our drinks, we retreated to one corner of the kitchen. Silvia pulled out a packet of *Gauloises Blondes* cigarettes from her shoulder bag.

"Care for a smoke?" she offered. I shook my head. I knew, from Johan, that once you're on hormones, smoking is a definite no-no. That said, Silvia was an adult. She didn't need my opinion or advice on smoking and I wasn't going to give it.

"Hey, ladies," the barista called out, "no smoking in here."

"I'm going out for a sec. Want to join me?" Silvia dropped the half-smoked cigarette onto the slate floor and stubbed it out with her stilettos.

"Sweetie, you go ahead. I'll see you back in the dance hall." I liked Silvia but didn't fancy standing in the chilly air inhaling someone else's smoke. That, Jules, is not the kind of solidarity I'm into.

Alone in the kitchen, I checked the time on my smartphone screen. *Goodness, it's almost midnight already.*

"Hey, Cinderella. You're not leaving us already, are you?" I looked up. It was a ridiculously handsome young man, dressed as a mariner, with a striped white and blue tight-fitting shirt and white flared pants. A classic look, straight out of a Jean-Paul Gaultier *Le Male* advertisement.

"No, sailor. Not yet."

"Good." He winked.

"Would you like another drink?" he offered.

"Sure! Another vodka-orange. Thanks!"

We chatted for a while. He was definitely a smooth talker and body-wise, rippling hot. As we chatted, I couldn't help but notice that he kept creeping closer and closer up to me, until his face was only a few centimeters from mine.

"Can I taste your vodka-orange?" he asked.

"Nope."

"Playing hard to get, are we?"

"You're playing. I'm just having a drink!"

As he moved in for a smooch, I turned my face away and his lips landed on my cheeks. Sloppy and wet. Before he could make his next move, I crouched down and swiveled around him. Quite lithe and agile of me, I must say. I'm sure Pantera would have been proud.

"Goodbye, sailor, and don't follow me. I mean it!" I called back, raising my right hand high above my head and made the diva-like hand gesture of 'back off'. Before he made his move to kiss me, I had read his eyes – they had SEX written all over them. I wasn't going to go there. I had already decided: no sex until after my sex-change operation.

Back in the dance hall, I rejoined the colorful platoon of trans women, who were now showing off their Voguing[16] skills. With a few drinks inside me, it was time to boogie. There was just one thing missing – a track that I could really groove to. That was easily remedied – I went up to the DJ and whispered one of my favorite tracks in his ear.

16 Vogue or Voguing: a dance style, started by the trans and gay community in New York City in the 80s, consisting of a series of highly stylized poses struck in imitation of fashion models. This dance style was allegedly appropriated and made famous by Madonna in the 90s.

"Sure, chica. Coming up next," he smiled while nodding his head repeatedly. He was a cool dude, but golly was he high – I mean stratosphere high. Marihuana seeped out of every pore in his body.

By the time I rejoined the girls, I heard Filippo Neviani's (a.k.a. Nek) sexy male voice declare in Italian, *"Sei solo tuuuuu, dentro me"*. That was my cue; I quickly grabbed Silvia's hand and moved to the middle of our group, which slowly began forming a circle around us.

"C'mon, sweetie. Let's give everybody something to talk about." As I swayed sensually and rhythmically to Nek's song, Silvia put her hands around my waist and pulled me closer to her. *Exciting. Yeah, baby. I like that!* I interlocked my hands around her neck and looked deep into her steely gray eyes. Soon our bodies bonded tightly as we swayed from side to side, deliciously in unison. Before the last note fell, I felt Silvia's sweet lips on my mouth. I parted my lips and she pushed her tongue inside. Trans on trans. That's hot! That's exotic! That's sexy! *Mmmm… you're delicious, Silvia. Bring it on! Let's rock the night!*

16

Brother, Where Art Thou?

Journal entry # 717$
Rotterdam, Oct 2015
🎧 Cock Robin – The Promise You made

I was over the moon with the love, support and solidarity which my sister, Nadine, bestowed upon me when I came out to her as transgender. Do I dare hope that Zachariah, my brother, will be equally supportive and *solidaire*? Today was his turn to demonstrate, in person and face-to-face, what I meant to him.

Zachariah and Nadine arrived at my apartment a little

after one o'clock in the afternoon. His customary way of greeting me was to give me a bear hug; something he reserved for close male friends and relatives, and of course, me. As for close females, he'd kiss them on the cheeks three times, the Dutch way.

"Welcome, Zachariah. It's been a while since you came to visit me in Rotterdam."

"Yeah," he nodded nervously, all the time avoiding eye-contact with me.

"Are you okay? You seem a little nervous," I asked.

"Just tell me what it is that you need to tell me, Maher?" His eyes wandering restlessly around the living room –any which way but me.

"Alright. I was going to offer you some coffee and cake, but since you seem to be in a bad mood and in a hurry, let's get down to it."

"Maher, I already know," he blurted out. "You want to tell me that you're gay. It's your life. Nothing to do with me."

"Zachariah, I'm not gay. I'm transgender."

His eyes stopped shifting, and he made solid eye contact with me, for the first time today. To say he looked puzzled and confused was an understatement. *Let him simmer in his confusion for a little while longer. Give it some time to sink in – I wasn't in the mood to be nice or polite to him anymore.* A few minutes had passed by and he was still silent. Now I was the one who was agitated by the silence.

"Zachariah, do you understand what transgender means?"

"I know what transvestite means," he fired back with a silly smirk on his face. With this, I felt my body temperature rise and my blood start to boil. Jules, to equate 'transgender' with 'transvestite' is about the worst insult you can give any trans woman.

"Listen, Zachariah. I don't know which rock you've been living under but you are clearly misinformed. Never call me a transvestite again, ever. Do I make myself clear?"

"Okay, I understand! Keep your knickers on," he mumbled.

"No, you clearly do NOT understand. A transvestite is a man who wears women's clothes for fun, sensation, show and occasionally for sexual kicks. That has absolutely nothing to do with being transgender."

"Okay. So, what is transgender then?" he asked, anger and irritation in his eyes. At this point I wasn't sure if I wanted to answer him or throw him out of my apartment. Thankfully, just in time, I recalled Johan's cautionary note that I needed to be patient and yes, accommodating when coming out for the first time to others. I slowed my breath down and mentally counted to ten.

"Transgender is when a person is born with a mismatch between their mind and body. Please understand, Zachariah, that all my life this disconnect has turned my life into a living hell. Since I was a child, I've fought against myself, trying my utmost to suppress my true identity. But I can't anymore. I'm tired; I'm exhausted. If I want to save myself, I have to do this."

"Do what?" he asked, his tone at once combative and gruff.

"I have to transition. I have to alter my body so that it reflects who I am inside."

"You're not seriously suggesting a sex-change operation?" He looked at me incredulously.

"Yes, that and more," I fixed my eyes on his, resolute and defiant in my riposte.

"Really? On top of all our miseries, this is the last thing our family needs. A scandal to bury all scandals." At this point, Nadine tactically intervened to calm things down. I'm grateful to her that she did this right in the nick of time because I was two degrees from boiling over. I was flabbergasted at his lack of empathy and downright rudeness toward me.

"Zoë, why don't you explain the medical urgency of your situation to Zachariah? I think that would put things into perspective for him."

I agreed with Nadine's proposal and proceeded to explain, with all the calmness I could muster, my condition to my brother, emphasizing all the time that this was about survival, nothing else. Furthermore, the whole process of transitioning would be under the control and supervision of medical experts. When I finished talking, he seemed unmoved.

"Okay, I get it, Maher." He paused. "Or Zoë, or whatever your name is. But you should understand that I'm rather conservative in my values. I'm finding all this really bizarre." I was incensed by his remark.

"Really? You, conservative? I could easily list ten things about you and your life that would thoroughly disqualify you from even remotely qualifying as a social conservative. If that's what you call yourself now, then it seems to me that you're being selectively conservative, only when it relates to matters of diversity of the human race." Alas, no matter how hard I tried, I simply wasn't getting through to him.

An uneasy, awkward silence fell upon us like the mist on a cold Dutch winter's morning when it shrouds the grazing animals in the fields just outside the city. Finally, it was Zachariah, who broke the silence.

"Mama won't survive this," he stated, as a matter of fact.

"Of course, she will," I countered. "You underestimate her strength. You should have more faith in her."

"No, she won't survive this," he repeated. "Having recently had open-heart surgery, her physical condition is very weak. Once you come out to our parents, Baba will psychologically terrorize the hell out of her, you know this, for what he sees as her failings with us. He'll do this for the rest of her living days. No, I'm telling you, she won't survive his relentless mental onslaught."

I looked at Nadine for some support. My eyes begging her, imploring her, to come to my aid.

"Zoë, Zachariah is right about Mama. She won't be able to cope with Baba's constant psychological aggression. In his eyes, all that's wrong with us (her children) is ultimately her fault."

At this, my heart sank to a new low as I struggled to internalize what all this meant to my situation.

"Are you both asking me to not transition, in other words to sacrifice myself?" I cried out. "Haven't I already suffered enough for the past twenty-five years?"

"No, Zoë. Of course not," Nadine calmly interjected. "We'll need to find a way to keep all this a secret. They must never find out. Ever!"

"A secret? How? It's not like I can hide all the changes that will happen to my body when I start taking hormones. There's absolutely no way I can fake being Maher for long."

"Well then, we'll just have to figure out an alternative plan."

Jules, today didn't go well. The meeting ended with a feeling of one step forward and two steps back. Nothing's been resolved. Deep down I know that my brother has more or less abandoned me. That hurts to the bone. My younger brother, whom I love dearly, can't find it in himself to accept me for what I am. The same brother to whom I gave my all ten years ago, when he was going through a major crisis. For months on end, I bent over backward, day in and day out to help him out of the black hole that almost devoured him. That he can't find it in himself to at least make an effort to be by my side, in my moment of desperation and need, truly depresses and infuriates me. It's like he's completely absolved himself of a promise he had once made to stand by my side always, come what may. That said, on one crucial point, I do concede he's undeniably right: we can't let my parents know that I'm trans.

17

Tramline 8

Journal entry # 719$
Rotterdam, Oct 2015
🎧 NINA – Beyond Memory

At the tram platform adjacent to the side entrance of Rotterdam Central Station, I warmly kissed and hugged my sister as we bade each other goodbye. When tram 8 to Spangen arrived, the sun was already very low on this chilly October Sunday. I stepped in and took a seat next to the window at the third to last row in the tram carriage. The seat next to me remained unoccupied. I leaned my head on the cold window pane. Thankfully, my scarlet woolen cap acted as a warm barrier between my skin and the window.

As I reminisced about the last few hours, which I had spent with Nadine in the city center, I couldn't help but feel a sense of satisfaction about how smoothly it all went. Except for that one time, when the waiter at the Little V restaurant stared at me for a while too long, there were hardly any hiccups. No people doing the dreaded double-takes, asking out loud, *"Is that a man?"* or worse, trying to publicly shame me.

I smiled as I acknowledged to myself my growing confidence and the tremendous progress, I've made in presenting as a woman in public since I first ventured out as Zoë back in April. I can't complain. Things are looking up; my intake appointment with the *Genderploeg* at Westeneinde Hospital was just around the corner, and I was impatiently counting down the days when I could finally start the medical process.

Of course, as Johan keeps reminding me, the intake interview has to go well, otherwise everything could come to a sudden and crashing halt. Oh, heavens. If that was to happen, I would be completely lost and utterly devastated. No, Jules, that won't happen to me, I have to keep the faith that it will go fine and the hospital will admit me into their comprehensive program for treating gender dysphoria. A medical program which will last three years, at the minimum, but more realistically four to five years. Contemplating being on this program, I felt a warm and serene happiness radiate throughout my body. I can only imagine how wonderful it would be to be on female hormones and, of course, the holy grail of transitioning, i.e., to undergo the sex-change operation, or SRS (Sex Reassignment Surgery) as I'm repeatedly corrected by my peers. To have a vagina after all those years of pain and torment would be the most incredible and important transformation in my life. Actually, it's way beyond 'important'; it's existential. It would be like finally seeing the light, for the first time in my life, after decades of slowly decomposing in a seemingly never-ending dark tunnel.

I was awoken from my reverie by a sudden pull on my scarlet woolen cap from the back. *Huh! Did that really happen or am I imagining things?* No, it must have been my imagination playing tricks on me while I was daydreaming about the surgery. It can't have been anything else. I rested my head on the window pane, hoping desperately to reconnect with my happy thoughts. However, that was once again interrupted as I felt a second tug on my cap from the back. This time it was quickly followed by a third. The third tug sent my cap flying from my head. It fell on the tram floor somewhere behind me.

I turned around and was disgusted to see the passenger, seated behind me, lewdly licking his lips and gesturing with his eyes for me to come sit next to him. The young man, let's call him hooligan or thug because that's what he really is, couldn't have been older than twenty years.

I picked up my shoulder bag, stood up and took a step toward the hooligan. I saw that my cap was lying on the tram floor, next to his left foot. When I stooped down to pick it up, he kicked it away and laughed out loud.

"Hey, baby. Come sit next to Daddy!" he uttered obscenely, while continuing to laugh.

I could hardly believe what was happening. Disgusted,

I picked up my cap and took a step toward the hooligan. I was definitely going to tell him what I thought of his juvenile behavior. I leaned in toward him and was about to give him a slight but firm push on the shoulder, when the tram jolted to the right. I lost my balance and my hand skidded his left cheek instead. Although the impact was laughably soft, he was clearly enraged. Mostly, I believe, by the fact that a woman dared to confront him. His alpha-male ego was compromised. He briskly stood up and shoved me backward upon which I stumbled and fell hard, landing straight on my bum.

"Fuck you, you stupid bitch! Who do you bloody think you are?" he shouted at me, while spittle foamed at the sides of his mouth.

The moment I made contact with the tram floor, I felt the socks, which I had stuffed in my bra, become dislodged. At the sight of my breasts vanishing, the hooligan quieted down while his pea-sized brain tried to process this information. At that moment, I realized that the hooligan was not alone; he had two of his buddies with him.

One of them shouted out, "That's not a woman; it's a bloke; it's a faggot!" At this proclamation, the hooligan's eyes turned red with venom and hatred and his face rippled with rage. In a flash, I picked up my stuff and made a dash to the front of the tram. On my way, I came across the elderly conductor who, upon hearing the commotion at the back, was making her way in that direction. I felt too embarrassed as well as afraid to speak to her, knowing the hooligan and his buddies were within earshot. Furthermore, I was aghast that not a single fellow passenger moved a finger to help me.

My body trembled with panic and anxiety, while I waited for the tram to reach my destination, just two stops away. *Please, Heaven, don't let them hurt me!* I prayed that they wouldn't follow me when I stepped off the tram.

My stop was up next, when doubts about my 'escape plan' started to cloud my judgement. Perhaps it was wiser to stay in the tram and to share my concerns for my safety with the conductor. The tram door opened and impulsively I darted out like a coiled spring suddenly let loose.

Fuck! The thugs jumped off the tram, as well. I calculated that a mere twelve meters separated us. I turned around, and like a terrified fox being chased by a pack of pit bull terriers, made a dash for my apartment block. I sensed them gaining ground on me. Miserably, I tried to control my erratic breathing and the panic, which was about to paralyze me. I knew that if I didn't take my high-heeled boots off, in a second or five they would be all over me. *Shit! Shit! Shit! Why didn't I take those damn boots off in the tram?* The adrenaline continued to pump ferociously in every vein in my body. I felt my legs were on the verge of buckling, when I decided to stop for a split second to kick off my boots. I bent down and zipped down the boot on my right foot. I switched to my left foot, and then it happened.

I felt something sting me with full force between my shoulder blades. A pang of intense pain flared up my spine as the impact sent me flying, face down toward the ground. Upon contact, my reflexes caused my body to curl up in a fetal position. I covered my head with my hands, in anticipation of the imminent violence.

The first kick landed on the side of my ribcage, the

second on my lower back. I cried out in pain and agony as an avalanche of kicks and punches pulverized my body. One of the thugs, like an animal possessed by demons, grunted thunderously that he was going to urinate all over my body and break my neck. So, this was what senseless hatred and violence sounded like. Surely, this was it – the end of my miserable existence. 23, 24, 25… I lost count. The lights were going out before I had even had a chance to start living as me. In an instant, everything seemed so far away, like I was no longer in my body. Little by little, it became darker and darker. I continued to drift away, oblivious to the blows landing on my body. In the distance, I heard a cacophony of sounds: a dog barking, male and female voices shouting, a car's claxon honking. Finally, the lights went out.

''

I woke up in a darkened room in some place I did not recognize. I tried to move, but a spasm of pain like an electric current immobilized my body. Suddenly, I felt it – the excruciating injuries all over my body, especially on the left-hand side of my ribcage and my back. Panic-stricken, I moved my right hand to my head – it was heavily bandaged. As I regained more and more of my senses, the smell of disinfectant hit my nostrils. At last, I realized I was in a hospital. Relieved and alarmed in equal measures, I scrambled for the buzzer, which I instinctively knew would be dangling from a cable somewhere alongside my hospital bed. In the dark, I heard the approaching sound of muffled feet as the door opened to let in a faint mustard yellow light from the corridor. A nurse in green scrubs walked to the foot of my bed.

"Where am I?" The tremor in my voice betrayed my anxiety and nervousness.

"You're in hospital, Mr. Shibli. This is Erasmus Medical Center in Rotterdam." She took my right hand and felt my pulse.

"Actually, it's Ms. Shibli. I'm—" I cut myself short.

"Sorry, what did you say? Something about Miss?

"Nothing! It doesn't matter."

"You need to rest, Mr. Shibli. Early tomorrow morning, the doctor will come and see you."

Indeed, in the small hours of the morning, the doctor, a handsome looking forty-something man with a blond moustache and toffee-brown wavy hair, checked on me. He explained that I had suffered two fractured ribs, heavy bruising over my whole body, especially my back, and a concussion. However, my breathing was normal, indicating that luckily there was no damage done to the lungs.

Two police officers came in later that day and took a statement. They didn't exude any sympathy, let alone any serious intent in catching the perpetrators. I'm assuming that they were simply following bureaucratic procedure.

After two more days of rest and monitoring at the hospital, I was discharged with a stash of painkillers to further recuperate at home. Jules, they gave me ibuprofen. Can you believe it? Seriously? Fuck them and those miserably weak painkillers! I have much more effective pain relief 'medicine' at home.

18

Red Flags

Journal entry # 720$
Rotterdam, Oct 2015
🎧 All Saints – Red Flag

Nadine went ballistic and came running to my apartment when I told her about the hate-driven attack by the hooligans. As if that wasn't enough, her anger and frustration with me hit the roof, when she realized that the incident had taken place four days earlier and that I didn't call her when I was in hospital.

All my explanations and arguments that I didn't want to unduly alarm and concern her fell on deaf ears.

"Please, Nadine, don't shout. Go gentle on me. I'm not fully recovered. My fractured ribs still hurt."

"For all intents and purposes, Zoë, please get it into your thick, obstinate head that I'm the only family you've got left. So how dare you not reach out to me right away in an emergency like this!"

There are no two ways about it; obviously, she was right and I was wrong. After a million apologies, I managed to placate her.

"Listen to me, Zoë. You've got to wise up quickly about the big bad world out there. As a woman, you need to sharpen your wits, especially when using public transport. Do you realize that you missed four clear red flags in that tram?"

"Huh, what do you mean? What red flags?" I was dumbfounded.

She continued, "Let me spell them out to you. One, you didn't scan the tram for potential troublemakers. What on earth were you thinking taking a seat at the back, where the bad boys usually congregate? Two, you overheard the main attacker talk about forcefully kissing a girl, regardless of whether she approved or not. How your radar didn't light up like a Christmas tree when you heard that, I don't understand. Anyway, didn't it occur to you that the girl in question was you?"

"Okay, I get it. I fucked up."

"Zoë, I'm not finished yet. Three, when you felt the second tug on your cap, you should've picked up your stuff and headed as far away from them as possible. And four, what in sweet Mary's name were you thinking confronting that bloody hooligan like that? Do you think you're some kind of cool superwoman? That was foolish at best and damn fatalistic at worst. You need to reverse all those years of being conditioned to confront things head on. Simply put: you do not directly confront bullies like that alone. If ever." I protested that change will never happen if and when, faced with such bullies, women mostly opted for flight instead of fight.

"Dear Zoë, there's a time and place for fighting. Then and there in the tram wasn't it. A woman, especially a trans woman, needs to choose her battles wisely.

After an eerie silence, I asked, "What did you mean by *especially a trans woman*? I'm intrigued why you think that?" Nadine was lost in thought for a while before she replied.

"The way I see it, a lot of people will readily intervene to help a woman in an emergency, but considerably less will extend that help to a trans woman, if they're aware that's what she is."

Jules, the last thing I want is to become a person who's captive to some kind of victim mentality. That's just not me. I'd rather look at the positives, even from a shitty incident like this. Nadine's red flags are definitely lessons learned. I promise I will be more careful in the future.

19

Transition Doldrums

Journal entry # 722$
Rotterdam, Oct 2015

Zoë, get on with it already! Today, Jules, I'm feeling anxious and agitated. I feel that I should have been further down the road with my transition and more specifically with my coming-out process, especially with friends and acquaintances. My procrastination is starting to really bother and stress me out. When I'm feeling *shit* like this, I start to eat more, and before I realize what's happening to me, I'll find myself in the tight clutches of that vicious circle of weight gain and depression. The more depressed I feel, the more I eat, and the more I eat the more depressed I get.

This week I'm determined to break the cycle and stop procrastinating – I'm coming out to my BFFs, Willem and Ashok.

20

Hoi Willem

Journal entry # 723$
Rotterdam, Oct 2015

I took advantage of Willem's short visit back to Holland to invite him to my home. He'd taken a week off his pilot project in India to take care of some family-related business.

On the phone, he sounded quite tense when I told him that there was something personal and private which I needed to share with him quite urgently.

I hadn't seen him in ages, and there he was in my home, sitting diagonally across from me; he took the sofa while I sat on the Marcel Wanders armchair. I initiated *the* conversation with my customary opening question.

"Willem, do you have any idea what it is I want to share with you?"

"No," he answered, as cool as a cucumber.

"Well, there's something which I've kept secret from you and everybody else because I was deeply ashamed of it. It's something I thought I could hide for the rest of my life, but I can't."

He fixed his eyes on me but kept a poker face.

Typical Dutch, never allowing any facial expression to betray how they feel inside.

"Are you going to tell me, Maher? Or am I supposed to guess?" This time the slightest of tremors in his voice betrayed an uneasiness. I never thought I'd see the day when ice-cool Willem would be nervous, even just a little.

"Willem, I'm transgender!" I blurted it out. In reaction to this, Willem exhaled a sigh of relief. "Am I mistaken, Willem, or are you actually relieved to hear that I'm trans?"

"Maher, you read that right. Yes, I am actually relieved. I thought you were going to tell me that you are gay and that you are *in love with me*. Although I didn't want to let you down, I don't feel the same way." I rolled my eyes and couldn't help but react to the irony and comedy of the situation with boisterous laughter.

"Well, I'm so sorry to disappoint you, my dear friend, because I'm neither gay nor in love with you." Now we laughed out loud in unison.

I filled him in on all that had transpired in my life in the previous few months since our last get together. He was alarmed, frustrated and concerned when I informed him about the recent hate attack. Like Nadine, he berated me for not reaching out to him earlier.

"Maher, listen to me carefully." Willem pointed with his right hand's index finger back and forth at me and himself. "I want you to know that this, I mean you being transgender, does not change a thing between us. You were, are and will always be, my best friend."

Tears of joy and relief streamed down my cheeks. Finally, not able to contain our emotions, we both stood up and gave each other a hearty bear hug.

A few hours later, after mac 'n' cheese and several bottles of *Jupiler Blonde* beers, he bade me goodbye and all the strength in my journey.

"Goodbye, Maher! And see you soon, Zoë." He leaned in and kissed me the customary three kisses on the cheeks. This is something heterosexual Dutch men reserve for female friends only.

21

Calling Shiva to Ashok

Journal entry # 724$
Rotterdam, Oct 2015

D ue to a plethora of family issues, Ashok couldn't make it to Rotterdam in the foreseeable future, so reluctantly I came out to him on the phone. Upon hearing the word 'transgender', he went eerily silent for what felt like a very long time. This prompted me to ask if he was still on the line. Although he tried to maintain the semblance of being cool and unaffected, he was clearly irate about the whole thing.

He kept suggesting that I was jumping to conclusions.

"Let the medical experts make that call," he insisted, "and not before a full psychological evaluation has taken place." The fact that I had already been evaluated and diagnosed by Dr. Johan de Zeelander, one of the most highly rated and respected gender psychologists in the country, didn't make much of an impression on him.

Exasperated and feeling that I wasn't making any headway with him, I changed course and tried to appeal to his Hindu heritage.

"Ashok, you're still a practicing Hindu, aren't you?" I asked.

"Yeah, what's that got to do with this?" he shot back.

"Everything," I exclaimed.

"Huh, I don't follow your logic."

"Well, as a Hindu, I expected more openness from you. Transgenderism has been part of the Hindu religion and culture since time immemorial. Transgender women, locally referred to in India as *Aravani* or *Kinnar,* were very much a revered part of Indian society all the way up to colonial British rule. It is the occupying British administration from 1858 to 1947 that ultimately lead to the marginalization of Kinnars to the fringes of society. Ashok, you yourself once told me that Lord Shiva, the highest divinity in the Hindu religion, is part male and part female. So that makes Shiva both or neither. In today's terminology, Shiva would be considered bi-gender or non-binary. Furthermore, Ashok, and correct me if I'm wrong, according to sacred Hindu scriptures, Hindu gods and goddesses frequently switched to the opposite sex. That makes them transgender!" To this, Ashok grumbled and sounded not at all amused, so I decided not to push this line of reasoning with him any further.

"Okay, Ashok. Frankly, I'm feeling frustrated, and I don't believe we're going to agree on anything today, so let's just give it some time to sink in."

Jules, I'm hoping the next time I speak to him, he'll be more receptive to the idea that I'm trans.

22

Intake

Journal entry # 727$
Westeneinde Hospital,
Amsterdam, Nov 2015
🎧 Colbie Caillat – Try

I opened and clenched my right hand several times in a futile attempt to relieve the stress. It was by now covered with a thin, sticky film of perspiration. The waiting in this hospital reception room is slowly killing me, and if that knot in my stomach gets any tighter, I won't be able to breathe anymore.

Reception Q at Westeneinde is, by Dutch hospital standards, quite a small waiting room. On three sides, the walls were covered by wooden panels, giving it a retro 70's feel. Benches with orange faux-leather cushioning were lined up against the wood-panel walls. In the middle of the room, there was the customary reading table surrounded by petite chairs. Judging by the Tin Tin and Suske & Wiske comic books on the table's surface and the size of the chairs, I guessed that this table was primarily meant for younger trans patients. By the entrance to the reception room, there was a vending machine which dispensed a variety of cheap, bland coffee and tea.

Reception Q was almost full with all manner of quirky looking individuals, including myself, who physically defied heteronormative labelling. Age-wise, according to my guestimates, the patients varied from five to seventy-five. When it came to the trans women in the room, generally the younger they were, the prettier and more feminine they tended to look.

From time to time, a medic in a white coat would walk into Reception Q and call out a name, meticulously avoiding the use of any gendered titles like Mr., Mrs., Ms. and Miss. After someone's name was called out, a patient in the room would robotically stand up, shake hands with the medic and follow him or her silently into the long corridor at the other end. Something about this mechanical sequence unnerved me. In my mind, the patients seemed like domesticated animals tethered to a shepherd, being led to the unknown.

By now, I was seriously questioning the quasi-wisdom of arriving way too early for my appointment. Of course, it wasn't to subject myself to this tortuous wait but out of acute anxiety and paranoia about not making it on time for the most important appointment of my life – the intake interview with the *Genderploeg*. After all, it was more than an hour and twenty minutes' drive from Rotterdam and that's if there's no traffic.

The medical part of my transition starts here. In a little less than ten minutes, a medic will walk in, call my name and usher me into a sterile, whitewashed office, where I will be subjected to a lengthy interview with Dr. de Jager, a psychologist who is an uber-specialist in gender issues. The previous week, Johan had explained, in detail, the process to me. If the psychologist is convinced by the merit of my case, I will be admitted into the first phase of the program – the comprehensive psychological evaluation. On the other hand, if the psychologist is not convinced by my case, i.e., if he or she does not believe it is related to gender dysphoria, then I will be referred to a different department of psychology.

Five minutes (and counting down) to go till my appointment and I feel the urge to go to the bathroom for the fourth time already. Jules, why didn't I just wait for my appointment on the pan, instead of this to and fro from reception room to restroom? Do I risk it? The medic could arrive a little earlier than scheduled, or all the stalls could be occupied. After a little hesitation I made up my mind to go, otherwise the pressure on my bladder would be unbearable. On top of that, I reasoned that asking to go to the restroom ten minutes into the interview wouldn't look good.

I walked back into Reception Q just as my name was being called out. A short fifty-something woman with intelligent blue eyes and ash-gray hair, cut in a bob style, extended her right arm and curtly shook my hand.

"I'm Dr. de Jager, senior psychologist at the *Gender-ploeg*. Please follow me." She escorted me into a small, bland office room with a wooden bureau table and three chairs. *So, this is where I'm going to be grilled by the uber-gatekeeper for the next hour or so.*

"Please sit down, Zoë. It's Zoë, isn't it?"

I nodded my head without uttering a word. My mouth was parched by now.

"What's wrong, Zoë? You look pale. Are you nervous to be here?"

"Yes, I'm feeling somewhat nervous."

"Why? What's wrong?" Her concern sounded more deliberate than genuine.

I decided to carefully navigate around this question. I didn't want to jump straight into the content just yet.

"I've been waiting a long time for this appointment. All the while the anticipation has been steadily building up. That's why." I looked into her eyes, but her face remained devoid of any expression.

"So, Zoë, now you are here, what can we do for you?" she asked in that nonchalant demeanor which is so typical of medical professionals.

In response to this ridiculous question, I almost rolled my eyes, but stopped myself just in time. *God, woman, you know why I'm here. I know that Johan has already sent you a copy of his medical assessment as well as my Life CV. So why ask me this question and in such a condescending manner?* I bit my tongue and decided to play dutifully along.

"I've been referred to you by Dr. Johan de Zeelander.

I've been seeing him for a while now. He believes it's time that I should come see you. That it's time to move to the next phase in my transition."

"And what do you believe, Zoë?"

So, she's continuing with this charade.

"I believe that I should have come to you a long time ago, but I stopped myself, time after time because I felt deeply ashamed and I didn't want to hurt my parents."

That was my opening salvo and before she could ask a follow-up question, I gave her an abridged account of my life in the past few years. What I did not mention is that I felt my whole life was hanging in the balance on the outcome of this one horrendous appointment. If the *Genderploeg* were to deny me this medical path, it would be tantamount to a death sentence.

"I read your Life CV, Zoë. Dr. de Zeelander sent us your medical dossier a few weeks ago. There are a few things in your Life CV that actually puzzle me." She let her question hang in midair, while her gaze roamed around the room.

I parried this rhetorical question with a polite smile but remained silent. I definitely wasn't going to say a word until she asked me an explicit question. Reading my thoughts, Dr. de Jager allowed a smile to grace her pretty face for the first time.

"So, I understand that you are big fan of Laura Jane Grace, the singer who transitioned recently?"

"No," I replied.

"No?" She echoed my answer. "Did I misunderstand something?"

"Yes, you did misunderstand. Although I admire and

respect her, I don't consider myself her fan. Until that radio interview earlier this year, frankly I hadn't even heard of Laura Jane Grace or Tom Gabel as she was known before her transition. That radio interview triggered me to write what was to become my tipping-point poem. A week after hearing that radio interview, that poem forced me to confront myself and accept, for the first time, my true gender identity, something which I'd put off all my life."

"And when you came out to yourself as transgender, how did you feel? I can imagine you felt extremely happy, even ecstatic."

"No."

"I don't understand. You're telling me you were not happy to finally accept that you're transgender?" She looked quizzically into my eyes.

"No, I wasn't happy; I was relieved, incredibly relieved, but not happy. After I accepted my true self as a woman, I broke down and cried for three days in a row. The pent-up pain, agony and sorrow of more than two and half decades came pouring out of me like a tsunami."

Hereafter, Dr. de Jager continued her line of questioning, however her questions were now more specific and more explicit. I felt for the first time during this interview that she was no longer playing mind-fuck games with me. I kept my answers concise and to the point and always with a polite, civil tone. Not once did I adopt a sarcastic tone of voice with her. *Just stick to the questions, Zoë! And never be impolite!* Johan had instructed me well.

"Zoë, before we wrap up this interview, is there anything else you would like to ask?"

"Yes, there is."

"And what's that?"

"There's a question that has vexed me profoundly since my self-acceptance as transgender. Do I have the right to be happy at the expense of others, in this case, my parents?"

Dr. de Jager paused to think for a few seconds as she pondered her answer.

"It's very noble of you, Zoë, to be pre-occupied with the happiness of others. However, that's not the crucial question you should be asking yourself. The question you should be asking yourself is: Do I have the right to be myself?"

Once or twice in a lifetime, someone asks you a (simple) question that changes your perspective so comprehensively, it triggers a paradigm shift. Dr. De Jager's question did just that for me.

"Of course, doctor, I have the right to be myself. That's a no-brainer. Everybody does!"

"Well then, Zoë, welcome! You are as of this moment a patient of the *Genderploeg*. You've come to the right address."

23

Reflections on Intake

Journal entry # 729$
Rotterdam, Nov 2015
🎧 Bernward Koch – Under Trees

J ohan was really pleased with the outcome of my intake appointment with the *Genderploeg*; he was genuinely happy for me. That touched me deep inside – to see a professional like him so dedicated and committed to my wellbeing and future. That said, he warned me (again) that the road ahead with the *Genderploeg* wouldn't be an easy one. He reminded me that once the psychological assessment began,

I shouldn't expect a warm bath. Genderploeg's psychologists are not there to support the patients but to evaluate them. He explained that they can and will 'interrogate' me thoroughly. Like a medical FBI, they won't leave a stone unturned in their search to establish the facts. That's their job, and they are very good at it.

Thank you, Johan. Your intentions are good but no need to psyche me up even more; I'm already a ball of nerves as it is.

Eleven months ago, give or take, I made an existential decision to save myself. For this to happen I needed to find a way out of the long dark tunnel that has been my life since birth. After the intake appointment, for the first time ever, I see the tiniest speck of light far away in the distance. I'm not so much feeling happy about reaching this milestone as I'm feeling relieved. Relieved that I live to fight another day. Jules, I shudder to think what would have happened to me, if the *Genderploeg* had blocked me. Okay, it's behind me now, so I don't want to dwell on that thought too much. Let's move on!

Yes, I'm daunted by the uncertain prospect of the long and arduous road ahead, not to mention the anxiety and stress that will bedevil me every step of the way. God, there are times when I feel so utterly exhausted, mentally and physically. On those occasions, I feel like throwing the towel into the ring and just letting myself waste away into oblivion.

By now, it's imprinted in my mind that the path ahead will be something akin to a war of attrition – surviving one day at a time, week after week, month after month, for the next three years, at the least. All that so that one day, Heaven willing, I will finally make it to the end of the tunnel, to the other side of the gender divide. I have to believe that one day, someday, I will feel the warmth of the early morning's sun on my face, breathe sweet fresh air and walk with bare feet on moist green grass. I hope.

24

Psychological Assessment Nº 1

Journal entry # 901$
Westeneinde Hospital,
Amsterdam, Jan 2016

H *ere we go. Again!* I followed Dr. Dominic van den Broek, a forty-something psychologist at the *Gender-ploeg* with cobalt-blue eyes and cropped walnut brown hair, from Reception Q to his office at the end of a long white corridor of anonymous white doors.

"Please take that seat." Dominic indicated with his left

index finger while he lithely maneuvered around a large wooden bureau to his seat on the opposite side.

I dutifully followed his instructions and positioned myself like a seated mannequin. I blinked my eyes a few times indicating that I was ready. However, he didn't take notice, or deliberately ignored my signals.

"Zoë, is that your name?" He picked up a stylo pen and opened a mauve-colored folder on the table in front of him.

"Officially, I'm still Maher Shibli. Zoë is the name which I choose for myself after I accepted myself as transgender. I hope one day in the not-too-distant future to legally change my name to Zoë. Something I understand I can only do after you've given me the required medical certificate."

"Oh, I see you are well informed about our process here at the *Genderploeg*. Do you know how this is going to work?" He opened his rather small palms upward as if balancing two invisible plates on each hand.

"You ask me a lot of questions and I answer." I was being cheeky. I shouldn't have.

"No, I was referring to our approach here at *Genderploeg*. Do you know how we will proceed?"

Okay, so we've established that you're as dry as dust. Pedantic and humorless. Great! Just what I needed to make my day.

"Please, I would appreciate if you explained it to me?" I assumed the attitude of a docile student, who had just asked her illustrious professor an important question.

"Our program consists of three phases: 1) Psychological assessment, 2) Hormone Replacement Therapy and

Real-Life Experience, and 3) Sex Reassignment Surgery. At the end of each phase the patient will be given a red, orange or green light, based on the results of our evaluation of their case. Red means the *Genderploeg* is not convinced that the patient is suffering from gender dysphoria and the patient will be referred to a different medical department or back to his or her GP. Orange means we have diagnosed the patient as having gender dysphoria but he or she is not yet ready to proceed to the next phase. And finally, green means that we have diagnosed the patient as being gender dysphoric and are satisfied that he or she meets the required conditions to move to the next phase."

I looked blankly at him. "What do you mean by *required conditions*?"

"It means the patient has the necessary social support structure and is of sound health and can therefore start taking hormones."

I wanted to continue this line of questioning, but Dominic raised his hand to stop me, as if to reinforce the point that he was the one in charge here and also the one who does the questioning.

"Zoë, to be honest, when I look at you, I see a young person who is largely passable as a woman. Not only in your appearance but your body mobility, movement and mannerisms. With the simple application of some makeup and women's clothing, you are already there. It seems to me that that is sufficient. Why put your body through the extremely grueling and punishing process of physically transitioning?"

Did you really just have the nerve to ask me this ridiculous question? I felt my blood start to boil just underneath the surface. I closed my eyes and took a deep breath. *Keep calm, Zoë, this is just a test.*

"Thank you, Dr. van den Broek, for the compliment. I truly appreciate it, as well as your concern. However, it has never been about the makeup and female clothing. I'm not a cross-dresser or a drag queen. I'm transgender; I'm desperate to feel at one with my body all the time, with or without clothes. I want to look in the mirror and just see me, a woman, and not this male vessel my female essence is caged in. This is not a show, Dr. van den Broek, which I put on for society." I had lifted the lid on my emotions slightly. I wanted him to notice my anger and exasperation.

"Zoë, are you presenting as a woman all the time?"

"No, not all the time. Professionally, I mean at work and to my parents, I still present as Maher, as a male. In my private life, however, to my friends and acquaintances, I present as a female, as Zoë."

"Why haven't you started presenting as female at work?"

"Once you give me the green light to legally change my name and gender, I will. I inquired about this at my company's HR department. They can only change my name in the company's administration after I'm legally registered at the municipality as a woman. That can only happen if and when the *Genderploeg* grants me a medical certificate that states that I'm transgender."

"And what if we don't?"

"Don't what?" I feigned incomprehension.

"Don't give you the green light, and don't provide you with the required medical certificate."

Do you realize how irritating you are getting to be?

"Correct me if I'm wrong, Dr. van den Broek, but my understanding is that the *Genderploeg* is here to help me, not hinder me."

"Of course, Zoë." He basically ignored my comment. "May I ask whether you've suicidal thoughts?"

"No!" I lied. "I'm the eternal optimist. As long as there's a chance I will make it to the light at the end of the tunnel, I will never give up. I truly hope you will help me reach that light."

"And what about your parents? Why haven't you come out to them already?"

"I'm not afraid of their expected utter and complete rejection of me. I can deal with that. However, the point that really matters to me is that I don't want to cause them any pain, especially my mother. Their child being transgender is something beyond shocking for them. It's beyond taboo." I went on to explain to him the delicate dynamics at my parents' home as well as my mother's fragile health.

"Zoë, I would still like to see your parents, as part of my evaluation."

You just keep pushing the wrong buttons. Don't you know when to stop, you little fuck?

"I'm sorry but that won't be possible. You are welcome to speak with my brother or sister or both."

Through Johan, I knew perfectly well that I could hold my position on this point. The *Genderploeg* has no right to force a meeting with my parents. Furthermore, this shouldn't have any negative consequences on my evaluation.

"Alright, Zoë. Let's discuss this point another time."

No Pandejo! There will be no concession on this point. You are not going to see my parents. Period.

"Dr. van den Broek, my parents are not Dutch. They are from the Middle East and have deeply entrenched conservative values. Their antagonism and fear of everything LGBT is probably beyond your comprehension. Your approach with regards to this point needs to be culturally sensitive, tactful and delicate. Please!" I pleaded.

Dominic looked down at his Omega Seamaster wristwatch and laid down his pen.

For fuck's sake, Dominic! Are you listening to me?

"Zoë, our time is up for today. I will ask the hospital administration to schedule an appointment every three weeks for the next six months. Before you leave the hospital, please inform our secretary to issue you with a hospital card."

"Thank you, Dr. van den Broek, for the care."

Dominic, you're an asshole!

25

Sex and All That Jazz

Journal entry # 904$
Westeneinde Hospital,
Amsterdam, Feb 2016

"Zoë, during today's appointment we'll be shedding some light on sex, in other words, your sexuality," Dominic explained.

"What about it would you like to know?"

"Basically everything." His cold eyes meticulously scanned my face. They were trying to penetrate deep into my soul.

That irked me but I decided to fight fire with fire. I matched his intense scrutiny with an equally intense gaze.

Dominic, I'm not a kid! Your psycho-shrewd techniques don't intimidate me.

"It's a broad subject. Can you be more specific?" I countered. "It would be helpful."

"Why don't you start with the first thing that comes to mind."

"Okay." I smiled meekly and cleared my throat.

"Please continue." Dominic gestured with his hand to emphasize the point.

"I hate my male genitals, with a capital 'H', to the point that if I touched them, I would quickly wash my hands."

"Really?"

"Yes, really. I recall, as a teenager, once telling my brother the disgust I felt when I saw boys fondling and touching their genitals. His reaction to this was one of surprise and confusion: 'Why shouldn't boys touch their genitals? Why do you think that way?' I didn't dare answer him back.

"This hate was sometimes so overpowering and overbearing that I wondered what the consequences of severing my genitals from my body would be? Half a dozen times, while I stood alone in the bathroom, doors locked, tears streaming down my cheeks, my hands shaking violently with the penis caught between scissor blades, I would find myself at the center of a nauseating whirlwind of questions: 'Will I faint after?' 'Would I survive the bleeding?' 'Am I really such a coward that I can't complete what needs to be done?' Luckily, I was never crazy or foolhardy enough to see it through."

My hand started trembling under the table that separated us. I loathe recalling this particular childhood trauma that was literally inches away (pun intended) from ending with a bloodbath between my legs.

"Zoë, are you okay? You look pale. Shall we take a break? Or can we continue?"

No, dickhead, I'm not okay. I just gave you access to a childhood trauma and that's all the emotion and empathy you can muster? I know you're supposed to be this detached and cold-hearted professional but frankly this is bordering on the ridiculous.

I took a deep breath and exhaled. I felt sick. *The sooner we finished this interview the better.*

"I'm okay. Let's continue."

"You do realize that the surgeons actually need your male genitals, especially the penis, for the Sex Reassignment Surgery?"

"Yeah. I became aware of that much later. That's why I say, luckily I stopped myself from carrying out the deed."

"Zoë, you do masturbate, don't you?"

"Of course, I masturbate. I'm human."

"I thought you said that it disgusted you to touch yourself there?"

"Yes, that's correct. Do you really want to know how I masturbate?" Dominic nodded.

"I put a pillow between my legs and rub my genitals vigorously against it until I cum. All the while I'm imagining I have a vagina."

"What about your sexual experiences, Zoë?"

So, you're not going to back off, are you?

"I've never actually had a satisfying and fulfilling sexual

experience with anyone in my entire life. How can I when I am not being honest with them or myself about my true nature? Don't misunderstand me – I was genuinely interested in and wanted the full intimate companionship with a woman, but ultimately, the sex was a charade."

"What do you mean by 'charade'?"

"Well, it was all make believe. The women in my past thought they were with a heterosexual man, and I tried very hard to be that for them. I am a very good kisser and very sensual with my hands and tongue. However, sexual intercourse was always very complicated and ultimately hugely frustrating for me. In my mind, I longed to be touched like a woman. That, of course, never happened."

"So how did you achieve intercourse or orgasm?"

There's no stopping you today, Dominic. Johan was right about you – 'Genderploeg's psychologists are not there to support the patients but to evaluate them. They will not keep a stone unturned.'

"I'm not impotent, if that's what you're thinking. However, to maintain an erection and reach orgasm I needed to use a great deal of imaginative power and fantasy. Basically, I would induce my mind to imagine myself to be in a female body and my partner to be male. Role reversal, I guess, but all in my head."

"How did this make you feel?"

"After orgasm, instead of feeling euphoria, I would secretly feel revulsion, disgust and anger with myself. I also felt a great deal of sadness for my partner – she deserved to be with a real man, not with one pretending to be one. Funny, isn't it, how sex is ultimately the great equalizer."

"Equalizer? What does that mean?" Dominic shot back.

"I'm not sure if 'equalizer' is the right word. What I meant to say is that sex will always reveal to you your true nature. It's humankind's most primary and basic of instincts. It can't be forever subdued by dogma, religion, culture or, for that matter by anything else, really."

"And what about your sexual orientation?"

"Are you asking me if I'm still attracted to women?"

"Are you?"

"Yes, but not exclusively. Ever since my coming out, I can't help but feel physically drawn to men as well. I believe I'm bisexual. That said, I haven't had sex since coming out. And I won't for a while, not until after the sex-change operation."

"In this hospital, we prefer to use the term Sex Reassignment Surgery or SRS for short."

Oh! How mighty humane and progressive of you!

"Sorry, as a transgender, I should know better."

"What about fetishes, Zoë?"

I felt my eyes cloud and my soul darken a few shades.

Fuck off, Dominic! Now you've crossed a red line. What a hypocrite! If a cis woman were to tell you she gets a kick from wearing her stilettos or thigh-high boots during sex, you wouldn't hold that against her. So why the prejudice toward trans women when it comes to fetishes and kinks? That somehow it delegitimizes us. No, Dominic! Pantera is off limits to you and the system.

"No, Dr. van den Broek, I don't think I have any fetishes. I've always preferred sex *au naturel.*"

26

Psychological Assessment Nº 4

Journal entry # 906$
Westeneinde Hospital,
Amsterdam, Mar 2016

N adine accompanied me to my fourth appointment at Westeneinde with Dominic. After much ado about nothing, he succumbed to the option of meeting my sister, instead of my parents. According to the Standards of Care as stipulated by WPATH (World Professional Association for Transgender Health), the assessing psychologist should have the opportunity to interview a close relative or friend of the patient, provided they have known the patient for an adequate length of time. Nadine and Zachariah both fit the bill perfectly, so why Dominic insisted and subsequently made a fuss about seeing my parents, I don't know. I did ask him once to clarify, but he wasn't forthcoming. I'm left guessing he's someone who's set in his ways and opinions, professional or otherwise.

Anyways, it finally fell upon Nadine to provide him with the third person's views and insights. Consciously, I did not discuss the appointment with Nadine beforehand. I wanted her to respond to Dominic's questions without being influenced (or tainted) by my own take on things. Jules, my notes on how today's interview went:

- Nadine was visibly nervous and defensive. Although she wasn't the person under the spotlight, her cramped body language and verbal terseness gave off the vibe of being the one who's being analyzed.

- Nadine indicated that she had no inkling to think that I might be transgender (before my coming out). She did, however, suspect that I might be gay. When asked why she thought this, she replied that it was because of my tendency to wear tight and colorful clothes in addition to my mannerisms, which tended to be rather elegant and delicate.

- She has embraced me completely as her sister and supports my transition wholeheartedly.

- After my coming out, she felt that we had grown even closer to each other than we were before my transition. When asked why, she responded that it was because I'd become a much more open person.

Maher was always wearing a mask which obscured things; Zoë isn't. *Isn't what?* She isn't wearing a mask.

Thank you, Nadine, for being there for me, especially during those dark and tough times. I love you with all my heart.

27

Psychological Tests

Journal entry # 909$
Westeneinde Hospital,
Amsterdam, Apr 2016

For the fifth psychological assessment, I was given a hefty bundle of multiple-choice questions to answer. I didn't count how many questions, but judging by the thickness of the physical pile of paper, I guess that there were more than three hundred questions in total.

I was allocated three hours to complete the tests. A student (after all Westeneinde is an academic hospital) was given the task of keeping an eye on me. I completed the tests within an hour. To be more exact, it took me fifty-seven minutes from beginning to end.

28

Le Charming Postman

Journal entry # 924$
Rotterdam, Apr 2016
🎧 Carpenters – Please Mr. Postman

I confess to you, Jules, that it's a weird time in my life. At work (and the few hours directly before and after), I present to the world as Maher. Outside of work, I present as Zoë. On a few occasions this has resulted in comic moments. To illustrate, this week the following transpired:

On Thursday:

- *DING DONG!* It's the postman with a package.

- I open the door; the postman sees Maher.

- I say hello to him cheerfully.

- His face goes from indifferent to grumpy.

- He shoves the package in my hands, mumbles something unintelligible and walks away.

- I think to myself: *How Rude!*

One day later:

- *DING DONG!* It's the exact same postman with a package.

- I open the door; the postman sees Zoë.

- His face lights up. He smiles from ear to ear and greets me warmly.

- I do not reciprocate. My face remains expressionless – I can't even be bothered to say hello.

- With a soft, kind voice he asks me to sign for the package and then ever so delicately places it in my hands as if they were made of Dutch China.

- He thanks me and wishes me a good day.

- I think to myself: *You bastard! Yesterday you treated me like shit, and today you treat me like I'm a princess.*

Jules, with this example, you might be misled to think that women are treated better than men. The stark truth is: the advantages of being a woman pale into insignificance compared to the advantages of being a man, especially in the realm of safety. As Maher, I never think twice about my safety when I'm in the public domain. As a woman, in the same space, I feel sometimes uneasy, less safe and yes, on a certain level, threatened. In other words, being outside is, for Zoë, definitely not spontaneous and carefree, the way it is for Maher. And this is just one example.

29

Psychological Assessment N° 6

Journal entry # 1001$
Westeneinde Hospital,
Amsterdam, May 2016

The sixth appointment with Dominic was mainly for the purpose of discussing the results of the psychological tests which I had taken the previous month. It would also provide him with the opportunity to ask for further clarifications on some of the answers I had given.

I was stunned to learn that Dominic hadn't evaluated my test papers. We ended up rehashing points which we had already covered in previous appointments. What a disappointment! I was genuinely looking forward to this appointment as it marked a symbolic and important milestone of phase 1. The evaluation of the psychological tests is one of the last pieces in the puzzle, leading up to the 'traffic light' decision at the closing stage of the psychological assessment phase. To add insult to injury, it wasn't just time wasting but money wasting, as well. It costs me almost forty euros to travel to Westeneinde and make use of their ridiculously overpriced parking garage.

30

Psychological Assessment N° 7

Journal entry # 1003$
Westeneinde Hospital,
Amsterdam, Jun 2016

"Zoë, I've analyzed your psychological test results. I need you to clarify something for me?" Dominic asked.

"Yes, of course. What's that?"

"You mentioned that sometimes you felt like you're intersex[17]. Anatomically speaking, you're not intersex, so why do you say that?"

17 Intersex: a person born with both male and female genitalia

You're sharp, Dominic, very sharp. I grant you that.

"Since childhood, in my sleep, I've had this recurring dream, wherein I'm conscious of my vagina. I believe that this incessant dream is trying to tell me something."

"Which is?"

"That underneath the skin, I have a vagina. It's there. Just hidden."

Dominic's eyes sparkled and for the first time since the start of our sessions back in January, a semblance of a smile gleamed on his good-looking face.

"Zoë, I believe we are done here."

"Huh! I don't understand. What are you saying?" I froze, sensing an incoming panic attack.

"Calm down! I wanted to say that as far as I'm concerned you are ready to proceed to the next phase. During the upcoming General Assessment Meeting, I will strongly recommend that the *Genderploeg* gives you the green light to move to the next phase, the 'Hormone Treatment Therapy' phase."

"Oh, my goodness, Dr. van den Broek. Really?" Out of sheer joy, I jumped out of my chair and thought about running around the desk that separated us and giving him a big hug. Fortunately, I stopped myself – I don't think Dominic would have appreciated that.

"Really, Dr. van den Broek, thank you so much." I giggled and hugged myself instead.

"The upcoming General Assessment Meeting is on July 12. After the meeting, I will call you to inform you of the *Genderploeg's* decision. It should be a formality." Now Dominic had a full-blown, hearty smile on his face, one which mimicked mine.

31

Revolving Door

Journal entry # 1006$
Rotterdam, Jul 2016
🎧 Melanie Martinez – Carousel

"I'm gobsmacked, Dr. van den Broek. I don't know how to react to this news. Orange! Why? What happened?"

"The *Genderploeg* does not dispute my assessment that you are suffering from acute gender dysphoria, but they are of the opinion that you are not yet ready to move on to the next phase."

"Huh? But why? I don't understand this decision?" I felt the ground beneath me shift. I wanted to throw up.

"Because you've not yet come out to your parents."

"What? Seriously?" I shut my eyes in disgust and agony for a few seconds. "But I explained the reasoning behind that to you in detail."

"The *Genderploeg* has made its decision. Based on this, we've concluded that we can't let you move on to the next phase."

"But that's not what you told me last time. You said that—"

Dominic interrupted me. "Stop, Zoë! I stand by the *Genderploeg's* decision."

Of course, you do! You spineless iguana. Volte-face! This is nothing short of a blatant U-turn.

"So, what now?" I was grasping at straws.

"The *Genderploeg* is going into summer recess for the entire month of August. I've scheduled an extra session with you in September. We'll take it from there. Until then, goodbye." Dominic hung up.

I stood there, suspended in disbelief, staring at my smartphone's screen. I was shocked, lost and devastated. *For fuck's sake, Dominic, at least have the decency to say sorry or express some sympathy for me after this totally unexpected U-turn. You said it was going to be a formality…*

Feeling the strain of being on my feet for what felt like hours, my legs finally buckled under me. 68, 69, 70, 71. I collapsed on the sofa in my living room, buried my head in my hands and cried for hours.

32

Detour

Journal entry # 1007$
Rotterdam, Jul 2016

Today, Jules, I relayed yesterday's horrible news from the *Genderploeg* to Johan. I reached out to him for guidance and support. On both accounts he was there for me, and then some. Although my existential journey has hit a serious road-block, Johan urged me to keep the faith.

"With a little help from me, Zoë," he said, "you will get to the light at the end of the tunnel."

Further to his feedback:

- Dominic bungled the job causing unnecessary

distress and delay. My dossier should have been easy pickings.

- Johan is really disappointed in Dominic's performance, considering that he firmly believed that Dominic was one of the rising stars of the *Genderploeg*.

- With regards to my parents, the *Genderploeg* should have definitely taken into consideration the cultural dimension. Their standard template, which is primarily designed to deal with patients of Dutch or Western-origins, does not adequately address this matter.

- Johan instructed me to prepare and subsequently email a document detailing the arguments why I have consciously, after consulting with my brother and sister, chosen not to inform my parents. The arguments should focus on two fronts:

  1. The protection of my mother.

  2. My parents are not part of my support structure.

- In my upcoming appointment (in a week's time) with Johan, we will start preparing for my coming out at work. According to Johan: "The train keeps moving on – that will be our next station."

33

Psychological Assessment N° 8

Journal entry # 1020$
Westeneinde Hospital,
Amsterdam, Sep 2016
🎧 Michelle Gurevich – First Six Months of Love

Dominic sat opposite me in his office at Westeneinde.
Gone are the verve and enthusiasm, which he displayed during our last face-to-face appointment just before
he presented my dossier to his colleagues in the *Genderploeg*.
The positive vibes and energy of that meeting seem like a
long time ago.

"I've read the document you emailed me, Zoë. Thanks for the detailed information. I would like to go through it with you now."

"Of course. That's why I am here. Your success at the next General Assessment Meeting is my success. We are allies in this."

In the following half hour, we went through my document line by line. From time to time, Dominic would highlight some of the text with a bright yellow marker.

"I'm going to put your dossier on the agenda for the General Assessment Meeting in October. I will recommend that *Genderploeg* give you the green light to proceed to the next phase. With this extra input, we're in a stronger position than last time."

"Thank you, Dr. van den Broek. Both Dr. de Zeelander and I are convinced that you will succeed this time." I intentionally dropped Johan's name, knowing full well that the *Genderploeg* held him in high esteem.

"There's one more thing, Dr. van den Broek. Please do not take what I'm going to say as some kind of coercion because I assure you it isn't. See it as additional relevant feedback from your patient."

Dominic blinked a few times.

"Yes, Zoë, what is it?" There was a discernable note of apprehension in his voice.

"Doctor, if the *Genderploeg* blocks me again, I will start self-medicating. Testosterone blockers and estrogen pills are easily obtained online. Yes, they are generic, and I'm aware they could be of substandard quality and therefore potentially harmful." I paused for a few seconds. "All this time, I've been an exemplary patient, but you forget, I'm also a patient in terrible pain. What other patient in the medical system needs to wait more than six months for a prescription?"

34

3rd Key

Journal entry # 1029$
Rotterdam, Oct 2016

Jules, if you could make your smartphone catch fire by simply staring at it, mine would have been reduced to a smoldering pile of ash by now. In anticipation of Dominic's call with the result from the *Genderploeg*, I've been doing just that for the past three hours. It's *make or break* time for me. Literally!

Yesterday night was one of the worst in my life. I was consumed many times over by agitation, restlessness and multiple bad dreams. I can't recall the substance but they felt bad, very bad. *If you can't sleep, get out of bed and distract yourself by reading a book or watching a movie,* Johan had advised me on more than one occasion. I tried it but couldn't get my mind to let go.

When my smartphone finally started buzzing, I almost had a heart attack.

"Hello, Zoë. This is Dominic, your assessing psychologist from the *Genderploeg*."

God, I know who you are, Dominic. Please just tell me the result.

"Good morning, Dr. Van den Broek."

"As you well know, this morning the *Genderploeg* discussed your dossier for the second time."

Fuck it, Dominic! Tell me the result before I self-combust.

"Yes! And?"

"I'm happy to inform you that the *Genderploeg* has endorsed my recommendation and has given you the green light. You can now proceed to the next phase. I've already scheduled an appointment for you with one of my endocrinologist colleagues. She will prescribe you the necessary medication."

I wanted to say something meaningful, but nothing came out of my mouth. I was simply flabbergasted!

"Zoë, are you still there?"

"WOW! Dr. van den Broek, I can't find the words to express my relief and happiness."

"You can pick up the medical certificate in a month's time. It's going to be alright, Zoë. I wish you all the best."

"Oh, Dr. van den Broek, before you go. I want to say a very big thank you to you and your colleagues at the *Genderploeg*. Thank you with all my heart." I was utterly sincere in my sentiment. It was as if with one swift stroke, all the pent-up anger I harbored for the *Genderploeg* had completely dissipated.

Besides accepting myself as transgender, the *Genderploeg's* decision to give me the green light is probably the most important development in my journey, so far. It is the key that unlocks so many doors that hitherto were bolted shut in my face. Jules, it is the key that unlocks the doors to:

1. Hormone Therapy Treatment and the start to body feminization.

2. Legally changing my sex and name at all government organizations and public institutions.

3. As a consequence of number 2 above, the change of my name and title from Mr. to Ms. at my company and all other companies, e.g., utilities, transport, banks, shops, etc.

4. Voice-feminization sessions with a logopedics expert.

5. Coverage by my medical insurance company of facial electrolysis costs. Until now, I've been paying for this out of my own pocket. It has cost me an arm and a leg. I still need upward of fifty electrolysis sessions to eradicate all the beard follicles in my face and neck.

Later down the line:

1. Sex Reassignment Surgery, and possibly,

2. Breast Enlargement Surgery.

That dim light at the end of the long dark tunnel just got markedly brighter. Jules, on this day I decided to stop all 'pizza mutilations' on my arms. I will also start applying medical-grade silicone gel on the most recent scars. Can't have the hospital people find out about this.

III

TRANSFORMATION

1

Cold Turkey

Journal entry # 1032$
Rotterdam, Oct 2016
🎧 Michelle Gurevich – Poison in My Mind

I doubled over the toilet bowl and after a few violent con-vulsions, threw up the entire contents of my stomach. The thick fog of nausea and the acrid smell of vomit hung heavy around my head. My temples throbbed with a sting-ing pain as if *kobolds* had descended from the ceiling above me and with their pickaxes and hammers gave my head a proper whacking.

Acidity burned the back of my throat and pharynx.

I can't clear my throat – it's too sore. I took a few deep breaths, hoping that would help me find my balance again. Alas, the hiatus was short-lived as the convulsions flared up again; I doubled one more time to send a torrid of filthy orangish brown fluid out of my mouth. One more upheaval like that and I swear the innards of my entire digestive system will end up in the toilet bowl.

Every muscle, every sinew in my body ached with an intensity I'd never experienced before. Had I not collapsed onto the bathroom floor out of sheer exhaustion, I'd be in bed shivering and sweating out of every pore.

It's been three days since I stopped taking the prescription-grade codeine mixture cold turkey. I'm not naïve – I was expecting withdrawal symptoms but nothing as disgusting and painful as this.

Gradually weaning myself off the opioid was not an option. In a little over ten days, I have my first appointment with the *Genderploeg's* endocrinologist. If all goes to plan, the endocrinologist will prescribe me the hormone treatment, and the feminization process of my body can start in earnest. From trusted sources, I understood that the *Genderploeg* would conduct a very extensive blood and urine test to check for any anomaly that might complicate the intake of hormones. I wasn't going to let anything sabotage that process – no way anything is coming between me and those hormones. Anyway, the worst of the withdrawal symptoms is probably behind me. My body should slowly adjust to life without that deliciously venomous opioid.

2

Office Inner-Circle

Journal entry # 1034$
Company HQ,
Amsterdam, Oct 2016

Waiting for an appointment to take place, while a hefty dose of nervousness and anxiety consumed the innards of my stomach, seems to be the leitmotif of my life right now. I sat alone in the meeting room on the fifth floor at my company's corporate headquarters.

Is it cold or is it just me? My fingers are freezing. I rubbed my palms vigorously trying to get the blood flowing in them. *What's that I hear?* I heard the muffled voices of Lieselotte and my manager, Daan, just beyond the closed door. Any second now this door will swing wide open and we'll all flash wide, toothy, but contrived, smiles.

"Hello, Maher. How are you? It's been a while since we last spoke." Lieselotte walked in, beaming.

That's not entirely true, Lieselotte! Just the other day I asked you how you're doing in the office kitchenette but you were too busy to answer me, let alone acknowledge I was there.

"Yeah, it's been a while, but always nice to see you, Lieselotte." Once more, I flashed my corporate smile at her, for perception's sake.

Lieselotte is one of the HR officers assigned to my division. In her late forties, tall and athletic, she had an extremely well-toned body and the agility to match.

"Hey, Maher. How was your vacation? Did you enjoy Spain?" Daan tried to make himself relevant.

Wonderful, Daan. Thank you for asking. I spent most of it on my knees, with my head in a toilet bowl, vomiting.

"It was great, Daan. I flew down to Andalucía for a bit of sun, tapas, and sightseeing," I lied.

With all three attendees seated, Lieselotte was the first to get down to business.

"Maher, you asked to see me and Daan together. It's not entirely clear to us what the subject matter is? Something to do with private issues?"

"Correct. But before I expand on that, let me be very clear this does not involve any colleague at the company. It's just about me." This statement clearly had the impact I had hoped for. They both relaxed visibly. Lieselotte's frown was replaced by a smile. This time it was genuine.

"How can we help you, Maher?"

"The information that I'm about to disclose is of a

medical nature and must remain confidential until further notice." Concern clouded both sets of eyes opposite me. Daan turned to look at Lieselotte. Lieselotte kept her eyes fixed on me. "There's a major and significant development in my life, which I need to share with you. Since January of this year, I've been in the care of the *Genderploeg* at Westeneinde Hospital."

Daan looked somewhat puzzled. However, Lieselotte maintained a cool and professional facade. She nodded her head a few times.

"Please continue, Maher."

Okay, here it comes, folks.

"I've been formally diagnosed by a medical team specialized in gender issues as transgender."

Daan's eyes almost popped out of his head and was about to say something when Lieselotte lifted her right index finger to cut him short.

"Continue, Maher," she said, her voice calm and reassuring.

"After a lengthy and exhaustive psychological evaluation, the *Genderploeg* has concluded that I have a condition called gender dysphoria. Soon I will commence with hormone replacement therapy, and once I've legally changed my name and sex, I will start with what's called the *Real-Life Experience* phase."

"And when you're in the Real-Life Experience phase, you will be presenting fulltime as a woman. Isn't that correct, Maher?" Lieselotte interjected.

"Huh!" It was my turn to be surprised. "Are you familiar with transgenders?"

"Until now, not directly, but I have a Master of Science

in Psychology and am familiar with gender dysphoria and its consequences."

Really! This is an unexpected piece of good luck. I couldn't conceal my satisfaction.

"Lieselotte, I'm truly grateful to hear this and consider myself lucky to have you as my HR contact person on this matter."

"When will you be coming out at work?"

"Soon after I've arranged a new passport and national ID card. With my new name and sex, of course."

"That's good, Maher, since we're legally not allowed to change your name and gender details in the company's administrative system until you provide us with a new ID."

"What about my email account? Once I start presenting as a woman, I will need a new email account with my new name."

"Yes, that's possible. We'll take care of that together with the administrative change."

"Once again, I need to stress that this information is strictly confidential. I trust that you and Daan will not share it with any other colleague outside this room."

"Agreed," Lieselotte affirmed. "However, I would advise you to inform Marcus Ockermann, head of our division, as soon as possible. We're going to need him on this."

Wow, Lieselotte! It's like you're reading from Johan's script on how to come out at work. Amazing! I'm starting to wonder if you've done this before.

"Lieselotte, you seem very knowledgeable on how to deal with this matter. Are there any other transgenders in the company?"

"In the company, yes. In our division, no!"

"Hmm, is it possible for me to contact this colleague?"

"I will see what I can do for you. I will consult with an HR colleague of mine without mentioning your name."

"Super! That would be amazing!" I thanked her.

"Don't count your chickens, Maher. There's no guarantee that the transgender colleague will be forthcoming. Worth the shot though."

"One more thing, Lieselotte, Daan?"

"Yes?"

"Until my official coming out to my team and colleagues, please continue to interact with me as Maher."

"Of course!" Lieselotte smiled. "May I ask about your new name?"

Foxy! Lieselotte!

"No. Not yet. But soon. I promise. What I can tell you right now is that it won't be Middle Eastern. I'm going to change both my first name and surname to western names."

"So, you're dropping your family name, as well? That's unusual." Lieselotte was intrigued.

"No. Not from where I'm sitting."

3

Marcus Ockermann

Journal entry # 1035$
Company HQ,
Amsterdam, Oct 2016

Kurt, my nemesis at Megalaar, walked across the hall toward me with a big, crafty smirk on his face.

"Hey there, Maher. Heard from Daan you've been to Spain for a short vacation?"

Fuck off! I know you better, Kurt. As usual you want to take a dig at me.

"Yes, Kurt. Do you need anything?"

"Where did you spend your time in Spain? In a tunnel? You look as pale as death." He laughed out loud.

Bugger off and get out of my way! I don't have time for your nonsense.

I ignored Kurt and turned my back to him to address Marcus, who'd just walked past us. He was probably on his way to the management assistants' room.

"Good morning, sir! Can I have a few minutes of your time?"

"Sure, Maher. What's it about?" Marcus looked a little surprised that I had approached him.

"I'd prefer if we did this somewhere more private."

We stepped into an empty meeting room. Marcus took a nearby seat and swung an arm over the backrest. At 1.92 meters, he is a giant of a man, who carries himself with uber confidence and the swagger of a man who knows he's made it. Marcus oozes power and privilege, and for that alone, some of company's wannabees, or management high-potentials as the company like to call them, hang on his every word as if he's already achieved the status of 'Captain of Industry', which he hasn't, yet. On top of everything else, to rub salt into the wounds of a lesser mortal, he is very smart, eloquent, good looking and seems to always sport a healthy bronze glow. For that alone, I disliked him.

"Is this about the Ancillary Revenues project?"

"No, sir. It's something private and personal."

"Are you going to come out?" Marcus smiled. It was a sly, foxy smile, which unsettled me, somewhat.

I can't believe it. That idiot Daan must have blurted out my secret which I had shared with him and Lieselotte in confidence.

"Huh! What makes you say that?"

"My apologies, Maher. It was just a hunch, a passing thought. Do continue with what you were going to say."

"Actually, yes, I am going to come out. I've been diagnosed as transgender by the *Genderploeg* at Westeneinde Hospital."

There I said it. Are you shocked now? Marcus continued to smile warmly.

"I've always perceived something feminine about you, yet it was not gay-like. So, no, Maher, this does not surprise me."

If this is true then I'm really impressed with your strength of perception, Mr. Marcus Ockermann. I'm starting to think I'm the one who has misperceived you. You are not at all the egomaniac I convinced myself you were.

"Thank you, sir. That's really perceptive of you. I must admit that I'm impressed." Without intending it, I was starting to sound like one of his corporate groupies, which I had sworn never to be.

Marcus waved his hand as if to suggest he's not *that* special. "I'm a people's manager, Maher. I make it my business to understand what makes a person tick. And in your case, I've always felt that you're an enigma, like you were holding something back and that this something, in turn, was holding *you* back. Now, finally, I understand what this something is."

I was totally gobsmacked. I had utterly misjudged him.

"Can I ask you for a favor, sir?"

"Sure, Maher. Feel free to speak your mind."

"Thank you. In a few months, after I get my new passport and national ID card, I intend to come out to all my colleagues at the company. When that happens, I would appreciate it if you could send an email, in your capacity as head of this division, to our colleagues to inform them of my personal development."

Marcus nodded in agreement.

"Send me a draft with the most important points you wish to be communicated. Separately, make a list of things I should avoid."

Funny this! Johan and I were already busy working on such a draft.

"Yes, sir. I will do that. Thank you so much for your help."

"And when?"

"Sorry, sir. When what?"

"When do you want me to send this email on your behalf?"

"On the day I come out to my team. The best estimate I can give is that it will be in January next year."

"Good. Oh, and send the draft to my private email account." On a piece of paper, he scribbled down an iCloud email account. "More than one management assistant has access to my business mailbox. I assume this is to remain our secret till then." He winked.

"Yes. Sir, this really means a lot to me. I can't express how grateful I am." I couldn't help but feel deeply touched.

"Don't mention it. I'm a staunch believer in personal freedoms. In my opinion, a transgender person's right to express his or her true identity, and transition to it, is the ultimate manifestation of those principles. I'm proud of you because you have what it takes to go through this enormous change. Just half an hour ago, Kurt from Customer

Experience was telling me that you're someone who's afraid of change. He has no idea how wrong he is about you."

"It's unfortunate that Kurt said that about me. He and I do not see eye to eye on how to execute the project we're working on, and he hasn't been exactly a team player, to put it mildly."

Marcus understood the message I was trying to convey to him diplomatically.

"You're doing a good job, Maher, on the Priority M project. Keep it up!"

Sir, if only you knew. Work is the only thing in my life I'm still good at. Once upon a time I would have gone as far as to say that I was a stellar project manager. Today, however, with my health failing, I'm at best okay. On top of everything, it doesn't help that I have to work twice as hard to achieve half the recognition of a Dutch colleague, like that snake, Kurt. But, sir, you wouldn't know anything about that. About how hard it is to get recognition – would you?

4

My Hormones are Raging

Journal entry # 1039$
Rotterdam, Nov 2016

For the second day in a row, I woke up in the middle of the night in a puddle of sweat. My pajamas and the bedsheet underneath me were soaked to the point that they clung to my body like a soggy second skin. *Yuck!* And there is more: my head, especially at the back, as well as my neck were as hot as coal embers in a fire-burner on a cold December night. Jules, I haven't the least doubt that this a consequence of starting with the hormone replacement therapy.

Three days ago, I started taking the hormone pills, which the *Genderploeg's* endocrinologist had prescribed for me. For the greater good, i.e., the feminization of my body, I'm willing to accept this and any other physical inconvenience the transition will throw my way.

If all goes well, those two prescription pills, which go by the clinical names of cyproterone acetate[18] and estradiol, will respectively block testosterone (male hormone) and boost estrogen (female hormone) levels in my body. Like a two-pronged attack, they are my ticket to a more feminine body. They should trigger the development of bigger breasts and buttocks, a smaller waist, wider hips and overall smoother skin. All this is down to the fact that those pills will start redistributing the fat in my body. My face, especially the cheeks, should also start to fill out, giving my face a more rounded and plumper look, as opposed to the rather gaunt and angular look I have today. It will also lead to a loss in muscle volume and lesser hair all over. Unfortunately, they won't have any impact on my facial hair. Those hairs will still need to be lasered or electrically epilated.

Oh, sweet mother of Jesus! I pray and hope that my body will respond well to the medication, and soon I and others will see significant physical changes.

In any case, the first victory, noticeable within a few hours from starting with the pills, is already in the bag. The penis (for I will never call it mine!) has gone *totalmente* limp. Hurray! No more erections. *Zero! Zilch! Nada!* What a massive relief that from now on, when I wake up in the morning, there will be no more raising of the man-

---

18 In the United States, trans women are usually prescribed Spironolactone as a male-hormone blocker.

hood flag. I can only imagine that for some men, morning erections are experienced as some kind of phallic triumph – a manifestation of masculine strength and potency. For me, however, erections have always had the exact opposite effect. They were the tragic manifestation of the mismatch between my brain and body, and a reminder (in the worst possible way) of my captivity in a body that's not mine.

According to the endocrinologist, it will take up two years to see the full results of the hormone therapy. I will also need to be on the pills for at least one and half years, before the hospital will consider the next big step in my transition, i.e., the sex-change operation, or Sex Reassignment Surgery, as Johan keeps reminding me.

5

Parlez-Vous Cher?

Journal entry # 1041$
Rotterdam, Nov 2016
🎧 Sara Bareilles – Little Voice

"Go on, Zoë dear, push that voice higher. Higher! Higher!" Bianca instructed while raising her right hand upward.

Goodness me, woman! Have mercy on me! If I push any higher my vocal cords are going to snap.

"AaaaaAAAAAA." I was completely out of breath and my throat stung. I paused to take in a much-needed gulp of air. "I'm doing my best," I protested.

"No, dear, you're not doing your best. What you are doing has nothing to do with Voice Feminization whatsoever," Bianca countered.

Well, duh! That's why I'm here. So that you can teach me.

"I'm here to learn from you. Bianca, I desperately need to do something about my voice. It's too deep and masculine. These days I find myself being extremely reluctant, if not downright terrified, to speak to strangers, especially on the phone. I feel once they hear my voice, they will *clock me*, misgender me with the dreaded 'Mister'."

Jules, if you were to picture a big, strong, blond, blue-eyed woman, the archetypal 'Helga' from the former Democratic Republic of Germany, then probably you'd visualize more or less accurately Ms. Bianca Grossmeyer, my new and highly rated logopedic therapist. Her practice was a small two-story house based in a leafy neighborhood of Rotterdam, close to the zoo.

"Pay attention, dear. I'm going to demonstrate four characteristics of the human voice, which play a significant role in how others perceive your voice as male or female. By the way, would you like a cup of tea? It will help lubricate those strained cords of yours. Never coffee. That'll dry out your mouth and throat."

"Sure. A cup of tea would be nice. Do you have English Breakfast or Earl Grey?" I wanted something other than lemon-green tea, which tends to be the default tea at such venues.

After a few minutes, Bianca came back with two mugs of Earl Grey tea.

"Earl and Lady Grey are my favorite." She winked. "So, where were we? Ah, yes. The four basic components of the human voice. 1. Pitch, 2. Resonance, 3. Articulation, and 4. Intonation.

"Listen carefully dear. Number one! Pitch is the frequency of your voice. The higher the frequency, the more feminine it will sound. You need to start pushing your voice upward by relocating *the source* of your voice away from your chest and into your mouth. Men's voices mostly start in their chest area. Women's voices, on the other hand, start in the mouth. The further upward you push your voice, away from your chest and throat, the higher your pitch will be. But be careful not to push your voice into your nose. If that happens, you'll start speaking in falsetto, something like Mickey Mouse voice. Number two, resonance! You need to consciously resonate the letters, especially 'm' and 'n'. Have you noticed how women usually extend and resonate their 'm's and 'n's? Listen carefully to how I say, '*Namen, Numen, Nemen*'.

"Number three! Articulate! Pay close attention to how women articulate their words. Generally, consonants sound crisper and more precise, with every word well-articulated. Men have a lazy tendency to mumble and swallow some letters, especially the last letter of a word. And four, intonation. Notice how melodic and colorful women's voices are, with considerable variations upward and downward, while men's voices tend to be flat and monotonous."

"That's quite a list, Bianca." My facial expressions betrayed my lack of confidence in achieving a feminine voice in the foreseeable future.

"Don't worry, dear. With my help, you'll get there, but it's going to require lots of effort and daily exercises on your part."

"I'm in." I breathed in deeply and tried to visualize in my head the information Bianca had just shared with me.

"Tell me, dear, what are your ambitions and expectations with regards to feminizing your voice?"

"Well, I would be extremely happy if one day I had a voice similar to Cher's. Meaning a voice that's deep, darkish but unmistakably feminine."

"Fine, Zoë. I'm glad you said that. If you'd said that you wanted to have a voice like Britney Spears, I would have kicked you out of my practice." She lifted her mug to her mouth and smiled. "I'll see you next week."

6

Van Vixenhoven

Journal entry # 1049$
Rotterdam, Dec 2016

The large Philips TV screen, mounted on the wall opposite me, indicated that they were now serving numbers A28, A29 and B16 at the counters. In my cold hands, I was holding a ticket with number A32. That means there are only two customers ahead of me in the queue.

The elegant waiting room in Rotterdam's Stadhuis, a grand, neo-Renaissance building dating from 1914 which served as its Town Hall, was already half full with the good citizens of the city going about their legal business.

Even though I find myself unable to stop my feet from thumping, I'm actually not nervous, just excited. After all, I've been anticipating this moment for a very long time and dreaming about it like forever.

DING DONG! No kidding, Jules, that's exactly the sound the Queueing Management System produced, indicating that counter 5 was now serving customer A32. I jumped out of my seat like a spring which had been recoiled to its maximum and set free. I walked (more like ran) to counter 5 as if my life depended on it. A young man, smartly dressed in a dark navy suit, white dress shirt and official green and white Rotterdam Municipality tie politely smiled as I handed him my ticket.

"I'm here to pick up my new passport," I announced merrily.

"Please, take a seat." He gestured with his hand for me to sit down. "Do you have your old passport with you?"

"Yes, I do." I took it out of my shoulder bag and handed it over to him. "And I also have this for you. It's a letter from the Municipality explaining my legal name and sex change."

He took both documents, checked them carefully and started typing in some commands on the keyboard in front of him.

It's all in there, handsome. Just check the additional info tab in my digital record.

"What is the name in your old passport?"

"Maher Shibli."

"Date and place of birth?"

"Beirut, Lebanon, December 28, 1980."

"And your new name?"

"Zoë van Vixenhoven." I could read his mind thinking *that's an unusual name*. "One of the few privileges we have, after being certified as transgender, by Westeneinde Hospital in Amsterdam, is the possibility to change our names," I added.

Using a mechanical device that resembled a staple gun, he punched a big hole in my old passport. "Do you want to keep the old passport?"

Are you kidding me? Of course not! Please burn it, incinerate it, shred it to a thousand pieces.

"No, thank you. Please dispose of it securely and as quickly as possible."

"Miss van Vixenhoven, here's your new Dutch passport. Have a nice day."

Oh, handsome, you can hardly imagine what a beautiful day it already is.

A while ago, dear Jules, I concluded I need to go for a new surname not only to emphasize a new start and a new me, but also to put even more distance between me and my homophobic/transphobic father. As of this December day, I'm legally and officially Zoë van Vixenhoven. *Christmas has arrived early this year, Jules. Merry Christmas, luv.*

7

Maher, Sayonara!

Journal entry # 1055$
Company HQ, Amsterdam, Jan 2017

"This concludes the first part of our weekly team meeting. You are well aware that this meeting has been extended by half an hour for a specific reason. Maher, the floor is all yours." Daan gave me a thumbs up. I moved to the front and connected my laptop to the beamer.

I've never felt comfortable giving a presentation sitting down, so I wasn't going to start now. I stood before seventeen of my colleagues, who were seated around a large circular table. In their eyes and on their faces, I could read signs of surprise and puzzlement.

Guys, I wish I was in your shoes right now and not the one under the spotlight.

My vision blurred slightly as I started to feel a little woozy. *Not now please.* I pinched my upper right leg as hard as I could. Thankfully, that helped, and I started to regain my orientation. The air of anticipation hung heavy in the room, as Daan urged me to get on with it. I took a deep breath and prepared to utter the opening words of my presentation, when the meeting room's door flew open and Lieselotte and Marcus stepped in. After apologizing for their slight delay and the interruption they caused, they settled down in two chairs close to where I stood. Heavens! The looks of puzzlement on my colleagues' faces had now morphed into expressions of anxiety and alarm. I had to diffuse this situation and very quickly.

"Dear colleagues, I noticed the look of alarm on your faces when Mr. Ockermann and Lieselotte walked in. Please, I would like to assure you that this extra agenda point is in no way related to the reorganization and cost-cutting plans of our company. I requested this extension to our weekly meeting so that I can share something personal with you. To that end, I've prepared a presentation, a few PowerPoint slides. Most slides contain one image; one image only and no text. I will explain the significance of each image. All questions are welcome; however, may I suggest that you wait until the end. Chances are that you will have your question answered by the information which I will provide during my presentation."

Nineteen pairs of eyes, including those of the Vice

President, were now firmly planted on me, and you could hear a pin drop. *OK, kid. Give it all you have!* I clicked open my presentation.

<u>Slide One</u> – shows one image, that of the facade of Westeneinde Hospital.

"As you all are undoubtedly aware of, Westeneinde is one of the major and most prestigious academic hospitals in the Netherlands. For more than a year now, I've been a patient at this hospital."

A few eyes in the room widened, some mouths gaped open and one of my female colleagues couldn't help but cry out in panic, "Maher, please, don't tell us you have cancer?"

"No, Odette, rest assured I don't have cancer." I moved on to the second slide.

<u>Slide Two</u> – contains an image of a manila file folder. In the top left corner of the file folder the words 'Diagnosis: acute gender dysphoria' are stamped in bold red letters.

"Within Westeneinde, there exists a specialized medical team made up of psychologists, endocrinologists, surgeons and researchers, all focused on one thing, and that is to provide the best care possible for patients with gender dysphoria. Dear colleagues, I'm one of those patients. I'm transgender!"

A buzz of electricity crackled around the room. Some faces frowned. Some eyes widened, contracted and widened again. Some colleagues, whom I've known for several years, were clearly trying to connect the dots between the past and this present moment. I pushed forward with my presentation.

<u>Slide Three</u> – contains the image of a Dutch passport, with its classical burgundy cover, in the foreground and a row of data-servers in the background.

"This photo is meant to represent the Dutch government's databases, which contain the data of every single citizen and resident of our country. If you had access to the databases on those servers and were to look up the record for a Mr. Maher Shibli, the result of this query will be zero, i.e., 'No records found'. Because, my dear colleagues, legally, Maher Shibli does not exist anymore."

More confused looks in the audience. I pressed 'Page Down' on the keyboard.

<u>Slide Four</u> – depicts an abstract image of a man. The man is casting a long shadow on the wall behind him, except the shadow is that of a woman.

"Dear colleagues, my new name is Zoë van Vixenhoven. I am a transgender woman and it is my pleasure to make your acquaintance."

A cacophony of sounds rose and fell in the room. A few faces were now adorned with a smile as if to say, 'Well done, you!' Others conveyed the message, "I still don't get it. Is Maher trying to pull our legs!?"

<u>Slide Five</u> – contains a collection of images and snippets of articles, which have been widely distributed by the media:

- A review of the film *The Danish Girl* in *Rolling Stone*

- A picture of Caitlyn Jenner, on the cover of *Vanity Fair*

- An article in the Dutch daily newspaper *De*

Volkskrant about Loiza Lamers, a transgender woman, who won first prize in the TV show 'Holland's Next Top Model' in 2015

-   A photo of Lisa Williamson, author of the book *The Art of Being Normal*

"Uhmmm!" I cleared my throat. "Now that you're all acquainted with the real me, I'll move on. The message I wanted to convey with this slide is that the mainstream media is giving more and more coverage and attention to all things transgender. For a vulnerable minority group, which let's face it, is still very much marginalized and stigmatized, the attention is largely welcome and is a positive development. That said, in my opinion, the lion's share of their attention is still being given to the physical aspects of transitioning and less on the human story of the transgender individual. In the next few slides, I will shed some light on the question 'What is a transgender person?' and give you some insights into my own transgender story."

Slide Six – I'm sorry, this slide does contain text.

Transgender: *a person with a mismatch between their mind and their body, as with regards to their gender identity. The neuro-biological condition which causes this mismatch is called gender dysphoria.*

"Ask any trans woman, what is the definition of a trans woman and nine out of ten will tell you: she's a woman trapped in a man's body. Although this statement doesn't sound very scientific, actually it's very accurate. In my case, my brain is continuously, day in, day out, at war with my body and is non-stop bombarding me with the message 'this male body is NOT mine'. Dear colleagues, please excuse my bluntness! According to medical science, a person's gender identity is not defined between their legs, but in their brain. How you feel about yourself, whether you are a man or a woman, or neither. This is determined by your brain. It's hardcoded. It's not something you can change.

Slide Seven

"Here we see an image of a six-week-old human embryo in its mother's womb. According to the great monotheistic religions, the emphasis of creation is put on 'Man'; after all, Adam was created in God's image whereas Eve was created from Adam's ribs, meaning she's a derivative. This is grossly inaccurate according to science. Actually, according to biological science, it is the female that's the blueprint of humankind. After conception, in the first six to eight weeks, all embryos are physically female. I stress the word 'physically' and emphasize that this is not to be confused with 'genetically'. That's why we all have nipples, for example. Also, the fact that males have two testes is not a coincidence. Those testes started their lives as tiny ovaries!" I paused for this latest statement to sink in with my audience.

"If you want to learn more about the evolution of embryos, I recommend the website Livescience.com as an excellent source of information. Moving on, around approximately the seventh week, embryos carrying the Y-chromosome will start with the process of masculinization, as testosterone (the male hormone) kicks in. This masculinization takes place in both the brain and the body. That's how those embryos start to develop male characteristics. Scientists still do not understand fully why and how a tiny minority of embryos become transgender. However, the prevalent theory, and I must stress it is a theory, stipulates that in those transgender embryos who carry the Y-chromosome, this masculinization process of the brain is interrupted – I'm convinced this is by design and not due to an accident. This leaves their brains partially or mostly in the original state, i.e., female."

<u>Slide Eight</u> – depicts a vivid and disturbing painting. In this painting an adult has a child pinned to the wall with one hand around its neck. The other hand (of the adult) is about to strike the child's head. The child looks horrified and frightened at what's to come. Blood is trickling down from the child's nose.

"All those rainbow-colored Pride celebrations around the world, and you'd be forgiven for thinking all is hunky dory with the LGBTQ community. Nothing could be further from the truth. What this painting portrays is unfortunately very much the reality for far too many queer and transgender kids and individuals. And you wouldn't have to look hard to find them.

"Dear colleagues, trans persons are being beaten up to a pulp, whacked, bullied, spat at, terrified out of their wits, ridiculed, humiliated, raped and killed for no other reason than being different, for being transgender. Let me be very clear, if someone is transgender then they are born transgender. It is NOT a choice, a hype, a lifestyle or a phase. When I was four years old, give or take, I was already aware of the fact that I'm not a boy; I felt very much like a girl. For example, I demonstrated girl-like behavior and wanted to be with girls all the time, because I could feel that's what I am. My environment, meaning my family and school, strongly and aggressively rejected this. Into my little head, they drilled the message that *this is obnoxious and forbidden. It's against the rules. Against our norms and values.*

"From a very young age, I internalized this destructive message and instinctively understood that in order to survive and be accepted by my environment, I had to bury my feelings about how I felt deep inside me. Basically, I grew up with the belief that there's something fundamentally wrong with me. It was something shameful. Something which I should never talk to anyone about. It's strictly taboo. All my life, I've been forced to live in fear and contempt of my deepest feelings and the never-ending conflict within me.

"As I grew up, I tried to convince myself that this terrible pain would one day go away. That it was a phase, but in reality, gender dysphoria never goes away. Left untreated, it will only get worse and more painful, turning the lives of transgenders into a hell, a living nightmare. So, in my case, how does it feel to live with gender dysphoria? It's horrible and excruciatingly painful! The pain, which I've endured and still do, manifests itself in a never-ending cycle of anxiety, panic attacks, distress, depression, insomnia, fatigue and exhaustion.

"For more than thirty years, I managed somehow to contain this pain, which not unlike cancer, is progressively eating me up inside. In January 2015, I reached my 'tipping point'. At that point, it became crystal clear to me that if I continued to resist and refuse medical treatment, gender dysphoria would kill me."

<u>Slide Nine</u> – depicts the image of a busy operating theater at a hospital.

"As regards the medical process, usually this process takes three to five years, from start to finish. I'm in my second year at the hospital and have at least another two years to go. The only medical solution to gender dysphoria is to match the body to the brain, through hormone therapy and surgery. Never, ever let anyone mess with your brain! Tragically, in the past, that's what some medical institutions did. For many years, transgender patients were subjected to disgusting practices like electric shock therapy and lobotomy. They were electrified and their brains butchered, reducing them to vegetables."

<u>Slide Ten</u> – contains an abstract image of a heart made up of two hands clasped together, as in a handshake.

"I do not expect any of you to hoist the Rainbow flag high up in the air, but I do expect that regardless of our differences, we continue to interact with each other with respect and dignity. That is the bedrock of our society and civilization. Our company (and I have checked this with Lieselotte) will not tolerate any transphobic language. Words like 'tranny', 'transvestite', 'cross-dresser' and 'she-male' are definite redlines when talking to or referencing a transgender person. These derogatory words are not only hurtful, they are despicable. They are heavily laden with negative connotations which imply that trans women are 'fake' and are somehow 'in it' for the sensation and sexual thrill. Unfortunately, some imbeciles in this world prescribe to this dangerous nonsense. Can you imagine telling a four-year-old child: 'Listen up, not only are your feelings fake, you are a sexual deviant and a danger to society for wanting to wear your sister's clothes.' A four-year-old child, for goodness' sake! I ask you: 'Who is seriously sick and disgusting in this picture?'

Slide Eleven – has an image of a winding road stretching to the horizon. In the foreground, there's a yellow road sign with words 'Change Ahead'.

"So, what lies ahead? Today, is the very last day you will see me in men's clothes. I'll be taking two weeks off and when I return, I will return to you as Zoë. She will be wearing makeup and female clothes. I do respect and accept that you will need some time to adjust to this new reality. Though, if I may use an animal metaphor, I do promise you that Zoë is a cat. She is not a dog pretending to be a cat. I hope that you understand what I'm trying to say." A few heads nodded in agreement, so I continued to the next slide.

Slide Twelve – Questions?

"Now I think we have five minutes for questions."

"Yes, here!" Henri, a male colleague, indicated he wanted to kick off the questioning.

"Yes, Henri. Go ahead."

"You talked about the masculinization process of the brain being interrupted or cut short and that leads to an embryo becoming transgender. If that is true, how does it explain children who are born female and feel they are boys? There's surely no masculinization process involved there?"

"Wow, Henri, you ask me as if suddenly I'm a world-class researcher in the field of gender dysphoria. Again, I stress that what I shared with you is a plausible explanation, but is still a theory. Science simply hasn't figured it out definitively. Some scientists are convinced that a transgender gene or genes exist in the embryo, and are actively looking for those genes in labs across the world. However, if I understand correctly, the majority of scientific opinion seems to be conflating around the possible impact of the male hormone, testosterone, on the embryo's brain, while still developing inside the mother's womb.

"In my case, my brain was spared the testosterone treatment and, in the case, you mentioned, it could be that the embryo's brain is subjected to a burst of testosterone in its mother's womb. All humans, including pregnant females, have organs which produce to varying degrees both testosterone and estrogen. This last part is not theory; it's scientific fact. Furthermore, all human body cells have receptors, which can interact with both male and female hormones, testosterone and estrogen." I cleared my throat. "Excuse me! My mouth is almost parched from all the talking. Yes, Claudia. You have a question?"

"Yes, Maher. Mmm… sorry, Zoë. I'm not sure how I should address you?"

"Maher is okay for now. From February onwards, it's Zoë."

"Yes, I just wanted to say what a super presentation you just gave! A big compliment to you. And for me personally, I've always struggled in trying to figure you out. You were always a riddle to me. Were you gay? Were you straight? And now, finally you've answered my question. Now it's all starting to make sense."

"Thanks, Claudia, for the compliment. Sorry for being

so secretive, but I hope now you understand the reasons why I was the way I was. Yes, Robert. You have a question?"

"Earlier in your presentation, you mentioned chromosomes. Is it not biological fact that XY means male and XX means female?"

"No. It's not biological fact because nature is *not* black and white or zeros and ones. Science has already established that chromosomes are not an ironclad indicator of whether someone is male or female. Chromosomes have multiple mutations and variations. For example, there are cis women who carry the male Y-chromosome. Are you suggesting, society excludes them from being classified as women, Robert?"

"Uh, no of course not." Robert tried to gather his thoughts.

"I'll take one more question and then we'll wrap things up. Yes, Ellen. You have a question?"

"You said that as of February you will be wearing women's clothes, right?"

"Yes, that's correct."

"Well, just to be clear, I expect you to wear shoes with heels no shorter than three centimeters."

"Dear Ellen, I didn't wait thirty years to wear shoes with three-centimeter heels. Girl, you won't ever see me in heels which are less than eight centimeters high. At the minimum!" I wasn't intentionally trying to be funny, but the whole room burst out in laughter. Especially, Marcus Ockermann – he laughed the loudest.

On this light-hearted note, I decided to conclude the presentation. Most, but not all, of my colleagues stood up and rushed to congratulate me on this courageous step and wished me the best of luck. Marcus, Lieselotte and Daan were among the well-wishers. Jules, thank heavens for their public display of support. In the coming weeks and months, I'm going to need it.

Until today, I led a double life: at the office I presented as 'Maher', outside the office I'm just me, Zoë. Today marks the end of the road for Maher. From now on it's Zoë 24/7. Only Zoë. Johan believes I should be thankful to Maher for bringing me so far. I'll suffice with saying goodbye: Sayonara, Maher.

8

Marcus Honors His Promise

Journal entry # 1056$
Rotterdam, Jan 2017

Within an hour of my coming-out presentation at work, Marcus sent out the following email to approximately three hundred colleagues:

Dear colleagues,

With regards to our colleague, Maher Shibli, I have the following news to share with you:

Since November 2015, Maher has been a patient at

Westeneinde Hospital under the medical care of the Genderploeg. In October 2016, the Genderploeg diagnosed Maher as being transgender.

As of February 1, Maher will be living and presenting fulltime as a woman. Her new name is Zoë van Vixenhoven. From that date onwards, you are to address her and refer to her by her new name and use female pronouns (she/her). Furthermore, per the given date, her email address will be:

Zoe.van.Vixenhoven@megalaar.nl

Zoë has shown significant strength and courage in taking this step, and I know that I'm talking on behalf of all professionals at Megalaar Logistics when I say she *will* receive our respect and support.

I want to remind you that our company stands 100% percent for Diversity and Inclusion within its workforce. This company has a zero-tolerance policy for any type of discrimination, including transphobia.

If you have any questions or comments, don't hesitate to reach out to Daan Westerveld, Lieselotte Holten (cc-readers) or myself.

Best regards,
Marcus Ockermann
VP Air Logistics
Megalaar Logistics Group

Later on that day, Marcus sent me a second email:

Dear Zoë,

Best of luck with the next phase in your transition. Should you need our help, let me know.

Best regards,
Marcus

P.S. Jena was disappointed (I would even say hurt) that you didn't invite her to your coming-out presentation at work.

Ouch! Stupid, stupid, me! I'll call and apologize to Jena first thing tomorrow morning.

9

Zoë's First Day at Work

Journal entry # 1061$
Company HQ, Amsterdam, Feb 2017
🎧 New Order – True Faith

There's a scene in *Casino Royale* in which Daniel Craig as
James Bond stabs himself with an antidote-filled syringe
to stabilize his heart. Right now, I swear if I had such an
injection in my hand, I would do the same, because if this
ticker of mine doesn't slow down, it's going to explode.
*Should I press '8' on the numbers panel in the elevator and exit
one floor earlier?* Too late, we've arrived at the ninth floor.

Okay, Zoë, just smile, say hello and go straight to your

usual work area. But don't overdo it with the smiling, otherwise, your colleagues will think you're nervous. *Well fucking excuse me, here's a news reel: Zoë is so nervous she could actually pee her pants right about now.*

Okay, take a deep breath and walk. Don't stand here like a stupid flagpole. You're starting to attract attention to yourself.

"Can I help you? Are you looking for someone?"

"Manon, it's me, Zoë." I took off the red beret.

"Oh my God, Maher. Oh. I'm sorry, Zoë. Is that really you?"

"Yeah, that's what I just said."

"Welcome. Should I introduce you to everyone?"

"No, no, Manon, don't be silly. I work here. It's not like I'm a new employee."

"Hello, Zoë. How are you?" Anton waved from behind a desk.

"Oh, hi Anton. Finally, you see the real me."

"Hey there, stranger! I don't believe I know this lovely young lady!" Chris touched me a little inappropriately.

"Stop it, Chris!" I grit my teeth while trying to remain polite.

"Good morning, Miss van Vixenhoven!" Daan called out. "The other day I looked up your new surname; it's not exactly Dutch, is it?"

"It's Dutch inspired. I'll explain later."

"You look amazing, dear. Look at that eye shadow. Did your sister teach you how to apply makeup?" Ellen inquired.

"No, actually, it's the other way round; she comes to me for advice. I taught myself on YouTube."

"I'm so glad you chose to go for your own happiness. Good for you!" Henri gave me a manly slap on the back.

"Happiness had nothing to do with it," I protested. "I did this to save myself. This is the only way I can continue living."

"What about your family? Your parents – do they support you?" Bart asked.

"My sister, she supports me. The others, it's complicated."

"Do you feel safe travelling on public transport? Do you get harassed?"

"People say I'm passable. I mean that most people don't notice that I'm different from other women. But sometimes, yes, there are those who do stare at me. That does make me feel very uncomfortable and unsettles me. Please, I need to start preparing for my next meeting."

"Wow, Zoë. I've never seen your eyes sparkle like they do now. With Maher, they were always dull and lifeless." Claudia offered her endorsement.

"Well, that was because I was never myself as Maher."

"Hey, Zoë," Jena called out. "Alright, everyone, I think it's time to give her some space. Chop-chop! Off you go! Work beckons." Jena locked arms with me and gently but firmly pulled me out and away from the circle of colleagues who had congregated around me.

"Thanks, Jena. Always there to rescue me."

"You don't have to answer all their questions at once, you know. There's a time and place for everything."

"You're right, I know. Just trying to be friendly and accessible. Not like Maher was – a closed book. You understand?" Jena nodded.

Even though it was still early morning, exhaustion, both physical and emotional, finally got the better of me. I slumped down onto the closest office chair.

"What, Jena? Why are you staring at my legs like that? Is there something wrong? I thought I looked okay in skinny jeans."

"Zoë, where on earth did you get legs like those. I never noticed them before."

"I never wore skinny jeans to the office before." I winked.

"Girl, if I had your sexy legs, which seem to go on for miles and miles, I'd quit my job, move to Paris and join Crazy Horse or Moulin Rouge."

"Ha, ha, ha, Jena. There's a time and place for everything, remember."

Johan had warned me that the first two weeks at work would be emotionally draining due to the (expected) bucketloads of attention and curiosity that I'd get. However, as a cautionary note, he did add that by the third week the hullabaloo would die down almost instantly, and then even for an introvert it will feel like a massive dip and leave an eerie emptiness inside.

10

New World Job Seeker

Journal entry # 1066$
Leiden, Mar 2017

"Mama, Baba, I'm sorry but I need to share some bad news with you." I took the chair next to the sofa where both were sitting. My mother's eyes shone with dread and alarm while my father remained, as per usual, poker faced.

"What is it, Maher?" My father picked up the TV remote control and lowered the volume a few decibels.

"Well, as you're no doubt aware, through the news on the telly, my company is going through a very hard time, financially, right now. They're currently executing a radical re-organization and cost-saving plan. Around four thousand jobs are being axed. I'm sad to say that I'm one of the four thousand who will have to leave by May 30," I lied.

Aghast, my mother raised her hand to cover her wide-open mouth. "Love, I'm devastated for you. I know how important your career is to you."

"What are you going to do?" inquired my father, still keeping all his emotions under wraps.

"Being unemployed and being without an income, even for a short while, is not an option I can afford. I have fixed costs including a mortgage, which I have to cover." I paused for a few seconds. *Here comes the punchline.* "Unfortunately, the job market in Holland is still very much in the doldrums after the financial meltdown. I've had no choice but to look for job openings in other countries, including the United States and Canada. Actually, I'm already in serious talks with a company based in New York. They seem very interested. Next week, I have a second online interview via Skype with two of their managers. If that goes well, chances are I'll be moving to the United States before the start of the summer."

My mother's eyes teared up and she started sobbing quietly. I stood up, walked to her, took her hands in mine and kissed them warmly.

Mama, I love you. If only you knew that I'm doing this to keep you safe.

"Don't cry, Mama, please." I hugged her. "Things will one day get better and I promise you I will return to you." Deep down, I knew I shouldn't have promised that.

"C'mon, Liza, stop crying!" my father scolded her.

"Don't lecture me, Bashar. Leave me be," she snapped back at him.

Yeah, you miserable fuck. Stop pushing her around for once.

"I'm terribly sorry, Mama." Try as hard as I wanted, I couldn't stop myself from tearing up with her. We cried together.

I swear to you, Mama, if there was another way, I would have taken it.

A while back, my brother, sister and I concluded that Mama wouldn't survive the shock, trauma and severe consequences of my coming out as transgender to them. After much thought and deliberation, we decided that the only viable option was for me to exit my parents' lives indefinitely. The moment I started taking hormones, the clock started ticking down to the day when others will start to take notice that my body and face are changing. Jules, I'm barely able to conceal those changes from them right now, and come the summer, it will be downright impossible. This is heart-wrenching for me to do. It's literally tearing at every fiber in my body, but there's no other way out.

11

Serial Killer

Journal entry # 1070$
Dutch Railways, Mar 2017
🎧 Slash's Snakepit – Serial Killer

As always, Johan was right – once the circus of curiosity around me died down, I did miss it. It's terrifying how one quickly becomes addicted to all that attention.

Having hardly slept last night, due to the night sweats, I wasn't feeling particularly hunky dory today. I decided to leave the office early and headed back home to Rotterdam.

In the train carriage, some twenty minutes into my journey, I became aware that a group of teenagers, two boys and two girls, were talking about me. With all the stares, finger pointing and weird faces, sadly there was no denying this.

"I'm telling you that woman over there is a man," the teenage girl with frizzy hair announced.

"Are you sure? She looks quite normal to me," the teenage girl with freckles answered.

"I think Lona's right. She's a man. It must be a *travo*," the teenage boy with glasses remarked.

"Hell, what the fuck ya mean, she's a travo?" the teenage boy with baseball cap worn backward asked.

"You know! Travo as in transvestite, crossdresser."

"You mean she really is a man?"

"Yeah, look at her. Look at that face. Look at that masculine jawline. No woman has a jawline like that, as wide as a bus. I bet ya if she takes off 'em scarfs, we'll see his Adam's apple."

"Be careful, y'all. That man may be a killer. You know, a serial killa disguised as a woman," the teenage girl with frizzy hair giggled.

"Eewww! Creepy it is." The teenage boy with glasses glared and pointed at me as if I was the most disgusting thing alive.

Jules, I would never willingly injure a soul, but at that moment, I wished I had Darth Vader's Force choke powers. I would have force-choked them to teach them a little lesson that would make them think twice before they pestered or ridiculed a queer or transgender person again. *Wishful thinking, Zoë! Darth Vader is in a galaxy far, far away.* Realistically, the only thing I could do was to pack my stuff and look for another seat in another carriage.

As I stood up, to my astonishment, the boy with the baseball cap confronted me.

"Hey, mista. Where you goin'? To kill someone?" A guttural laugh came out of him, and the whole delinquent group exploded in hysterical laughter. At that moment, something inside me snapped. I grabbed the boy by the collar of his shirt and lifted him up until his sneakers were barely touching the floor. With long-heeled boots on, I towered at least two heads above him.

"Let go of me, mista. Let go!"

"I'm not a serial killer, you little weasel. I'm much worse than that! I'm a demonic witch, and if you don't get out of my way, I'm going to rip your little heart out and feed it to my cats during mass tonight." I took a few steps forward, shoved him back in his seat, turned and left. At that moment, a group of elderly passengers started cheering and clapping. "Good on you, ma'am, for showing them." Oddly, that did not make me feel better.

Even though we weren't in Rotterdam yet, at the next stop, I stepped off the train. I felt so angry and agitated, I needed to cool down and settle my nerves away from the prying eyes of people.

God, I'm so furious right now. I can feel steam coming out of every pore in my body. Not only with those fucking brats but also with myself. *What if they had knives on them? What then, Zoë?"* You want to end up in hospital again? Or worse! *What was I thinking?* Not obviously. I shouldn't have let my anger and emotions take over like that. Even though, I admit, for a second it felt good to tower like an Amazona over that imbecile. It was really stupid of me to react that way.

God, I'm really pissed off with a section of society that's always nasty to transgenders and the rest who are silent. Most of all I'm disgusted with the writers, bloggers, TV personalities and celebs who pull the strings from the lofty comfort of their luxury offices and continue to spew out these transphobic lies, all under the guise of quote/unquote 'free thought and legitimate debate'. Your transphobia is killing lives. Innocent, vulnerable lives. This is not free speech – it's hate. This has got to stop. It has to stop now!

12

The Two Ps: Paranoia and Passability

Journal entry # 1073$
Amsterdam, Mar 2017
🎧 Against the Current – Voices

"In your initial psychological assessment of my condition, you mentioned that besides gender dysphoria, I have a slight paranoia as well."

"Yes." Johan nodded.

"Well, it's not so slight anymore."

"Would you care to elaborate?"

"In public, wherever I go, I imagine people are talking about me and always I hear (maybe in my head, maybe not) the same question. 'Is that a man or woman?' When this happens, I feel I'm just two steps away from *freezing up* in fear and three steps from a full-blown panic attack. It's driving me crazy to the point I'm not leaving my home anymore, unless it's to work or get groceries," I added.

"Zoë, listen to me carefully. I'm going to give you some advice which I need you to carry out every time you hear those voices in your head. Every time you imagine people are talking about you, I want you to stop, turn and look in the direction you think the voices are coming from?"

"Why?"

"Because by doing so, in nine out of ten situations, you'll get confirmation that nobody is looking at you, let alone talking about you. Whoever is your vicinity didn't even notice anything unusual about you or didn't care."

"So, what you want me to do is to step out of my comfort zone and confront my paranoia?"

"That's it exactly. You might hesitate at first and think if you stop and look you might get confirmation people are looking and talking about you, but don't let that feeling of discomfort dissuade you. I promise if you follow my advice consistently, your paranoia will decrease and hopefully in time it won't affect you anymore."

"Okay, I will do it. There's another 'P' I would like your advice on."

"And that is?" Johan asked.

"Passability. My face isn't really passable as woman's, is it?"

"You have an androgenous looking face, Zoë. Believe me when I tell you you're one of the lucky ones. Most trans women in your age group aren't that lucky."

"You're telling me I'm lucky," I scoffed back, "but since when has luck been a friend of mine? Never."

"Give the hormones some time. In a few years, it will soften up your face and make it look more feminine."

"Johan, I don't have a few years. In a few years I might be dead!"

"No, Zoë. Don't think that."

"Why not, Johan? I've already been to hospital once because of a hate crime. Why should it be the last?"

"It might not be, but look at the physical progress you've already made, and you've only been – what is it – only five or six months on hormones?"

"Five months and thirteen days."

"In a relatively short time, I can clearly see noticeable physical changes to your body. Your breasts and buttocks are fuller; your waist is getting smaller; your hair is thicker and longer; and your skin is smoother."

"But my face, Johan, my face. Please level with me. This Adam's apple, this masculine jawline. They're never going to go away, are they? You tell me that I have an attractive face, but that's not what I see. Every time I look in the mirror, all I see are the masculine features of my face. And I truly hate it!"

"Listen, Zoë. Today, your eyes are physically way bigger than before and have an attractive feminine almond shape to them. Your eyelashes are thicker and longer. Your cheeks have filled out. I assure you, those feminine features weren't there a year ago. All that is thanks to the hormone treatment. But, yes, I will be honest with you: hormones can only go so far. They're not going to change your angular jawline and chin or Adam's apple."

"So, what's the solution then, Johan? Please tell me. I'm begging you."

Johan left his chair, took a few steps to the gigantic bookcase, which spanned the entire wall to my right, and pulled out a green manila file folder.

"Last year, during an international conference on transgender health in Barcelona, I attended a presentation on Face Feminization Surgery by a French surgeon called Saint Martegny. There was a lot of buzz and interest around what he's doing. The before and after photos of recent transgender patients' faces, which he shared with us, were very impressive. I would actually go so far as to say the results were actually spectacular." He passed me a brochure of 'Le Clinique St. Martegny' in Cap d'Antibes, France. "A word of caution, Zoë. This type of plastic surgery is radical, extremely painful and very expensive. We're talking here about skull alteration, and health insurance policies don't cover any of the expenses."

13

(Pseudo) Farewell to Holland

Journal entry # 1076$
Leiden, Apr 2017
🎧 FM-84 – Goodbye

"Okay, it's time for me to go!" I announced to my parents. "Tomorrow, I have to catch an early train to Frankfurt and from there a flight to New York."

"How come you're taking a flight from Frankfurt? And not with KLM Royal Dutch Airlines from Amsterdam Schiphol?" my father inquired.

Well, your Infernal Highness, that's because if I had said

Schiphol, Mama would have insisted that you come with me to the airport. Knowing Mama, she probably would have insisted that you guys walk with me through every step of the check-in and baggage drop-off process in the terminal, all the way to the passport and customs control. As this is all mere theater for Mama's sake, to protect her from you, I decided on this plan, knowing you would never give me a lift to Frankfurt. That's a four-and-half-hour drive. I calculated with this plan, the worst that could happen would be you waving me goodbye at the train station. Staging that isn't difficult, a fake passenger with a suitcase bids you goodbye, boards the train and once you're out of sight, I disembark and head back home to Rotterdam. It's really as easy as A, B, C.

"The flight with Lufthansa from Frankfurt is cheaper," I lied.

"Do you want us to bring you to the train station?" Mama asked.

"No, thank you, Mama. I appreciate the offer, but it's a very early train. I prefer to say goodbye to you here." I looked into her sad eyes. *Please, Mama, please don't be sad. I don't think I can stop myself from breaking down in tears if you don't stop looking at me with those puppy sad eyes.*

"Mama, Baba, I love you. I promise to call once I've arrived in New York." I hugged them – my father for like two seconds, and my mother for what felt like two hours. She started crying again.

"Please, Mama, I beg you not to cry for me!" This time, I stopped myself from repeating the promise that we'd see each other soon.

I turned away from them and walked the short distance to where my Lotus was parked. Halfway, I turned around and looked back. There she was, standing alone in the doorway. My mother had the saddest look on her face, but in her eyes, there was something else, a dread, an anguish that this might be the last time. I waved goodbye and tried to force a smile, but every muscle and sinew in my face refused. I turned and ran to my car. Once behind the steering wheel, I couldn't hold it in any longer. *Fuck! Fuck! Fuck this!* I whacked the steering wheel repeatedly till my fingers turned pale purple. I cried my lovely and dearest Mama a river. Heartbroken. Soul shattered. Devastated. Hook, line and sinker.

14

Slipping Under the Radar

Journal entry # 1077$
Rotterdam, Apr 2017
🎧 Two Door Cinema Club – Undercover Martyn

I can't pretend (as part of the plan to protect my mother) to be Maher in America, while my online footprint says I'm Zoë in Holland. Today, I deactivated all my social media accounts - good bye Facebook, Instagram, LinkedIn and Pinterest.

LinkedIn is probably the one that I'll miss the most - it's been useful for my career and professional networking. However, my father checks my LinkedIn page regularly, so it's got to go.

15

Photo op at Work

Journal entry # 1078$
Company HQ, Amsterdam, Apr 2017
🎧 Avicii – Freak

To mark the successful completion of phase one of our project, I asked the project team members to take a photo with me. The photo was meant for the company magazine. It would accompany a short article, which I had already compiled.

"C'mon, Kurt. Please join us. I really would like to have all the project members in the photo." I was being sincere.

Kurt jerked his head to the side and rejected all my efforts. "No, I'm sitting this one out."

His reaction didn't sit well with me, so once the project meeting was concluded, I decided to address the matter head on.

"Kurt, can I have a word with you? In private."

"What for?" His tone was at once aggressive and aggravated.

"Kurt, I know we've never been friends, but I would really like us to make an effort to end this senseless rivalry between us." In an act of reconciliation, I stretched out my hand and laid it gently on his left shoulder.

"Don't put those uncouth hands on me. Ever!" His eyes flashed with anger as he shrugged my hand off his shoulder.

"Huh! Uncouth? Kurt, what on earth are you talking about?" I was dumbfounded by his choice of words.

"Just back off. I don't want you touching me."

"Kurt, listen to yourself. You are wrong about this, you know." I had a hunch that his reaction was religiously motivated and I wanted to see where it went.

"Wrong about what?" he countered.

"I'm not a freak, Kurt. God created me transgender, just like he created you the way you are. There are no mistakes. All this is by design."

"Sod off! I despised you when you were Maher, and now that you call yourself Zoë, I despise you even more."

"But Jesus is all about Love and—"

He broke me off and pointed his index finger straight at me. "Don't! You conniving imposter. Don't you sully the Lord's name. God is constantly testing us all the time. He was testing you to see if you are strong enough to resist

Satan's temptations, and you failed. Big time! You're a loser, Maher." Before I could utter another syllable, he stormed out of the room.

This outburst of hostility left me shocked and flabbergasted. The picture I had painted for myself, in which all my colleagues were accepting of me, began to show some cracks. In the next few days, I couldn't help but notice that a small but not insignificant minority of my colleagues deliberately avoided all eye contact with me, all the time. Something I'm 100% sure they didn't do with Maher. I felt that a few of them even began displaying passive-aggressive behavior toward me. I thought of confronting them about this, however Johan cautioned me that this would be counterproductive. They'll just deny everything and then it's my word against theirs. Where will that lead us? He advised that I should give them time to process the change, just as I needed time to rid myself of my inner demons about being transgender myself.

People are not inherently antagonistic. Some are just easily influenced by political and religious dogma as well as group pressure and all the negativity surrounding the subject of trans-rights on social media, right now. It takes time for attitudes to change and the best antidote to this vile poison is to be my authentic self. In time, they will see that nature and fate had intended for those women who are born transgender, to have a complex and winding road to womanhood. That doesn't make them lesser woman.

16

Spooky and Spotify

Journal entry # 1082$
Rotterdam, May 2017
🎧 Seal – Killer
Calogero – Je joue de la musique

S omething tugged at my right sock and pulled it down. I ignored the impulse to check what was happening until I felt a light scratching of my skin. I smiled and stretched down to pick up Spooky from the floor.

Spooky is my new and very playful black kitten. She's a furry gift from Nadine, who has been very worried at my lack of social contact and at what she calls my quasi-hermit existence, especially during weekends.

"Hey there, Spooky! Luv, can't you see that I am working on my laptop?" I kissed her ever so lightly on her tiny nose.

"Meow."

"Meow to you as well! Here you go!" I placed her on the laptop's keyboard. "Okay, Spooky, it's all yours. Now write me something nice. Tell me that you love me. Tell me that you'll never leave me alone. Tell me that you'll dance with me till the end of time."

"Meow." Spooky planted her little tush on the keyboard and made herself snug and comfortable.

"What? Are you hungry? Or you just want to play some more? Again."

"Meow." Spooky stared up at me with her over-sized lime-green eyes.

"Do you want to hear a secret, Spooky?"

"Meow."

"I'll take that as a 'yes'. Well, Spooky, you and Spotify are literally keeping me sane during those long days and nights of extreme solitude. For that and more, I love you."

According to Spotify's latest feedback on my use of the music streaming service: in the past twelve months I had listened to 1311 artists and more than 200,000 minutes. That's a staggering 3400 hours. Wow! I can't believe it. Must be some kind of Spotify voodoo. Well, actually, I can believe it. Unsurprisingly, George Michael is still (and probably will always be) the artist whom I've listened to most.

17

Things Are Alright in NYC

Journal entry # 2003$
Rotterdam, Jul 2017
🎧 David Bowie – This is Not America

"Hello, Maher! Sweetheart, how are you doing?" Mama's voice was all excitement on the other end of the line.

"Hi, Mama. Things are getting along well here in New York. Can you believe that it's already three months since I left Holland? Time flies, doesn't it?" I answered.

"Are you eating well, sweetheart?"

"Of course, Mama. I'm eating well. I'm not a child," I chided her. "I do miss your delicious cooking, though. A few days ago, I went to a Lebanese restaurant in SoHo. It was very expensive and came nowhere close to your delicious home cooking."

"We're all here today. Zachariah and Nadine are visiting, and we're about to serve dinner. It's your favorite Lebanese mezzes. I so wish you were here with us."

"I wish that too, Mama, with all my heart. *Sufra Dayma*[19]! Enjoy your dinner. I'm already very jealous."

"What about you? What are you having for dinner this evening?"

"Well, actually a few colleagues from work are coming over and we'll probably end up ordering some deep-pan pizzas with lots of cheese. Americans seem to have a culinary love affair with cheese; they put it in and on virtually everything." I continued to make things up.

"How are your colleagues treating you?"

"Really good. I must say that I love everything about New York. Its vibe, energy and especially its colorful mix of people. I feel like a fish in water. I kinda acclimatized right away."

"Well, don't get too acclimatized! Maher, I still want you back here with us, when things get better in Holland." Her voice took on a more serious tone.

"We'll see, Mama. For now, I have a work contract for one year. I'll finish the year and take it from there."

"Have you seen anything new in New York?"

"As I explained in our previous calls, work has a tendency to take up most of my time. I get back late from

19 Sufra Dayma – 'Bon Appetit' in Lebanese Arabic

the office and leave early in the mornings. That leaves only the weekends."

"Tell me what you did last weekend?" she asked. "I want to know everything!"

"Well, as you already know, I've already visited the major landmarks like Ground Zero, Statue of Liberty, Empire State Building and MoMA. Now I'm focused on discovering New York's different neighborhoods. Every weekend, I try to go to different area. Last weekend, I went to Brooklyn, walked around and went to a Yiddish deli, where they make the most amazing pastrami sauerkraut sandwiches." I continued with my fabrications.

"Listen to you! You're already speaking like a native New Yorker! How come you've never shared any photos with us yet?" she scolded me.

"I already told you that the camera on my mobile is not working. Once I get a new mobile, I promise to bombard you with photos every day of the week."

"You better do! By the way, I see you're no longer on Facebook. Or are you blocking your parents? Maybe we're not cool enough for your friends and acquaints, anymore." She added.

"Block you, Mama, never. And you're like the coolest mom ever. No. I've been thinking about closing my account for a long time. Now I finally did it, it's truly liberating." Those words definitely rang true when I said them.

"Sweetheart, I'm just teasing you. One second, your father wants to know something. He is asking when are you coming to visit us? Or perhaps, we can come and visit you? I would love a local to show me New York. Hint! Hint!"

"Ha, ha, Mama. It does take a little more than a few

months to qualify as a local. No seriously, I need some more time for things to settle down at work. Also, I'm looking around for a cheaper and hopefully bigger apartment. Soon I'll be checking out some apartments in Jersey City, just across the Hudson River from New York City. It's cheaper there and the view of the Manhattan skyline is breathtaking."

"Alright, sweetheart, but promise me, we'll spend Christmas together." I swallowed hard.

"Yes, Mama."

"Do you want to speak with Nadine or Zachariah? They miss you, as well."

"No, that's okay. My colleagues are about to arrive. I'll speak with them later."

"Love you, Maher. Take good care!"

"Love you too, Mama. Bye!" I killed the line.

My chest constricted and my breathing became shallow. I think I'm gonna suffocate. *Shit! Shit! Shit! I've always known these theatrics of pretending to be Maher in New York can only go so far, before they reach their fucking expiry date.*

My head started spinning around. A powerful nausea clenched its fists tightly around me. Fuck, I can't breathe. I rushed to the bathroom, doubled down and threw up.

18

Letter from America

Journal entry # 2006$
Rotterdam, Jul 2017

Via an acquaintance who lives in the United States, today my parents received my hand-written letter (complete with stamped US postage stamp).

New York, July 15, 2017

Dearest Mama and Baba,

Please forgive me for the pain this letter is going to cause you. What you are about to read is by far the most difficult thing I've ever written in my life. My hands are trembling as I scribble the words on paper. I'm writing to bid you farewell and to say goodbye for good. This letter is the last you'll ever hear from me.

In April, when I left for the United States, I didn't leave Holland just to start a new job. Indeed, I left Holland to start a new life – a life free of the chains, shackles and locks, which I could no longer bear.

For decades, I've lived my life for you. Basically, my life was about adhering to two objectives: to meet your expectations of me and never to cause you any embarrassment or pain. I'm sorry but I cannot continue to live like that anymore. I have to start living for me.

All my life, I've lived with a vicious inner conflict, which I'm no longer able to suppress and contain. It is literally tearing me apart. That's why I left for America, so that I can live an authentic and free life as me, without any guilt and shame. I will not say explicitly what it is about me that has driven me to all this, because I'm convinced that if I told you, this would cause you even more pain than if I remained silent about it. Please understand, all I want is to live as myself in peace and dignity. Nothing more than that. Leaving was the only option for me to do this and at the same time to not cause you any embarrassment, which I know is very important to you.

Recently I found a better job (elsewhere in the United States) and have left New York. Please do not pressure Nadine and Zachariah for more information – they know as much as you do.

I beg you not to think that it was easy for me to take this step; nothing could be further from the truth. This step is the most difficult thing I've had to do in my life. I'm 100% convinced that you would never accept me the way I am or the choices I've had to make to survive. We would be in perpetual strife and conflict till the end of our lives. I do not deserve this and neither do you.

I love you with all my heart, but can't continue to live a lie simply to satisfy you or the others.

I send you everlasting love,

Maher

19

Raw Poetry Nº 2

Journal entry # 2008$
Rotterdam, Jul 2017

A ll That's Left *by my sister, Nadine Shibli*
Tired face, tired bones
Still, more strength than I
Standing there alone
Any connection a lie
Happier with distance between
Not having to hear, to see
To pretend to mean

To be what we cannot be
All that's left is true
Past the lies we used to tell
I don't love you, Baba
But I wish you well

20

The Face Factor

Journal entry # 2011$
Rotterdam, Aug 2017
🎧 Daft Punk – Face to Face

W hat is it about a person's face, when looked at separately from the rest of the body, that tells us this is a man or a woman? I mean besides the obvious features like hair (or lack of it), beard or facial hair, Adam's apple and size of head? When we see a face, we subconsciously categorize it as being male or female. I use the word 'subconsciously' because we don't really have to think about it; the categorization happens automatically and almost instantly.

Take, for example, the American actress Rene Russo, who stars opposite Pierce Brosnan in the 1999 remake of *The Thomas Crown Affair*. Her jawline and chin are only slightly smaller and less angular than mine. I have a small head, which is definitely 'too small' by male standards and 'normal' sized by female standards. My hair is thicker and longer than Rene Russo's (in the film), and yet no one in this world would look at her face and have any doubt it's a woman's face. Whereas when some people look at my face, they are probably classifying it as male (or androgynous, if I'm lucky), especially if I don't have any makeup on. Why is that? This question has vexed me terribly, more so after that ugly incident in the train.

As a trans woman, when I'm misgendered, *it's killing*. Not only does this sicken me to the core, it triggers deep feelings of frustration and anxiety. Any incident of (perceived) misgendering can leave me in a panicked state of agitation, disgust and distress for days, if not weeks. That's not to say that this can only be triggered by external factors (i.e., by others); if I look at my face in the mirror for any prolonged period of time, I will obsess over all the male characteristics of my face, triggering a new wave of gender dysphoria.

Let me be frank, I do not want a superstar's face like that of Rene Russo. All I want is a normal female face, i.e., one that I'm comfortable with, and when people see it, they quickly categorize it as a woman's face and move on. Furthermore, every time I step out of the door, I want to feel safe and carefree, and not be consumed by lingering fear that today might be the day someone will want to smash my face in, just because they choose to classify me as a male freak in women's clothes. That day may or may not come, but I'm not going to wait to find out. I do not want to end up half pulverized and in hospital. Again. In the first week of September, I have an appointment with Dr. Martegny at his prestigious clinic in the south of France. Jules, based on all the online research I've done on him, he's considered one of the top three surgeons in the world in the field of Face Feminization Surgery. Fingers crossed!

21

Rendezvous in Cap d'Antibes

Journal entry # 2019$
Côte d'Azur, South of France, Sep 2017
🎧 Calogero – Face à la mer

Transavia flight HV5762 direct from Rotterdam to Nice-Côte d'Azur Airport (NCE) touched down right on time at 10:40 a.m. From the airport, I was whisked away by a chauffeur-driven white Mercedes to Cap d'Antibes, courtesy of Le Clinique St. Martegny. The handsome young driver, bless his heart, decided to take the scenic and winding coastal road. The scenery from the car's back seat, on this glorious end-of-summer day, was simply breathtaking – the natural beauty of this region is wowzers. I believe in French the expression is 'très agréable!'. Half an hour later, the driver pulled up to the cantilevered entrance of a sleek, ultra-modern glass, concrete, and steel structure, which housed the good doctor's clinic. Jules, I must say that the most eminent of Bauhaus architects, Mr. Mies van der Rohe himself, would have approved of this two-story building, such was its minimalistic elegance.

"Zis is it, madame," the driver announced cheerfully. "Pleaze have ze receptioniste call me after your appointment whis ze doctor has concluded."

I've never been called 'madame' before, but I'm not complaining – I'll take it. I walked the short distance to the reception desk and presented myself.

"Madame, I will let Dr. St. Martegny's assistant know about your arrival right away. You can wait in the reception room straight ahead and to the left."

"Is this entire building occupied by Dr. Martegny's clinic?" I was curious. The receptionist smiled.

"Non, madame. In total there are five private clinics in this building. As you will see, the building is U-shaped. The wing on the right houses the clinics. The wing on the left accommodates the operating theatres, post-operation patients' rooms and kitchen. For the care of our patients, we have everything under one roof." *End of infomercial.*

There were three other clients waiting in the reception room, who, by their looks, were probably here for the other clinics. They looked bling-bling, affluent, and had the air of the nouveau riche about them.

The reception room looked out at an impressive Mediterranean garden in neo-Roman style, which was reminiscent of gardens I had once seen in Tuscany while on vacation. The garden was surrounded by the building's structure on three sides; however, the fourth side stretched all the way to the edge of the coastline.

The beauty and elegance of this place and its contents started to disturb me. This place must be damn expensive. I'm guessing I'm way out of my league here – I probably can't afford any surgery performed here. *Zoë, what on earth were you thinking, coming here?*

"Mademoiselle van Vixenhoven, my name is Sophie. I'm Dr. Saint Martegny's assistant. Welcome to Cap d'Antibes." A very attractive, thin (of course), thirty-something woman with long cinnamon-brown hair and topaz-blue eyes welcomed me. "Please follow me to Dr. Saint Martegny's consultation office."

Does everything here need to be so uber beautiful? All this is starting to make me feel disorientated, inadequate and totally out of place.

"Okay, please lead the way." I gestured with my hand that I would follow her.

She led me along a brightly lit corridor.

"Please wait here!" Sophie smiled and opened a door to her right to let me in.

My thoughts continued to slide down the avenue of doubts and skepticism. I must have made a grave miscalculation coming here. *This is a place the Kardashians come to and well beyond me and my pay grade.* My thought train came to a halt, when the door opened and Dr. Saint Martegny entered the room.

"Mademoiselle van Vixenhoven, welcome to our clinic.

How can we be of *serveez* to you?" He stretched out his arm to shake my hand and gave me a million-dollar smile.

First of all, no way you're a doctor. Male doctors should be a little shaggy and have that comforting grandpa feeling about them. They shouldn't be heart-throbs straight out of a Hollywood movie-set. Dr. Saint Martegny, you're just too good looking. The last time I checked IMDB, Jim Caviezel was still busy making a living in Los Angeles. You must be his brother from another father, or something.

"Hello, doctor. I'm Zoë. I have come from Rotterdam to see you about Face Feminization Surgery." I briefly introduced myself and gave him a concise account of my transition so far.

"First of all, Mademoiselle van Vixenhoven, I only operate on trans women who have been officially certified as transgender by a reputable medical institution. And secondly, my clients must be on hormone treatment for at least twelve months."

"I've been officially diagnosed as transgender by Westeneinde. That's a well-respected academic hospital in Amsterdam. I have an official document from Westeneinde about my diagnosis, which I'm happy to share with you. As for the hormone treatment, in a few weeks' time I will complete my first year on hormones."

"Bien." From behind the desk, Dr. Saint Martegny nodded his head in acknowledgement. Then he left his chair and walked around the desk to where I was seated. "Please, may I examine your face and head."

I nodded. He softly cupped my head in his hands and, gently pushing it first to the left and then to the right, he carried out his examination. After a few minutes of talking to himself in French, he went back to his chair. With his aquamarine eyes, the color of the Mediterranean Sea just outside his office window, he gazed reflectively at my face. It seemed like he was consumed in deep thought.

"I can help you, mademoiselle," he finally declared. "However, please understand that Face Feminization Surgery is not cosmetic plastic surgery. We do not aim to make you more attractive, but *razer* as the name suggests to feminize your face. Your face will maintain its identity but become unquestionably more feminine."

I nodded in agreement. "Doctor, that's one of the reasons I've come to you. I have to remain recognizable as Zoë, but please bring out the feminine in me, which is currently being dominated by the masculine"

"That will definitely be the case," he interjected. "Also, I cannot make someone who is not attractive into a good-looking woman."

"Yes, of course. I understand." With sad eyes, I looked at him inquisitively.

"Oh, sorry. I wasn't referring to you. I meant in general. Non, mademoiselle, in that department, you have nothing to worry about; if I operate on your face, as a result you will have an attractive female face," he assured me.

"This surgery would dramatically change my life, doctor! A real game-changer; that's what I need."

"Please understand that this surgery is complex. It's expensive and you'll need at least six weeks to recover," he cautioned.

"May I inquire about the cost?" Finally, I had the courage to ask the dreaded question.

"My assistant, Sophie, will help you with the financial details." With his blue lacquered Montblanc fountain pen, he started scribbling down notes on a pad of paper in front of him. "If you decide to go with us, I will operate on five areas of your *visage*. Firstly, I will reduce the size of your Adam's apple. Secondly, I will soften your jawline by removing the square-corners of your jaw. Also, I will grind away some of your jawbone to give the lower section of your face a feminine V-shape. Thirdly, I will make your chin smaller. However, I can't do anything about the dimple in the center of your chin. If you ask me, I think it's an attractive feature, but that's my opinion."

"Absolutely! I definitely want to keep the dimple. It's like a trademark of my family. My mother, brother and sister, we all have it." Dr. Saint Martegny chuckled softly.

"I'm glad we're in agreement," he continued. "Fourthly, and most importantly, I will remove a significant section of your forehead above your eyes to open up your face. And that, mademoiselle, is the crucial factor in transforming your face from masculine to feminine. Have you not observed how women have a much smaller, dome-like forehead, while men have larger, more prominent and more boxy foreheads?"

Finally, the penny dropped. *Now I get it!*

"The feminization of the forehead," the doctor continued, "is by far the most complicated procedure. It will require that I make an incision behind the hairline, which will extend from ear to ear. I will need to roll back the skin with all the tissue, muscles and nerves attached, so that I have direct access to the bone. And then with a diamond-tipped surgical drill, I will start the structural modification."

OMG! This is starting to sound like a scene from CSI Miami.

"Sounds indeed very complex, doctor!"

"And, finally, I will do a rhinoplasty, to give your nose a soft, gently sloping bridge and reduce the size of the nostrils. *Et voila!* With those five interventions you will have a more feminine version of your face." Concluding the consultation, he shared with me before and after photos of several of his patients. I was blown away by what Dr. Saint Martegny managed to achieve with their faces.

I spent the next fifty minutes with Sophie, going through the financials, logistics and planning of the operation.

"Dr. Saint Martegny has a waiting list of six months. There's only one gap in that period. That's two weeks before Christmas. Do you want to go for that?"

In my head, I did some quick calculations. I gulped and nodded. "Let's go for it."

This surgery was going to cost me an arm and a leg. Jules, I'd be literally plundering my entire savings account and on top of that I would need a loan from the bank. To finance the surgery, I can kiss goodbye the month-long vacation in Thailand, Cambodia and Vietnam, the new SieMatic kitchen for my apartment and the major engine revision and refurbishment of my Lotus Esprit. To top it all off, I will be saddled with a pile of debt, which will take ages to repay. Is it worth this exorbitant price tag? If the good doctor can deliver on his promise, you betcha! Dear Saint Martegny, soon I will be making a very sizable donation to your church.

22

System Says No!

Journal entry # 2031$
Company HQ, Amsterdam, Nov 2017

In the fully packed auditorium on the eleventh floor, my colleagues from the Customer Experience department gave a broad presentation about the company's goals and ambitions for the next three to five years. Of particular interest to me was what Kurt had to share with us about the Priority M project, which I was (still) leading.

Kurt has this grand delusion that he's a young Steve Jobs waiting to be discovered. While in reality, he's nothing but a clown and a prick. A very bigoted prick, I had the unfortunate honor of discovering recently.

As the third speaker, Kurt took to the stage and immediately started mimicking the mannerisms of alpha male tech tycoons. He walked, talked and gestured like he was about to unveil that next big innovation that would change the world.

"Fellow colleagues, I'm purposefully keeping my presentation short and sweet. As a matter of fact, my roadmap for Priority M in the coming period consists of three slides and a video clip only. I've given my presentation the title 'Priority M – The Three Nos'. 'No' to Customer Delays. 'No' to Carbon Emissions and 'No' to System Says No." He took the remote control from the previous speaker and dealt with the first two slides in a rather effective and impressive manner. I was starting to warm up to his presentation.

Kurt is the only speaker, to my knowledge, that always uses the singular (I/my/mine) instead of the plural (we/our) in his presentations. With an ego as inflated as his, I guess it goes with the territory.

"Before I share with you my final slide, I want to play you a fragment from a TV comedy show." Kurt clicked open a video clip on YouTube. It was a scene from the British slapstick comedy called *Little Britain*. In this scene, male actor David Williams portrays crudely and idiotically a receptionist called Carol Beer. From her clothes, makeup, and wig, I'm assuming Carol is supposed to be transgender. Very much an offensive depiction of a trans woman, if ever there was one. After the YouTube clip had concluded, Kurt displayed Carol's caricatured face on the screen and with a final click of the remote control, a giant red X appeared on her face. The audience reacted with enthusiastic giggles and laughter.

"And the final 'No' is to the 'System Says No' attitude by some of our frontline staff. Our Priority M customer and our staff should never be the victims of our IT systems' failings. We need to get our basics right! Thank you for your time and attention." He swiftly concluded his presentation and handed the remote control to the next speaker. However, before leaving the stage, he abruptly turned to look at me and mouthed the words: 'Loser, I got you'.

That was a very Machiavellian performance by you Kurt, to camouflage the ulterior message of your presentation like that. In that final part of your presentation, what the majority in the audience perceived as a message about the deficiencies of our IT system combined with a touch of British humor, was in essence, way more sinister than that. By using the caricatured personality of Carol Beer from the *Little Britain* TV show, you sent two subliminal messages to those present. The first, ridiculing me as the project leader of Priority M and the second message, which is infinitely worse, is to ridicule me as a trans woman. Well, as far as I'm concerned, there was nothing covert about it at all – that despicable image of Carol Beer with a huge red X on her face sprang off the screen and punched me front and center.

Jules, as preposterous as this incident and Kurt's previous transphobic outburst are, they're still not enough for me to take him down. If, today, I was to put in a complaint about him at HR, he'd just deny everything and try to paint me as being hysterical and irrational. It would be my word against his, he'd be left off the hook and my reputation would be tarnished for good. But no worries, I've got him exactly where I need him to be, i.e., in my team, where I can keep an eye on him. With this latest stunt, the noose around his career at Megalaar just got a little tighter. In his delusions, he's got me down for a feeble and harmless pussycat, but what he did today is unleash the fiercest and darkest side of me. And believe you me, Pantera is coming for him, with the wrath and anger of a woman scorned.

23

Malbec in Juan-les-Pins

Journal entry # 2040$
Juan-les-Pins, Côte d'Azur, France, Nov 2017
🎧 Gotan Project – Diferente

"The paradoxes of life – here we are sipping on Argentinian Malbec wine in one of France's leading wine producing regions." I picked up my glass of wine to toast Nadine's health.

"Well, we are having dinner at an Argentinian steakhouse. C'mon, seriously, what else were we going to order with our rib-eye steaks? *Beaujolais Villages*?" She rolled her eyes at me.

"Touché, sis!" I stuck my tongue out at her. "Once more,

thank you for coming with me to the south of France for my surgery."

"You're very welcome. But for the umpteenth time, I implore you to tell me more about the surgery?"

"Dr. Saint Martegny mentioned something about making an incision from ear to ear and rolling back the skin to alter the shape of the frontal skull," I replied in a matter-of-fact tone.

"Sweet Mother of Christ, Zoë! You mean he's going to scalp you?!" Nadine's eyes popped out.

"Well, if you want to put it that way, yes." I nodded.

"I wish you would let me come with you to the clinic tomorrow. Why won't you let me?" she pleaded.

"Nadine, take a look around you! You're in the Côte d'Azur, for goodness' sake, the most beautiful region on the planet. Tomorrow is going to be a sunny, winter's day with clear blue skies stretching for miles. Go for a walk on the beachfront promenade, to the old-town, or take a bus to Cannes. I won't have you cooped up between four walls for hours on end. What's the use in that? Anyway, the clinic has your cell-phone number. If they need you, they'll call you."

"You're so bloody stubborn, Zoë van Vixenhoven, and so independent. You know that, don't you?" she snapped back, her face a picture of total exasperation.

"Yes, I know. Don't worry. Everything will be okay." With my best effort at a puppy-face impersonation, I tried to mollify her.

"The clinic better call me once the operation's over," she insisted.

"They will. It could be quite late though. Dr. Saint Martegny estimated that the surgery will last between eight to ten hours."

"And here you are, as cool as a cucumber! Sipping your glass of wine like there's not a worry in the world."

"No, sis. I just have a very calm exterior. Deep down inside me, my core is burning away like a smoldering volcano. That's how it's always been with me since childhood."

In Juan-les-Pins, a resort town a stone's throw away from Cap d'Antibes (where the good doctor's clinic is located), I rented us a modern two-bedroom apartment via Airbnb. The apartment is located a mere seven-minute walk from the beachfront promenade and, more importantly, just across the street from a Carrefour supermarket where we did a week's grocery shopping earlier this afternoon. I've been informed by the clinic that for the first three weeks after the surgery, I will only be able to consume soft foods. Basically, only foods that won't require much chewing.

"I'm so grateful to have a sister like you, Nadine, to take care of me after the surgery. And I'm so looking forward to your Risotto Funghi and Risotto Frutti di Mare."

Nadine raised her glass one last time.

"Here's to a speedy recovery, dear."

I checked the time on my wristwatch. "*Garcon, s'il vous plaît, deux cafés dulce de leche.*" I ordered us our favorite coffee concoction a mere half an hour before my food-and-drinks embargo kicks in. As of ten o'clock this evening, I have to cease all consumption. This includes drinking water.

After a few minutes of operating the gigantic espresso-machine contraption, the waiter came back with our Argentinian-style caramel sweetened coffees.

"To Argentina! And her love affair with *dulce de leche*."

"Viva Argentina," Nadine agreed.

24

Face Feminization Surgery

Journal entry # 2041$
Cap d'Antibes, Côte d'Azur, France, Nov 2017
🎧 The Beatles – Eleanor Rigby

"Take off all your clothes, mademoiselle, and wear this," the nurse instructed me.

"Everything. Including my underwear?" I inquired, though it sounded more like a protest.

"Yes, mademoiselle, everything. For the operation, all you need are this surgical gown and those non-slip socks. This will be your room for the coming two nights. You will be the only patient here. You can use that closet to hang your clothes. Please do not forget to remove all your valuables: watch, rings, earrings, bangles. There's a safe box in the closet. You can put your passport and cell phone in there too." She paused and looked straight into my eyes. "Do you wear contact lenses?"

"Yes."

"You need to remove those too. I'll be back with my colleague in about twenty minutes to take you to the operating theater."

I resisted the temptation to roll my eyes. *Theater! Really, why do they still call it that?*

What she called a surgical gown is nothing more than a flimsy, cucumber green-colored apron with short sleeves, which can be fastened by an even flimsier string at the back. I decided to wear the non-slip socks on top of my cotton socks. It was too chilly to take them off. After following the nurse's instructions (more or less), I sat on the bed and stared at the ceiling.

True to her word, after twenty minutes, the nurse returned with a male colleague who was pushing a stretcher.

"My name is Sergio. How are you feeling, mademoiselle?" the male nurse asked.

"Okay. A little nervous, I guess."

"Don't worry. Dr. Saint Martegny is the best in this field of surgery. You'll be in very good hands," he tried to assure me with sympathetic eyes.

I climbed onto the stretcher. It was clearly designed for shorter patients; my feet dangled from the edge.

"You're quite a tall lady, mademoiselle," Sergio remarked, stating the obvious. I liked him, though. He was the type who at least made an effort to make you feel at ease. This I couldn't say about the nurse. No, she was too rigid and austere. I didn't like her. Not at all.

"My name is Zoë. I'm from Holland," I smiled back at Sergio.

"Zoë, we're taking you to the antechamber. It's like a small room, where the head nurse will do some checks and administer the intravenous drip before you're taken to the operating theater."

In the antechamber, I waited for the head nurse to arrive, while I stared at the pole from which the IV-drip hung. *Fuck! I hate this part.* I don't like needles and dreaded the moment the needle would pierce my skin and be inserted into my vein.

"Zoë, please stretch out your left arm for me, and open and clench your left fist several times."

I followed the nurse's instructions while she massaged the vein on my inner left arm, just below the elbow. She tore open a sealed plastic wrapping and produced an ominous looking needle. *Heavens! That's a long needle. Pretty thick too.* Horrified, I turned my head in the opposite direction. I felt the temperature in my fingers drop to sub-zero levels. She continued to massage my veins and suddenly it happened: a pang of sharp pain at the spot where the needle broke the skin. I ground my teeth and a teardrop crawled out of my right eye.

"Please, continue to open and close your left hand. The blood is not moving. *Merde! Excusez moi*! I will need to remove the needle and try another spot. Maybe at the pulse of your wrist." She removed it and inserted it again a little lower than the initial spot. *Aaagh!* This time it was more painful, and both my eyes teared up.

"It's still not working," she exclaimed, exasperated.

Lady, fuck this. Are you kidding me! Are you new at this?

"Why don't you try my right hand? It gives better blood. In the hospital in Amsterdam, I've given blood dozens of times. The right hand always works," I intervened, beseeching her.

With the IV-drip finally secured (just before I reached the point of passing out), I was carted to the operating room. There were several nurses in green scrubs busy moving around like bees in a hive in this odd, oval-shaped room. *Jules,* w*hy do operating rooms have to be so cold and look so ominous, like something from a psychological thriller?* The nurses transferred me to a narrow operating table directly underneath a colossal metal disc containing at least ten circular lights. One of the nurses attached some kind of clip to the middle finger of my left hand.

"You have very cold hands, mademoiselle."

"I usually do. Even in the best of times," I offered by way of explanation.

"*'Mains froids. Coeur chaud!'* we say in France." She gently but firmly pressed the flesh in the center of my palm, as if to reassure me.

"Sorry. My French is quite limited."

"Cold hands. Warm heart. It's an expression in France." She clarified.

A fourth medic in scrubs, surgical mask and protective hair cap approached the operating table. *You must be the anesthetist. By the way – what a God-awful, tongue-twisting word! Anesthetist.*

"Zoë, you've been informed earlier that this operation will be performed under general anesthesia. Once I put this mask on your face, I want you to inhale and start counting down from ten to one. *D'accord?*"

I nodded and he placed the rubber mask on my nose and mouth. I took a deep breath.

"Ten, nine, eight…" I started to fade away and blacked out.

I heard lots of voices speaking in hurried French around me. There was an air of panic in those voices. *Guys, I don't think you've administered enough anesthesia. Somehow, I'm still awake (somewhat). I can hear you talking.* I thought I heard Dr. Saint Martegny's voice. Something about giving me more anesthesia, or that it's not working on the patient. So, it's not working. They're aborting the operation. They're starting to wake me up. Why in Heaven's name is it not working? Please, please try again. You must operate on me. I need this surgery.

The voices started getting louder and louder. Flashes of sharp artificial light in my eyes. Rapid movement. I was being moved on a stretcher to another location. *Guys, what happened? Why didn't you operate?* Suddenly, I felt extremely nauseous. I couldn't help but double-up and vomit. *Fuck! That yellow bile on the linoleum floor is last night's steak and wine. I will never have that again. Ever.* Someone wiped my mouth with a cloth. More hurried voices around me. I think there are three of them.

I'm now alone in a dark room, lying in bed. Crying. *Why did the operation fail? Why did they have to abort? What am*

I going to do now? The tears continued to stream down my cheeks. I could taste their sour saltiness in my mouth. My face is itchy. I need to scratch it. I lifted my right arm and put my hand on my face. *Huh! It's bandaged.* Except for my eyes and mouth, my entire head is wrapped in bandage. *Huh! How come?* And then the realization dawned on me. Underneath the bandage, I couldn't help but smile. *God that hurt! Zoë, stop smiling already! So, they did operate on me after all. Merci! Merci!*

The next morning, Dr. Saint Martegny came to my room looking like a Hollywood movie star, dressed in a striped navy-blue Armani suit, crisp white shirt (two buttons open from the collar) and platinum-plated cufflinks.

"Doctor, you look so elegant and so handsome!" I couldn't help but blurt out the words. To my embarrassment, I sounded like a groupie. His cheeks blushed.

"Bonjour, mademoiselle." He sat on the bed next to me and carefully removed the bandages from my head.

"You're a very brave woman, mademoiselle van Vixenhoven. The operation lasted more than ten hours. How are you feeling?"

"Groggy. Every part of my face and the top of my head, everything feels so stiff and hurts like hell." I tried hard to focus on his attractive face.

"The nurse will come soon with the medication. I've prescribed you some strong painkillers. Take the Tramadol pills three times a day for the next ten days. They will help you cope with the pain. I'm sorry to say this but the next two days are going to be excruciatingly painful and after that the pain should start to subside." He took my hand and pressed it warmly.

Fuck the pain, doctor!

"Doctor, how did the operation go? Are you pleased?"

"Your face is extremely swollen and bruised right now. There are also some scars, especially around the nose area." He gestured with his left hand toward the middle of his face. "I had to break your jaws into two parts to complete the surgical modification on your jawline. But don't worry! All of it will heal in time. You're young. It will heal quickly, I'm sure."

Doctor, answer my bloody question.

"Doctor, tell me, how do I look?" I said, my frustration finally boiling over. He smiled from ear to ear.

"You're going to look stunning. Still Zoë but a very feminine version of you." At that moment, all I wanted to do, but I didn't dare, was to hug him and return his million-dollar smile.

Dr. Saint Martegny wasn't exaggerating about the pain. It hurt like the nether regions of hell. I tried to distract myself by listening non-stop to music and watching one video clip after the other on my cell phone. Jules, not that that really helped much, but in this situation, when you're very much inclined to dig your fingers into your face and fucking rip it off your skull, every little bit counts, believe me!

On a quirkier note, in the seven days after the operation, every time I closed my eyelids, the world would light up with bright yellow, orange, red and green psychedelic patterns, like dense forest foliage ascending to the sky. For some odd reason, the continuously changing patterns reminded me of a cartoon film called *The Yellow Submarine*, which I had once seen, as a child, in Lebanon. It featured animated versions of The Beatles. Much later, Johan would explain to me that it wasn't that odd to think about *The Yellow Submarine*. He explained that The Beatles were allegedly under the influence of various hallucinogenic drugs, including anesthetic agents, when they created that iconic album from which the cartoon is derived.

IV

CULMINATION

1

Nutella Witchcraft

Journal entry # 2054$
Rotterdam, Mar 2018
🎧 Kylie Minogue – Chocolate

Thou shalt not be operated on! Westeneinde Hospital made it crystal clear to me that if I don't do anything about my weight, my Sex Reassignment Surgery (SRS), planned for end of April (2018) will be postponed. Why? Because according to their analysis, I'm borderline anorexic. To meet their strict health criteria for the SRS operation, I need to increase my BMI (Body Mass Index) to 20 (or 19 at the minimum). The other two criteria, which I'm required to adhere to are: 1) a complete halt to smoking; not an issue for me since I'm not a smoker. And 2) part of the pubic zone should be permanently free of all hair; already taken care of, courtesy of five laser sessions.

I'm thrilled that the surgeon, who will be operating on me, is none other than Ms. Laraki. She's considered one of the top four surgeons in the field of vaginoplasty in Holland, and that automatically makes her one of the best in the world. Not only is she the only woman at the top, she's also the only one from a minority ethnic group. Her parents are immigrants from Morocco; they arrived in Holland in the early seventies, like thousands of others seeking a better life for themselves and their children. Immigrants from Morocco are overwhelmingly Muslim and usually are considerably more conservative than the Dutch in their outlook and norms, which makes Ms. Laraki's journey to the top of this specific field of plastic surgery all the more remarkable. Way to go, girl! But, dear Jules, I do digress from the main purpose of this journal entry, i.e., preparing for the upcoming SRS operation.

To help me in my assignment to gain weight (and very fast), I've decided to summon to my kitchen no lesser a cooking goddess than Nigella Lawson, herself. *I wish! A mere mortal like me having Nigella in her kitchen – girl, keep on dreaming. That's never gonna happen.* So, I settled for her sacred cooking book *Nigellissima*. I leafed through the book until I found the section containing the recipe for Nutella Cheesecake. *C'mon, Zoë. You don't need the book. This recipe is literally hard coded in your brain.* I closed Nigella's cookbook and put it back on the shelf. Okay, here goes: 1) 250 grams digestive biscuits, 2) 2 tablespoons of unsalted butter, 3) 350 grams of Nutella, 4) a handful of chopped roasted hazelnuts, 5) a packet of cream cheese (I prefer Philadelphia), and 6) 60 grams of icing sugar.

Sorry, Nigella. Cooking goddess as you most definitely are, and as impossible a task as it may have been, I did find a way to elevate your divine recipe to an even higher level of divinity – we're talking here about Seventh Heaven heights. So, without further ado, I made the following changes to the original recipe: 1) I melted a bar of Lindt Swiss dark chocolate (69% minimum cacao content) in the microwave and added it to the bowl which contained the Nutella and cream cheese, and 2) reduced the quantity of icing sugar by half. *Et voila!* Witness the 'Bestest' (with a capital 'B') ever Nutella cheesecake.

A word of caution, be very careful when accepting a piece of Nutella cheesecake from La Vixenhoven – it's *sooooo* good she might bewitch you ;-)

2

Neo Vagina

Journal entry # 2059$
Amstelland Hospital, 25–29 Apr 2018
🎧 Alexis Ffrench – Reborn

<u>Day 1</u>

With more than half an hour to kill before my train to Amsterdam departed, I persuaded myself that I had an opportunity to stuff myself with an apple-crumble pie and wash it all down with a flat white at Dudok Patisserie at Rotterdam Central Station. No, dear Jules, I'm not giving in to gluttony; this extra boost of calories is called risk management. You see, I was still a little concerned that the hospital would refuse to operate on me due to my low BMI.

Standing at the long table along a glass wall overlooking the station's main hall, I gorged the delicious pie and couldn't help but lick my sticky fingers clean. I know, it's bad manners, but hell whatever. That was truly delicious. Mind you, not as delicious as my Nutella cheesecake, but delicious, nonetheless. I was contemplating having another piece, when I heard something being broadcast about the next train to Amsterdam. It wasn't clearly audible, so I checked my train on the Dutch Railways app, just to be sure. Thank goodness! All was well. No cancellation or delay. My train should leave in approximately eight minutes. I packed up my stuff and was about to leave when I noticed a sun-tanned, middle-aged man in a gray suit and creamy pink shirt staring at me. He flashed a toothy smile at me when our eyes met. I looked away. Why are you staring at me? Fuck it! I don't have time to ponder the reasons why? I took off.

On my way to platform 11, I couldn't help but notice someone shadowing me; it was the man in the gray suit. He noticed that I noticed him and walked past me. Out of the blue, he stopped just three meters ahead of me, turned around and extended his left hand. He held a small piece of paper between his thumb and index finger. I could see there was a telephone number scribbled on it. Again, he flashed a smile, as I walked past him.

"This is for you, guapa!"

"No thank you," I replied.

"Why not?" he reacted, disappointed.

"I can't. I'm taken," I lied. A second later, I stepped

onto the escalator to platform 11 and once there, to my relief I noticed my train pull onto the platform. I jumped into the closest coach and settled in a seat on the right-hand side of the train (i.e., the side furthest away from the platform).

Believe it or not, Jules, this is not the first time something like this has happened to me. I mean that someone tried to pick me up this way. Many years ago – way before my coming out – I was once walking down Place Vendôme in Paris, when I noticed a middle-aged woman (yes, woman) brush very close past me. A few steps later she tried to push a piece of paper (with a telephone number) in my hand. "*Pour un petit bijou comme toi.*"

Enough of that! I banished all thoughts from my head except one: my upcoming sex reassignment surgery. Tomorrow morning is the most important day of my life; a day which in many ways will mark my rebirth.

One and a half hours later, I checked into Amstelland Hospital on the outskirts of Amsterdam. Due to a shortage of beds, Westeneinde subcontracts some of the operations to Amstelland Hospital.

"Not a bad thing," Johan recently explained, "as Amstelland is much quieter and the kosher food is much better." Kosher? Yes, Amstelland has Jewish roots; it was previously the Joods Amsterdam Hospital. Walking across the wide hospital hallway to my room, I noticed the multitude of framed pictures of Jerusalem on the walls. How ironic was this? A Christian patient is going to be operated on by a Muslim surgeon at a Jewish hospital. I love it! Perhaps there's hope, however unlikely, for the Abrahamic faiths to make peace one day. Mind you, I hasten to add that both Dr. Laraki (I'm assuming) and myself are only nominally of our respective faiths.

In my hospital room, I met Adrienne, a fellow trans woman whom Dr. Laraki will also operate on the next day. Adrienne is a copper-orange haired, blue-eyed foxy lady, ten years my junior. On the 'passability' scale, she would score a perfect ten, and after tomorrow she will have completed her crossing to the other side. We had a nice rapport; we clicked right away and stayed up all night talking about our lives, and about the day after. After what? Well, Jules, the day after *the* surgery, of course. When both of us would have vaginas. Now is a good time to dispel some misconceptions: sex reassignment surgery does not involve any chopping off the penis. As a matter of fact, the penis is surgically reversed into the body, like a glove turned inside out. Jules, do you recall my journal entry about all humans physically starting out as female? The only organs that will be discarded are the testes, otherwise known as the balls or the bollocks. Goodbye and good riddance to those testosterone factories, which have been poisoning me all my life.

<u>Day 2</u>
Here we go again. Almost five months to the day, and once more I'm laid on a stretcher being pushed by a group of nurses to the operating theater's antechamber.

"Where are you from?" Nurse number 1 asked me.

Seriously! You are asking me this question right now? My eyes almost betrayed my disgust at this question that never seemed to go away. C'mon, after all these years of living in Holland, I'm still being confronted with this nonsense.

"I'm from Rotterdam." I decided to play it my way.

"I don't think so," Nurse number 2 interjected. "Your accent is much more southern than that."

Keep calm, Zoë, this is not the time to butt heads.

"I'm from Rotterdam!" I repeated, digging in my heals.

"Judging by your accent, I would say you're from Limburg," Nurse Number 2 continued. I rolled my eyes and wanted to burst out laughing. Limburg is Holland's most southern province. I recalled that Adrienne had mentioned that she's from Limburg. We talked all night. Some of her dialect must have rubbed off on me. Crazy! But happy crazy. Sorry, nurses, that I thought you were implying something else.

In the antechamber, when Nurse number 2 asked me to stretch out my left hand, alarm bells started ringing in my head. 9, 10, 11, 12. Last time, this did not go well, so I refused.

"Please, miss, stretch out your left hand so I can insert the IV line."

"No," I shook my head. "Sorry, nurse, you're going to have to trust me on this. Please put it in my right hand." No way was I going to back down on this. Nurse number 2 walked off to talk to Nurse number 1. A few seconds later, Nurse number 1 walked up to me and asked:

"What seems to be the problem, Miss van Vixenhoven?" I explained to her what had happened in France, when I had my Face Feminization Surgery.

"That's alright, dear. No worries. We'll insert the IV line into your right hand. Always listen to the patient. Usually, they know their bodies best," she reprimanded Nurse number 2.

A few minutes later, I was transferred to the operating

table. My legs spread wide and hanging up in the air on leg stretchers. In this position, I couldn't help but feel like a mom about to give birth (stupid of me, I know).

The anesthetist asked me to count down from ten as he placed a rubber mask on my face. I was gone by seven. Total blackout! And I'm happy to report that there were no hallucinations this time. Four hours later, I woke up, and although I was as groggy as a drunken sailor, I was all smiles. I'm a woman, now!

Day 3

Thank heavens for the morphine pump which the hospital gave me after the surgery. I don't know how otherwise I would have kept the pain at a manageable level. I administered the morphine liberally. Heavily sedated, I passed in and out of the Dreamworld. I was stepping out of the dark tunnel and into daylight for the first time in my life.

I lifted the blanket and looked down under. Heavens! That's one huge, bloody swelling between my legs, and with a plastic tube (a catheter) protruding out of my vagina (it still feels funny to say that) it looked like a dystopian battlefield. Bear with me, girl. No pain, no gain.

Talking about pain, I continued to bleed quite heavily throughout the day. At night, I saw the nurse remove what looked like a gigantic glass container full of blood (my blood) from under my bed. *Fuck! Where are they taking all this blood? To the blood bank?* Don't panic, girl. Trust the experts. They know best.

Day 4

Adrienne: 15 (and counting) Zoë: 2

There was a steady stream of visitors to Adrienne's side

of the hospital room. They just kept coming. I counted sixteen and then gave up. After all, it's quality that matters more than quantity, right?

I received two very special visitors. The first was Johan. He brought with him a beautiful exotic-looking flowering plant with oblong bluish-green leaves and an orange flower. *Goodness, Johan. How did you know that I adored Bird of Paradise.* I mused that only a very intelligent and perceptive person would have chosen such a plant. I was overjoyed that he came to visit me. Honestly, Jules, I don't think this is his MO with his patients. That really made me feel special. Thank you!

Second visitor was Nadine. She arrived with chocolates, a huge bouquet of flowers and an adorable stuffed black panther toy. Bless you, Nadine. I love you so much.

<u>Day 5</u>

This morning, Dr. Laraki herself, came to remove the tampon (which was inserted into my vagina, right after the surgery, to stretch the cavity) and that god-awful catheter.

"I'm going to remove the catheter now. This is going to hurt, Zoë," she warned me. Fuck, she wasn't kidding.

From a brown leather bag she was carrying with her, Dr. Laraki produced what looked like a very mundane looking dildo.

"This is a dilator, Zoë. You use it to keep the cavity of your vagina open. I want you to dilate twice a day, every day, for the next six months."

Uh-hu! Sure thing doctor!

"I see you're healing quickly. Well done! Just remember to take it easy and no physical activities for the next nine weeks."

"Well done me? No, Dr. Laraki, well done you. You did all the work. Thank you! You can't imagine how utterly grateful I am to you."

An hour later, my visitor counter went up to three as it was Willem, my only BFF, who came with Nadine in a rental car to take me home, back to my beloved Rotterdam.

3

Reflections on Being

Journal entry # 2070$
Rotterdam, Jun 2018
🎧 Isfar Sarabski – Planet

A Woman (with a capital 'W'). That's what I have always been. A woman – that's what my body's been for the past nine weeks, since the sex reassignment surgery. Yesterday, for the first time since my coming out, I dared to stand totally naked in front of the mirror. And what I saw was a woman, with a vagina, breasts, wider hips and smaller waist. A woman. For the first time in my life, I don't hate my body. For the first time in my life, I don't reject it. For the first time in my life, I feel calm and serene when I see a reflection of my body in the mirror. The raging tempest around me, which has been my companion since time immemorial, has at long last died down.

Dear Jules, I'm going to go ahead and say it. For the first time in my life, I feel one with my body. Yes, I feel alive.

4

It Takes
Two to Tango

Journal entry # 2074$
Amsterdam, Jul 2018
🎧 Narcotango – Mistela

"That's hilarious!" I recounted to Johan the incident with my neighbor, who recently accused me of flirting with her husband. When I confronted her and asked if she had actually seen this with her own eyes, she admitted that it was a friend who had seen me. All I had done was talk with her husband during a party. Yes, I was friendly with him, but definitely not flirtatious.

"Zoë, it's okay to flirt. But I will add an important caveat: when doing so, be conscious of it and its possible consequences."

"I'm not sure I follow you, Johan."

"For all intents and purposes, Zoë, you are just starting to learn about your sensuality and sexuality. Whereas a cis woman would have had years, if not decades, to fine-tune this side of herself, you are having to fast-track this process in a very short period of time. While you're now in your thirties, in many ways when it comes to your sexuality, you're just a teenager."

"So?"

"So, don't rush into anything. Take small steps. Promise me?"

I nodded. *Oh, Johan. If only you knew – I'm not that innocent.*

5

The Dominatrix and Her Whip

Journal entry # 2094$
Rotterdam, Sep 2018
🎧 Emmanuelle Seigner – Venus in Fur

He did exactly as she ordered. Bogdan lay spreadeagled on his back, anxiously waiting what came next. Although his back now stung and burned, and the skin color had changed into a darker shade of pomelo pink, he would do anything to please her. Especially after she had just spent the last thirty minutes flogging him with the cat-o-nine-tails whip.

With four neat bundles of Japanese hemp rope in her hands, Mistress Pantera walked to the bed where Bogdan lay. She teased his body with the ropes and then proceeded to tie his hands and legs to the four bed posts.

"Hmmm, I see your pathetic excuse for manhood went to sleep prematurely. Some stimulation is required," she hissed seductively into the night air. From a chest of drawers, she took out a pair of shoulder-length black leather gloves. The best gloves ever made – nobody makes them like Lanvin, anymore. Bogdan stretched and turned his neck until it ached, but he was desperate to see her pull on her gloves. Mistress Pantera swung her body just enough to offer him a glimpse, as she slid on the left- and then the right-hand glove excruciatingly slowly. This specific pair was very, very tight. Skin tight. With every little pull and caress of the buttery soft leather, Bogdan's manhood became harder. By the time she had finished, it was fully erect and as hard as a rock. *Et voila!* This pair of long leather gloves matched her Saint Laurent thigh-high boots perfectly. And in combination with the shiny black latex leotard, the stereotypical Dominatrix look was complete. The customer gets what the customer asks. Most of the time.

"Hmm, I'm going to enjoy torturing that ugly phallic thing." She struck the perfume-sweet boudoir air twice with her horse whip before teasing his manhood with it. "If you dare cum, I will throw you out. Is that understood?"

"Yes, Mistress Pantera," Bogdan whimpered.

Twenty minutes later, Bogdan felt his entire body ache in pain and ecstasy. Pantera wasn't finished with him though. She climbed onto the bed, straddled his body between her thighs and took his nipples in her gloved fingers.

"Permission to speak, Mistress."

"Permission granted."

"Please, Mistress Pantera, I have 7300 euros in the inside pocket of my jacket. The money is yours if you fuck my cock. Please, I beg you, fuck it to smithereens?" he pleaded.

"How dare you ask that! You know I'm not a prostitute," she barked at him and twisted his nipples so hard he yelled for mercy. "If you ever ask that again, it will be the last time you are allowed into my studio. Is that clear?"

"Yes, Mistress Pantera. I'm very sorry, Mistress. Very sorry. It won't ever happen again, Mistress."

"Now shut up! I don't want to hear a word from you anymore." From the bedside table, she took the XXL red block candle, which had been burning for the better part of an hour.

"You know what's going to happen now?" She looked down at him and smiled, a wicked smile.

'

Bogdan showered and put on his clothes. His eyes sparkled and radiated with an intense energy.

"Thank you, Mistress. I feel invigorated and energized like a million suns. Truly! After you take care of me, I feel I can take on the world and win."

"You're welcome, Bogdan, but I can't take all the credit. It's the endorphins. After the session, your body is literally flooded with them."

"Mistress Pantera, don't be humble. You're the real deal, unlike most of the others who are ludicrous clichés and silly stereotypes of what a Dominatrix should be." Bogdan's eyes were now soft and reflective.

"So where do you sail to next?" Pantera asked, knowing that Bogdan was the proud maritime captain (from Serbia) of a colossal Taiwanese freighter ship.

"In a few hours we sail to Shanghai via Suez and Singapore. I should be back in Rotterdam in two to three months. I would definitely like to see you again." Pantera responded with a terse but polite smile.

"Please check first with the boys at *Flooow*. They will let you know if I'm still around." *When I've finished paying off my mountain of medical related debts, I'm out of here, baby!*

"Mistress Pantera, you are my Mistress Amazona. Please, you can't stop. You are a natural talent."

"'Mistress Amazona', why do you call me that? Is it because I'm trans? I'm open about that fact on my website."

"Yes, Mistress, partly. And because I believe the mythical Amazona warriors were like you, trans women. Think about it? They're described as being very tall, fierce, exotic women who had the muscular strength of men."

"Hmm."

"Also, they were very reclusive. You know, because of their secret, they kept their distance from people. They must have been transsexual women. What else could logically explain that?" Bogdan seemed to be thoroughly convinced by his reasoning.

"Interesting theory." She paused for a second and extended her right arm toward him. "For now, Captain Pantović, I bid you safe journey to China. Take good care of yourself."

Bogdan bowed deeply in reverence and kissed her hand

with genuine affection. Secretly, he made a wish, kissed the Slavonic cross around his neck and let himself out of the soft red tones of Pantera's studio and into the deep inky blue of the night.

6

'Lenny Kravitz' Smile

Journal entry # 2099$
Rotterdam, Sep 2018
🎧 Luciano Supervielle – Perfume
Lisa Stansfield – In All the Right Places

Has he figured it out? That I'm trans. It's my second date with Jeronimo and still no sign that he's noticed that I'm different from the other girls. I wish I could throw this irritating, nagging question, once and for all, out of my head and just enjoy myself with this handsome hunk of a man.

Two weeks ago, I couldn't believe it when the dating app notified me that Jeronimo 'liked' my profile. Initially, I dismissed this as some software glitch, which AI would duly rectify. So, imagine my surprise (I literally fell off my chair), when Jeronimo texted me *Hello sexy lady* and suggested we meet in person.

Physically, Jeronimo ticked all my boxes – he's tall, athletic and sports a cool afro. His most endearing physical attribute, I would say, is his sexy lady-killer smile. I call it his 'Lenny Kravitz' smile. Suave and Swagger – he's got it all and in abundance. He's done really well considering that he's a second-generation Cabo Verdean whose parents had immigrated to Holland four decades ago from that remote archipelago in the Atlantic Ocean, with nothing to their name except the clothes on their backs and one suitcase between them. From very modest beginnings he had pulled himself up and through the system, graduating cum laude from the Technische Universiteit Delft, one of Holland's most prestigious engineering and technology universities.

On our first date, I deliberately tried to challenge his intellect, steering the conversation toward Literature, Art, Architecture, World Politics and Current Affairs. Hell, I even threw in some cooking-related questions, hoping to trip him up. He comfortably parried everything I'd slung at him (and then some). I was impressed – from what I'd seen and heard so far, this man was the real McCoy: he's got brains, looks, character and brawn. But would he be okay being romantically (and maybe later, physically) involved with a trans woman? Damn it! This question was hanging like a Sword of Damocles above my head.

"A penny for your thoughts, Zoë?" Jeronimo snapped me out of my little reverie.

"Nothing! Just enjoying the spectacular view of the

river and the port beyond. I love those vintage cranes just beyond the Lloyds and Müller piers. There's something strangely romantic about them – in a steampunk kind of way. Thank you for bringing me here. Hotel New York has always been one of my favorite spots in Rotterdam. Did you know this used to be the headquarters of Holland America Line? I'm referring to the company that owned the great ocean liners during the first half of the twentieth century."

"No, I didn't know that, and you're more than welcome." He lifted his beer bottle. "And here's to steampunk engineering!" We clicked our Leffe Blonde bottles.

"Would you like some *bitter ballen*?" Jeronimo offered me the plate full of crispy, fried Dutch finger food.

"No thanks! Excuse me, I have to powder my nose." I excused myself and walked to the restroom to touch up my makeup but mainly to think about things. Like, what am I going to do if he tries to kiss me? *Zoë, don't forget Johan's advice to not rush anything and take small steps.*

When I returned to our table, Jeronimo jumped out of his chair, took my right hand in his and with all the panache of a seasoned salsa dancer, he swirled me around a couple of times. When I was facing him again, he laid his hands gently on my waist and looked deep into my eyes. At this point, I thought he was going in for a kiss (and I would have let him) but he turned away and pulled out my chair.

"Mademoiselle, your chair!" he ushered me with a contagious smile.

"Oh, how incredibly gallant of you, sir!" I replied with an exaggerated smile of my own. "So, besides being a rascal, you're a gentleman too!" We both burst out laughing. There was definitely a click between us, and the chemistry was getting hotter and spicier by the minute.

Being the rascal gentlemen that he most definitely is, Jeronimo insisted on walking me home.

"This is me." I pointed to the main entrance to my apartment block. "Thank you for the lovely time and company, Senhor Viera da Cruz."

"You're most welcome Senhora van Vixenhoven. Hmm, by the way, is that Dutch? I thought you said you're from Lebanon?" He continued to hold my left hand.

"Long story. I'll tell you about it some other time."

"No time like the present. How about you invite me in for a coffee?"

"Hmm." I put my index finger on my right temple to indicate that I was pondering the question seriously. Before I could answer, he cut in.

"Do you know something, Zoë?"

"No, actually most things I haven't got a clue about," I said, putting on the most matter-of-fact voice I could conjure up.

"You're like a beautiful box of contradictions." He smiled.

"I'm a box, am I?" I continued to tease him.

"No. I mean, yes – a box of contradictions. I mean contrasts."

"Really? Would you care to explain?"

"I'll try," he replied. "You're so mature and yet child-like. You're classical, elegant and yet you have that rock-edge chic side too. You're flirtatious and yet reserved. You're modest and yet you have an arrogant streak or maybe it is pride. You're intelligent and yet naïve."

This guy has got some serious psychoanalytical prowess. Impressive. Very.

"You're calling me naïve?" I objected.

"I called you intelligent. And if you hadn't interrupted me, I wanted to say that you are beautiful but don't act it or maybe don't even realize it." I blushed and looked away. "But there's one serious glitch in your system."

Okay, now we've finally come down to the wire; from now on it's all about the 'trans' factor.

"I was a box and now I'm a system. Gosh, what a grand promotion you've given me, Senhor da Cruz?" I feigned incredulity.

"There's indeed a major glitch in your system. Meu amor, you think too much! You're totally over-thinking things. You stand in your own way." He looked down at me with smiling, love-infectious eyes. "Let it go, Zoë. Take a chance on me and live life to the max." I felt his sweet breath on my lips. The pulse of my heart quickened to red-danger levels and adrenalin rushed in blistering torrents into my brain. I wanted to withdraw, to protest, to run away and then it happened. Jeronimo's lips joined mine.

Those lips unlocked and unleashed a pent-up reservoir of intense, repressed sexual energy in me. I kissed him back. Ferociously. On the way to my apartment, we kept tripping on each other, refusing to let go of the other's lips. We started undressing each other even before I had opened the door to my apartment. By the time we reached my bedroom, there was a trail of intermingled clothes behind us.

Next to my bed, the moon's soft light fell on our naked

bodies. He lifted me up. I wrapped my arms and legs around him so tight like Christmas gift wrapping around a box. *Holy Moly! So that's what a man inside you feels like!*

He threw me onto the bed and took me over and over again. The sex was passionate, frantic, frenzied. It felt desperate, almost angry, like it was our last day alive. But it wasn't kinky, until I dared him to take me from behind, all the while pulling my hair and biting the nape of my neck, like a lion does when mating. That dare worked – it released the hidden nocturnal animal in him and Pantera in me.

7

Reality Check

Journal entry # 2100$
Rotterdam, Sep 2018
🎧 Heart – There's The Girl

The air in my bedroom was heavy with the smell of our sex and the vanilla, labdanum and musk base-notes of my perfume. Dear Jules, I know we will never again experience a night like the one we had on our second date. On that night, our stars and planets aligned in way that only happens once in a lifetime. After last night, deep down I know that I'm forever changed. I hope, for the better.

With satisfaction, I inspected Jeronimo's bite marks on

my body, and noted that Pantera had left some of her bite marks on him, as well. Only hers were deeper, more pronounced and outnumbered his by a ratio of 2 to 1. *Well, he's still got some way to go (to learn my kinky ways), but he's a fast learner.*

I heard my stomach grumble; I'm famished, and I bet you when he wakes up, Jeronimo will be too. I'm going to prepare him a breakfast fit for a lion king. I pulled some clothes on, leaned down and kissed his back between the shoulder blades. Last night I gave you something special – a very special and unique gift. I hope, when you wake up, you'll appreciate it. Oh yeah, there's one other thing: my vagina is so sore I can hardly walk.

❡

"What's that divine smell?" a drowsy sounding Jeronimo asked.

"What does it smell like to you? I'm preparing you breakfast."

"Breakfast?"

"Yes, sleepyhead, I'm chopping the potatoes and onions."

"What are you making?"

"Spanish omelet."

"Smells good. What's in the oven?"

"Milk butter croissants. There's OJ in the juicer, English Breakfast tea or Lavazza coffee and help yourself to fruit." I waved a hand at the bowl of strawberries on the table, then turned to fetch the West Country Cheddar (farmhouse, of course), the strawberry jam and apricot marmalade, then tossed the onions into the pan.

"Cheese?" he said. "For breakfast?"

"Why not?" I picked up the jar of Nutella.

"And this, because I'm the Nutella Queen."

"Fancy."

"Now you tell me – is this a breakfast fit for a lion king? Or what?" I waved my hands like a diva.

"Oh, it certainly is. Fit for a king and *his* queen." Jeronimo slid behind me and wrapped his hands around my waist, while I continued working at the kitchen counter.

"But you silly *bobinha*. When I asked about the divine smell, I didn't mean that?" He dug his nose deep into my hair and inhaled. "I love the smell of your pheromones."

"I see that your *bandeira* is not as sleepy as you?" I smiled from ear to ear.

"My *bandeira*, as you call it, is also addicted to you. You have this effect on us."

"Umm. How many girls have you told that to? Senhor rascal gentleman?"

"None. You completely misjudge me and your impact on me. Did I tell you that you're a beautiful box of contradictions?" His soft breath tickled my neck.

"Oh, that box again." I bit my lip to stop myself from laughing.

"Yes, indeed. That same beautiful box of contradictions. Before last night, when it comes to sex, I had you down as the girl-next-door type."

"Really? And what on earth does that mean?" I asked, irritation, audible in my voice.

"It means the kind of woman who prefers that the man takes charge and does all the work. But last night, after you cuffed my hands to the bedframe, you fucking obliterated me. You blew me away, body and brains. *Completamente*."

"That was Pantera," I blurted out without thinking.

"Who's Pantera?"

"Nobody. My alter ego. It's a long story."

"Well, for the record, just so that you know, I totally dig Pantera. She rocks my boat. I want more of her."

I turned around to face him.

"It's totally cliché but be careful what you wish for, darling." I smudged the tip of his nose with a little butter and licked it like a kitten.

His eyes, now filled with lustful intent, drilled deep into mine. He lifted me onto the kitchen counter and wrapped my legs around his torso. With his tongue, he parted my lips and slid it inside. I tasted the sweet saltiness of his mouth and then alarm bells started ringing in my head.

"Stop! Please. Please, I need to tell you something." With that snap declaration, I pushed him away from me.

"Huh! Did I miss something? What happened?"

"Sit down," I insisted. "Please."

He sat down on a nearby dining-room chair. I remained on my feet.

"Jeronimo, what happened yesterday took me by surprise. I surrendered to the moment. We both did. What happens next between us is entirely up to you. So, please, I beg you to think twice before you react to what I'm about to tell you." I drew a deep breath.

"Tell me what?" The lustful, sly smile of less than a minute ago evaporated from his face, replaced by puzzlement.

"Also, I want to apologize beforehand for not telling

you earlier and for any distress I may cause." My hands were now visibly shaking.

"Meu amor, whatever it is, we'll work it out, I'm sure." He tried to calm my nerves.

I opened my mouth, but nothing came out.

"Zoë, meu amor, what is it?" His voice was masculine gentleness personified.

"I'm transgender." It finally came out. Loud, crisp and clear.

"What do you mean, you're transgender?"

"I'm a transgender woman," I repeated.

"Huh?" He was lost in thought for a few seconds. "What the fuck! Are you telling me you're a man?" His voice was no longer sweet but crude and angry. Very angry.

"No!" I snapped back at him. "I'm NOT a man. I'm a trans woman. There's a huge difference between the two. Don't fucking insult me!"

In rapid sequence, his confusion changed into shock and from that into indignation and finally into outrage.

"But I'm not gay," he roared at me. "How dare you trick me like this, you fucking homo."

"Please, Jeronimo, baby. This anger, this hatred for LGBT folk, is not you. I've looked into your heart – it's beautiful and full of light and compassion. You are special. That's why I gave you *me* yesterday. That's why I gave you my virginity." My whole body was now shaking. Violently.

"You're a fucking man." He shook his head over and over again in total disgust and disbelief.

"Jeronimo, if you can't bring yourself to see me as a woman anymore, then please see me as something that is neither man nor woman, a third gender. But whatever you think of me, I'm 1000% NOT a man."

"You tricked me into sleeping with a man." His voice was now very different. Distant. Repugnant.

"You are a man, Jeronimo." I yelled at him. "Look at me! Do I look anything like you? Didn't you fuck my vagina, like a million times last night."

"You conniving she-male bitch. You bloody evil *bruxa*." He was now utterly possessed by the demons of wrath and loathing. Dear Jules, what happened next, will, unfortunately, leave a scar on my life till the day I die. With one swift motion, Jeronimo grabbed the hair on the back of my head and smashed my face, one, two, three times into the wall. My nose started gushing rivers of blood. Blood soaked my blouse and seeped between my breasts. When he finally loosened his grip, my knees buckled, and I crumbled like a house of cards onto the floor. A pool of blood quickly formed around my head. Few seconds later the front door slammed shut with a thunderous thud. 17, 18, 19, 20. In a flight of fury, exit Jeronimo.

8

Baccara Rose

Journal entry # 2129$
Rotterdam, Nov 2018
🎧 Secret Garden – Song from a Secret Garden

The light around me dimmed when a menacingly low column of charcoal-gray clouds floated above the cemetery. The last of the fall leaves rustled in the trees as the wind picked up and howled a melancholic tune.

A tall, statuesque woman stood alone and half-concealed behind a tree on a hilly slope. She was clearly in mourning – she wore a black dress with long black leather gloves. A black and red silk scarf wafted in the air from her neck. Her eyes were covered by Tom Ford designer shades. In her hands she held a dark, burgundy-red rose.

In the distance, she observed a small group of bereaved persons console each other as the casket was lowered into the earth. *Ashes to ashes. Dust to dust.* One by one, they dropped a rose onto the coffin as the cemetery workers started shoveling spades full of moist earth into the freshly dug hole.

When the group of mourners retreated out of sight, I took heavy, reluctant steps from my hiding place behind the tree, to where she had been laid to rest.

The golden lettered words on the dark-gray read: Isabella Amel Shibli beloved mother of Maher, Zachariah and Nadine. I laid the rose next to the gravestone, knelt down and kissed it. *Farewell, Mama. May you finally find peace in Heaven. Please forgive me for not being there for you. I love you more than you can ever imagine!* Rivers of tears meandered down my face.

Behind me, a pair of feet shuffled. It must be the cemetery worker come back for his shovel. I felt the tap of cold fingers on my left shoulder. I stood up and turned around. *What's wrong with your face?* I recoiled in fear and felt sick in the pit of my stomach. His face was warped, surreal and continuously changing like something macabre from a Francis Bacon painting. A flash of metal, a lightning movement of the arm, too quick for me to register what was happening and before I realized it, he had thrust a sharp blade, perhaps a bayonet, through my abdomen. I doubled in pain and cried out in horror. I knew that face.

"Why, Baba? Why? Won't you leave me be with Mama in peace?" I spat out blood from my mouth while clutching my gushing wound. In the ground, behind me, a new hole appeared next to my mother's grave.

"You want to be with your mother? Why not join her, you disgusting freak!" He took a step forward and pushed me into the hole.

In the calm, cold night air, I woke up shaking and bathed in sweat. 34, 35, 36, 37… Parasomnia. Another nightmare, two nights in succession. Heaven, won't you have mercy on me?

My mother's health has deteriorated significantly in the past week. Nadine informed me that Mama was rushed to hospital last Wednesday. The doctors' diagnosis is alarming: her heart as well as her kidneys are failing. Due to certain complications, surgery has been ruled out as an option. That only leaves medication, which can only slow things down, at best. Since the moment I received this news, I've been on a knife's edge. What does it all mean? Is this, Heaven forbid, the beginning of the end? That can't be. For goodness' sake, she's only in her early sixties. How long does she have?

Jules, what am I feeling, right now? Distress. Disbelief. Anxiety. Tension. Profound shock and immense sorrow. Sometimes the pain in my chest is so powerful, I can't breathe. To rub salt into my wounds, the fact that I can't be there for her in person is eating away at me. I can't bear to think that my mother might think that I had abandoned her. Mama, I only chose to disappear from your life because I love you so much and wanted to protect you. Piece by piece, I'm being undone, being unraveled by this forlorn ordeal.

9

The Dreadful D-word

Journal entry # 2133$
Rotterdam, Nov 2018
🎧 Arctic Monkeys – Do Me a Favour

"Zoë, Zoë, is that you?" The neighbor interrupted me while I was checking my postbox at the apartment-block's lobby this morning.

"Hi, how are you guys doing?" I tried hard to avoid making eye contact with him and his wife, especially his wife.

"Zoë, dear, what happened to your hair? Who did that to you?" the forever inquisitive wife asked.

"Nothing. I cut it short myself," I shot back, annoyed. Though, she did have a point – I grant her that. I cut it so crudely that it looked like a disaster zone. Well, at least it fits 100% with how I'm feeling these days.

"And why are you wearing men's clothes?" the interrogation continued.

Lady, don't you get it. I'm not interested in small talk right now.

"Just putting my old clothes to use." Listless, I looked away.

"Are you okay, dear?" the husband asked. His voice resonated with genuine concern.

"Zoë, dear, are you *de-transitioning*?"

"Ursula, shush. That's none of our business," the husband intervened.

"Don't you shush me, Pim. I saw a TV documentary a few days ago on transgenders who reverse their transition and go back to what they were." The relentless wife tried to reassert herself and regain the upper hand.

One stupid documentary and now you think you're an expert, you dogged nosey parker.

"No, Ursula, I'm not de-transitioning," I stared her down, "and I never will. Now, if you don't mind, I'll see you some other time."

Dear Jules, just to clarify my thoughts on de-transitioning, I believe those who de-transition, are either: a) under extreme pressure to do so and have no other choice; basically, their survival necessitates this dramatic course of action, or b) they are not (and never were) transgender, to begin with. They and the medical institutions involved made a colossal mistake. They should have never transitioned in the first place.

Currently some who are claiming to be transgender are definitely not transgender. They are hurting our cause. So, most de-transitioners are one example. Don't even get me started when it comes to transvestites and crossdressers being wrongfully identified as transgender. My heart sinks when I hear that. And it doesn't stop there: a few days ago, *Vogue* magazine featured someone on their Instagram channel, who claims to be a non-binary trans woman. WTF? Seriously, how can you claim to be two contradicting identities at the same time? Jules, I should know: I am a trans woman, and I definitely know that's not congruent with being non-binary. When push comes to shove, it's simple: those who do not feel trapped in their bodies and are content living with their anatomy at birth are NOT transgender. The waters are being muddied by too many at the moment. This suits the machine of hate, lies and vitriol which is working overtime to deny us our identity. Let's hope from chaos comes clarity.

As a trans woman, if given a choice between de-transitioning or death, I would choose the latter, without the slightest doubt or hesitation. Why? Because, for me, de-transitioning is a sentence infinitely worse than death.

10

Message in a Bottle

Journal entry # 2135$
Rotterdam, Nov 2018
🎧 IAMX – Song of Imaginary Beings

I stood for five (or was it fifteen?) minutes in front of the tangerine-colored PostNL drop box. The 'next pick-up time' indicator adjacent to the aperture, showed 18:30. That's in approximately forty minutes. In my sweaty hands, I held a large C4-sized envelope addressed to my solicitors. Enclosed within were two items: first, a smaller, dark blue-colored envelope addressed to my sister, and second, an A4 paper with instructions to my solicitors that upon certification of my death, they should forward the blue envelope to Nadine and to faithfully execute my testament.

ʹ

Contents of the blue envelope:

Dearest Nadine,

There's this team assignment, which I had once participated in with my colleagues at work, to write down and present (to the others) how he/she wanted to be remembered once they've passed away. To my embarrassment, in my naivety, I interpreted this assignment literally, and when it was my turn to give a presentation, some colleagues started laughing at what I had to say. It turned out that the assignment was meant to make you think about what it is that's very important to you and whether you were already busy achieving this important thing (or things) in your life! Well, when I reflect upon this question today, my answer is 'yes'. I have achieved the most important objective in my life: I have physically transitioned to a woman. I have freed myself. By doing so, I have lived a real and authentic life, no matter how short. I'm lucky – I actually got to see daylight as a woman; most trans women live trapped inside all their lives. Of course, I would have loved to have had more time, especially with you. But this is life, it's hard and it's brutal. Things don't always end up going according to one's wishes and dreams.

By now you might have started to suspect the purpose of this letter. My dearest, dearest, dearest Nadine, if you have received this letter (via my solicitors) then I have already passed away. I'm terribly sorry to shock you like this, but life has become totally unbearable since Mama's death and my realization that there's just so much hate and contempt toward trans women in this world. Believe me, it's not just verbal abuse and poisonous words which have finally broken my heart and soul.

Please take care of Spooky; you're her mother now. I've instructed my solicitors that all my possessions are to go to you. My apartment, my Lotus sportscar, savings, books (some of them valuable limited editions), everything I owned is now yours.

Many years ago, I had consented to all my organs being donated to medicine once I've passed away. Hopefully this way, I can contribute to alleviating the pain and suffering of a few fellow human beings. So, my life had more than one purpose, after all.

Please do not mourn me for too long. I beg you not to. I'm not sure what the procedure is when one donates their body organs to medicine. I mean I don't know how long it will take before the medical institutions release my body (for burial). To achieve some semblance of closure, after my passing away, please take the enclosed poem with this letter and put it in a glass bottle. The hand-written poem is my 'tipping-point' poem, 'A trans-Existential Crossing', the first of four 'keys' to my liberation. Take this 'message in a bottle' to the Lloyds pier in Rotterdam, say a prayer for my soul and drop it into the River Maas, my beloved Maas. Even though there's a lot of river traffic on the Maas, I'm sure like me, the bottle will make it to the other side.

Nadine, I want you to live a long and fulfilled life. C'mon, sis, push yourself to be the very best version of you, but always authentically you.

There are no words big and colorful enough, in any written language, to express my love for you. I'm so grateful for having had you in my life. You are and will always be the brightest star in my universe.

Thank you for everything.

Your sister forever,

Zoë van Vixenhoven

11

Curtains!

Journal entry # 2137$
Rotterdam, Nov 2018
🎧 Seal – Prayer for the Dying

Nadine opened the front door to Zoë's apartment and called out twice for her sister. No answer was forthcoming. Just an eerie silence. A small ball of short velveteen black hair came running up to her. She knelt down and picked up the cat.

"Hey, Spooky, baby, where's your mummy?" Nadine babbled while holding Spooky close to her face. "Let's get you some water. You look thirsty."

From the corridor, she turned left into the open-plan living room and kitchen. "Where's mummy g-g-g…" Nadine's heart skipped a beat she dropped Spooky and screamed.

Zoë lay face down and motionless on the kitchen floor. Littered beside her: a half-empty bottle of Absolut vodka, several dark-brown medicinal bottles and two dozen white pills strewn haphazardly across the floor.

"No, no, no, Zoë. What have you done?" Once the initial shock had passed, Nadine dashed to Zoë's lifeless body. She turned her sister's body around and placed her wrist close to Zoë's open mouth. She could only sense the slightest of breaths.

"No! No! No! Zoë, don't you fucking die on me. I won't let you." She snatched her cell phone from her shoulder bag and with hands shaking, dialed 112. "Please, operator, help. My sister is dying. I think she tried to kill herself."

"Madame, I need you to calm down and tell me what you see." The voice at the other end was calm and authoritative.

"My sister. I found her lying on the floor," Nadine stammered. "I can't feel any pulse in her wrist, her breathing is very, very faint, I can barely feel it, only just. It looks like she's tried to take her life. There's a bottle of vodka, some pills and bottles of what looks like some kind of prescription cough syrup. Please. Please send someone quickly. She's going to die."

12

Adieu

Journal entry # 2138$
Rotterdam, Nov 2018
🎧 Secret Garden – Sleepsong

The light around me dimmed when a menacingly low column of charcoal-gray clouds floated above the cemetery. The last of the fall leaves rustled in the trees as the wind picked up and howled a melancholic tune.

A tall, statuesque woman stood alone and half-concealed behind a tree on a hilly slope. She was clearly in mourning – she wore a black dress with long black leather gloves. A black and red silk scarf wafted in the air from her neck. Her eyes were covered by Tom Ford designer shades. In her hands she held a dark, burgundy-red rose.

In the distance, she observed a small group of bereaved persons console each other as the casket was lowered into the earth. *Ashes to ashes. Dust to dust.* One by one, they dropped a rose onto the coffin as the cemetery workers started shoveling spades full of moist earth into the freshly dug hole.

When the group of mourners retreated out of sight, I took heavy, reluctant steps from my hiding place, behind the tree, to where she had been laid to rest. The golden lettered words on the dark-gray read: Isabella Amel Shibli beloved mother of Zoë, Zachariah and Nadine. I laid the rose next to the gravestone, knelt down and kissed it. *Farewell, Mama. May you finally find peace in Heaven. Please forgive me for not being there for you. I love you more than you can ever imagine!* Rivers of tears meandered down my face.

Behind me, a pair of feet shuffled. It must be the cemetery worker come back for his shovel. I felt a gentle warm hand on my left shoulder. I stood up and turned around. My heart leapt inside my chest; it was my beloved mother. She was, once more, young and radiant. I wanted to throw my arms around her and with every ounce of energy left in my body to embrace her. But I hesitated, stopped myself and took a step backward. *Does she even recognize me, let alone accept what I am?*

A warm and heartfelt smile graced her face. "My dear daughter, my first-born child, let me look at you! You are a beautiful woman now! Always were."

I was flummoxed. "What? You knew?"

She took my hands in hers. "Of course, sweetheart. I've always known. A mother's heart always knows these things about her child. When you were conceived inside me, I secretly hoped and prayed to Heaven that my first child would be a girl. Well, after all, my wish, my prayer, has been answered."

Her revelation hit me like a rod of lightning and caused a million waves of electricity to ripple back and forth throughout my body. Feeling weak and wobbly, I was on the verge of collapsing when she held me in her arms and helped to steady me.

"Mama, please take me with you. I cannot bear this life anymore," I begged her.

"No, Zoë! No, sweetheart," she said, as her hand caressed my face, "it's not your time to go. Chin up, my daughter. I want you to stand tall and to honor me by living a long, productive and happy life. That is my parting wish. I want you to promise me this!"

"Mama, we will meet again, won't we?" I implored her; my vison blurred by the stream of tears.

"Sweetheart, so long for now but I promise you that this is not the end. We will meet again, in Heaven one day. But now it's time for you to awaken and continue with your life's journey on Earth."

V

ZENITH

1

Re-Awakening

Journal entry # 2139$
Rotterdam, Dec 2018
🎧 Lisa Gerrard – Now We Are Free

"Nadine, why are you crying?" I blinked my eyes a few times as the blurred outline of her face came into focus.

Nadine took my left hand in hers and pressed it to her lips. "Zoë, do you know where you are? Do you realize what happened?"

"By the smell, I'm guessing I'm in a hospital. Again! It's like my second home, you know."

"They brought you to Erasmus MC six days ago. Since then, you've been in a coma." She kissed my hand again. "Zoë, how could you do this to me?"

"I'm sorry." I closed my eyes and felt them swell with tears. "I'm sorry. I was gripped by a severe depression and saw no way out. It was Mama, you know, who saved me. She's sent me back." I gave Nadine an account of my vivid other-worldly encounter with Mama.

"Only this morning, the doctors were telling me that you might never wake up." Nadine sniffled and wiped her eyes with a Kleenex tissue.

"Did you get a blue envelope?" I asked.

"No. What blue envelope?"

Of course, it must still be with the solicitors. They didn't send it because I didn't die.

"Nothing. Something I wrote before I… So how did you know? I mean, to come looking for me?"

"Jena. She raised the alarm," Nadine replied.

"You mean Jena from-work Jena?" I looked at her, confused.

"Yes, that Jena. When you went AWOL for two days in a row, she tried to reach you but to no avail, so she looked up your company record and found that you'd left my cell phone number in case of emergencies. When she finally reached me, I rushed to your apartment." She took out another tissue from her handbag and blew her nose.

"Nadine, I'm truly sorry for hurting you and putting you through this terrible ordeal, but I can't lie to you – the truth is, I didn't want to come back. Mama made me."

"Don't you ever do this to me again." Nadine's voice trembled with anger.

"I promise I won't. I promised Mama that too." With my eyes and smile I tried to communicate as much warmth and affection as I could. Unable to suppress the incessant grumbles in my stomach, I beseeched Nadine, "Now, can we get something decent to eat. Please."

2

The Visitor

Journal entry # 2140$
Erasmus MC, Rotterdam, Dec 2018
🎧 Stereophonics – Maybe Tomorrow

A petite olive-skinned boy wearing spectacles ran into the room and hopped like a rabbit onto my hospital bed. *Do I know this little fellow?* I looked puzzled at Nadine.

She shook her head. "I have no clue either." The boy extended his hands toward me and offered me the bouquet of flowers he was carrying.

"Thank you, sweetie, but I think you've mistaken me

for the other patient." I pointed at the patient lying on his bed diagonally from me.

"No. He's not mistaken. That's David, my son." I looked up. It was Jena. A spark kindled between us.

"Hey, David, sweetie, would you like a muffin from the cafeteria?" Nadine reached out to David. His mother nodded her consent.

"What kind of muffin?" he inquired.

"Chocolate or raspberry. You can choose." Nadine took his small hand, and they left the room.

I stretched my arm toward Jena. I desperately wanted to touch her. She responded by taking my hand and interlocking fingers with me. I felt her energy in my aching body like a shower of electricity. "Are you feeling what I'm feeling?" I asked.

"Uh-hu! For an invalid, you sure have a lot of AC/DC!" She winked. I burst out laughing.

"Please don't make me laugh. It still hurts." I locked eyes with her. "If this wasn't a hospital bed, I would have asked you to climb into bed with me. Oh yes, it's true – I do bite!"

"I beg your pardon?" Jena was flustered, her cheeks blushing a dark hue of plum pink.

"I said that I do bite. In bed, I mean." I waited for her horrified reaction and for her to withdraw her hand in a jolt from mine. But to my surprise, the grip of her fingers strengthened around mine.

"Yes, I had a feeling you did. You're a foxy one!" she nodded, a sly smile on her face.

"No, not fox. Pantera," I corrected her. "I'm a panther."

"Darling, you're Pantera and Kitsune wrapped up in one."

With all the energy I could muster, I pulled her hand to my mouth and kissed it affectionately for a very long time. "Thank you, Jena! You and my mother saved my life."

"

Nadine returned with David. "Ladies, control yourselves. No misbehaving here. May I remind you you're in a hospital room."

3

Rehab

Journal entry # 2146$
Rotterdam, Dec 2018
🎧 Donna Summer – Stamp Your Feet

Dear Jules, this has been a long time coming. I'm ready to do this. Back in 2016, I thought I'd shaken off my codeine addiction, but when push came to shove, I relapsed, in a very bad way.

"Good morning, Rehab Center DNV, how can we help you?" the lady on the other end greeted me.

"Hi, my name is Zoë van Vixenhoven. I've been

referred to you by my family doctor. I'm a drug addict, and I need professional help to overcome my addiction."

"Of course, miss. We are able to help you with that. I'm going to need you to email me the referral letter and to provide us with access to your health records going back five years."

"Sure. I can do that."

"Can you specify the addiction?"

"Opiates. Specifically, codeine." I answered. "When can I check in?"

"The earliest possible is the first week of February."

4

Discharge

Journal entry # 2231$
Rotterdam, May 2019
🎧 Leela James – Mistreating Me

D ear Jules, today I was discharged from the addiction
treatment center. I've completed my 90 days of rehab.
How I'm feeling? Mostly good. Optimistic. I can hear music
again. At the same time, I'm a little apprehensive and nervous to be let out into the wilderness of mankind.

This morning at around 11:00, Willem and Nadine
were waiting for me in the lobby of the rehab clinic. Whenever I'm being discharged, whether from a hospital or a

clinic, those two beautiful souls are always there for me. Bless their hearts! My trusted social support structure of two (three, if I count Jena as well; she's a late addition, though).

Willem took us to a café on the outskirts of Rotterdam, right next to the take-off and landing runway of Rotterdam's Zestienhoven Airport. We updated each other on what had transpired in our lives recently, and naturally because we were at Zestienhoven, we couldn't help but talk about future vacation plans (or to be more precise, wishes, in my case at least). After that, Willem dropped us off at the Lijnbaan, in the center of town, as per Nadine's instructions.

"Zoë, I've booked us an appointment at Kinki's Hairdressers. I'm going to let them give you a tapered bob-style haircut, a la Victoria Beckham anno 2001. You're gonna rock, girl!"

Nadine was right. This hairstyle does suit me. Suits Pantera too.

5

Jena's Wisdom Redux

Journal entry # 2235$
Rotterdam, May 2019
🎧 Madilyn Bailey – Let It Go

J ena was right. I recalled her thoughtful, wise words during that short conversation at the company canteen so many years ago. As long as I keep seeking approval and validation about my worth as a human being, a woman and a professional from others I will never find peace. To the contrary, I'll be in a state of perpetual doubt and turmoil leading to self-harm and ultimately to self-destruction. Dear Jules, take, for example my mother: all her married life, she sought the approval of my father. The bastard knew it and used it to control and manipulate her; always keeping her on the edge until that beautiful rose withered away and died far too young. If I look at my own life, unfortunately I can give you dozens (if not gazillions) of toxic examples of how I sought the other's approval to my own detriment; the most recent time was when I was with Jeronimo. When he revealed his animosity toward LGBT people, I should have thrown him out of my apartment right away. But no, missy here tried very hard to regain his approval, and we both know how disastrously that ended. It's time to get off this road, once and for all. *Girl, let it go!* It's time to focus on one, and only one, kind of validation, and that's my own inner voice.

Rotterdam shone in her full maritime magnificence in tonight's full moon, but inside my apartment there were more pressing matters at hand. I turned away from the windowpane and glided like a seductive black panther toward Jena. I took the champagne glass from her hand, finished off her Mimosa and pushed her onto the sofa.

"Feeling amorous this evening, Miss van Vixenhoven?"

"Amorous, maybe. Wild, very."

"Ah, I see, it's the tigress, again. Am I in her presence now?"

"Grrrr… Pantera is an altogether different animal, my dear."

6

Letter from
Jeronimo

Journal entry # 2238$
Rotterdam, May 2019
🎧 Mike & The Mechanics – Don't Know What Came
Over Me

Dear Jules, this morning I found a hand-written letter
from Jeronimo in my postbox. My initial extreme hesitation to read it was overcome by curiosity (or something
else). Right now, I find myself shaken and too emotional to
write about my feelings regarding this letter. I do want, however, to include it in my journal. I've paired it with a song,

which I believe captures the essence of his message and some of the emotions, which he's expressed in his letter:

Querida Zoë,

I hate myself so much for the vile and unforgivable violence I've inflicted upon you. Every day, I relive the nightmare of the morning after we made passionate love. How could I have done it? Only a few hours after something so beautiful, I viciously attacked you. In that moment of madness, I don't know what kind of savagery took possession of me. Ever since, I've been consumed by guilt, disgust with myself, shame, regret and utter sadness.

Your kind and tender heart opened for me the door to the most wonderful place in the universe. A magical garden where I could have been the happiest man in the world, with you. And what did this idiot, this barbaric fool do? He desecrated and defiled this esplêndida, exotic flower called Zoë van Vixenhoven.

I know I have no right to ask you for your forgiveness, but I beg you to let these hands that hurt you so much, become the hands that from now on will only love you, support you, protect you and bring you joy and happiness.

I was so incredibly wrong. Not only are you all woman, but deep down in my heart I know that you are the most special woman I will ever meet. I have felt her, touched her, tasted her and made love to her. She took me inside her, as the first man in her life and wrapped me with her florescent female essence. I'm crying now like I've never cried before, for you and what I did to you. How could I have let prejudice and hate (both so foreign to

how I see myself) blind me, and like a disease, infect me
so catastrophically?

Today and for eternity, I pray for your forgiveness.
I do not deserve a second chance, and yet that's what I'm
audaciously asking you to give me.

Yours, com amor eterno,

Jeronimo

7

Flooow

Journal entry # 2249$
Rotterdam, Jun 2019
🎧 Jade De LaFleur – Shotgun

Flooow (with three 'o's) can best be described as a trendy Victorian-style cabaret café/club. With its dark mahogany wood, creamy beige leather upholstery, smoky-gray mirrors and shiny copper-pipe fittings, it wouldn't look out of place in a posh and ritzy 19th century London neighborhood. For a few years now, it has become *the* go-to place in our port-city for the well-to-do, middle-aged men looking for a particular kind of adventure, let's call it Sensual Magick (yes, Jules, its spelled with a 'ck'). Located in a leafy street in the heart of Rotterdam's bohemian quarter of Oude Westen, Flooow is a mere two streets from Pantera's SM studio. Jesper and Jensen, the club's two young and hip proprietors, also acted as Mistress Pantera's agents, for a handsome commission, of course.

After burning the midnight oil, Pantera liked to conclude her nights at Flooow's long bar with a tumbler of whisky-cola and a plate of pecan nuts. On this occasion, she invited Nina, a fellow Dominatrix, to join her.

For a few months now, Nina (or Lady Nina as she is known professionally) has been struggling to attract clientele to her studio, and to say business was lackluster was a blaring understatement. This was in stark contrast to Mistress Pantera, who's been fully booked weeks in advance, since her return from rehab.

Although Nina was not in the same league as Pantera (SM talent-wise), whenever possible, Pantera tried to lend her a helping hand, especially if the client asked to be dominated by two Mistresses.

On Tuesdays, after midnight, only a handful of customers, usually regulars, can be found at Flooow sipping their after-dark wines and liquors. The two Mistresses choose to sit alone at the far end of the bar, next to the dance floor.

"I love your leather corset. Where did you get it from? If you don't mind me asking," Nina inquired.

"It's a corsetry shop in Amsterdam called 'Black Steel & White Bones'. If you ever decide to go there, mention the names 'Verona', 'Aleera', and 'Marishka' and they'll give you a twenty-percent discount on any corset above three hundred euros." Pantera took another sip from her tumbler. "But don't tell them that I told you."

"Why 'Verona', 'Aleira' and 'Marishka'?" Nina took out her mobile to make a note.

"It's 'Aleera' not 'Aleira'. They're pretty fussy, when it comes to these codes; mispronounce one and you'll miss out on the discount all together. As to the why, have you never read Count Dracula? They're Dracula's three brides."

"Pantera, I couldn't help but notice you're always wearing long leather gloves – why is that?"

What the fuck is this? Pantera's fashion-reveal night?

"It's a fashion statement. Nothing more." When questions got too personal, Pantera's motto was 'Don't tell. Never Explain!' and she definitely wasn't going to reveal anything about Zoë's pizza-mutilation technique, which had left her forearms permanently scarred.

"Jesper, luv, could you turn on the dance-floor lights and put on an 80's playlist? We feel like dancing till the end of time. Pun intended." Pantera chuckled at her own humor.

"Sure thing, Pantera. For you, always. Any requests for the DJ?"

"Ain't Nobody – the original track by Chaka Khan. Please." Pantera blew Jesper a kiss. "C'mon, Nina. Let's give the boys something to drool over." She grabbed Nina's hand and led her to the dance floor.

Half an hour later, give or take, out of the blue, a group of five men joined the ladies and formed a circle around them.

"They must be tourists. Never seen them here before.

They look like foreigners to me." Nina kept throwing suggestive glances at the red-bearded one.

"I don't like this, Nina. We've both had a drink too many. You're already tipsy. Let's call it a night." Pantera grabbed Nina by the left shoulder. "C'mon let's go".

"Fuck off, Pantera! You don't call the shots here!" Nina turned her back to her colleague and moved closer to the red-bearded tourist. With a slight twitch of the head, *red beard* sent a signal to his chum, the one who was closest to Pantera. The chum, a burly man with short, cropped hair, nodded in acknowledgement and shoved Pantera to the side. After that, the men regrouped in a tight-knit circle around Nina.

Alarm bells started ringing in my head. This is definitely not good. It's classic wolf-pack tactics: isolate your victim, pressure her and then take her home, in this case, probably a hotel room. After that, Heaven forbid what will happen! No, this is not happening on my watch. I ran to the bar and from my bag I pulled out a nine-ft cowhide bullwhip.

"Jesper, Jensen, I need your help. Nina's in trouble with those mongrels," I pointed toward the dance floor at the back of the club. "Why on earth did Abdul let this rabble in? They're not exactly Flooow material, are they?"

I took a few steps toward the dance floor, reversed my right arm backward, swung the bullwhip twice above my head and unleashed it with lightning speed at the tourist closest to me, the one who just a minute ago had aggressively shoved me to the side. *SMACK!* The whip flicked, cracked and tore the back side of the man's shirt in two.

In pain and agony, he let out a shrieking scream. He turned around and once he'd registered what had happened, he charged at me like a raging bull. I took a step backward and flicked my bullwhip in Coachman style at his head. Reflexively, his hands reached out to cover his face, but it was too late. *CRACK!* The whip's tail hit him dead center between the eyes. He doubled in pain. I swooped down to the floor, pirouetted on my left foot in an anti-clockwise circular motion (not an easy stunt with high heels) and just as I faced the mongrel again, I unleashed my whip sideways. It flew like an Exocet a few inches above the floor, cracked the air, producing a *SONIC BOOM*, and coiled itself around his left ankle. Before he could move to shake it off, all the sinews in my arms tensed and I pulled as hard as I could with both hands.

His left leg thrashed frontward and upward into the air followed by the right leg, and in true technicolor slow motion he came crashing down on his back like a sack of potatoes, finally hitting the parquet wood flooring with a loud jarring thud. *STRIKE!* All ten pins down! All those hours practicing with the bullwhip, while I was alone in my room at rehab, had certainly paid off. I could already picture myself as a circus ring-mistress. With a red tail-coat, white equestrian leggings and shiny black thigh-high leather boots, I'd be a dashing figure under the Big Top, cracking my whip at clowns and animals all day. Actually, I quite fancy life on the road with a travelling circus. What, Jules? You don't approve of my hobby. What was I going to do with a zillion hours to kill at rehab – write a book? Nah! Not my style. This journal is enough ink on this girl's fingertips. Yes, Jules, you're right. Sorry, I do digress, back to Flooow.

Armed with baseball bats, Jesper, Jensen and Abdul cleared out the rabble and sent them packing home. Wherever home was.

I ran to Nina. "Luv, did they hurt you? Are you okay?"

"Fuck off, Pantera! You couldn't let this be, could you?" Nina lashed out at me.

"What the fuck?" I was dumbstruck.

"Just once, you were not the center of attention and you couldn't let it be?" Spittle flew from Nina's mouth in all directions.

"Really, Nina? That's what you think this is about?" I shook my head in disbelief. "That is simply incredulous."

"That's exactly what it's about! You selfish, egoistical bitch."

I locked eyes with her. "I'm going home. I have no time for this shit. Nina, if you feel the same way about me tomorrow, then we part ways for good. Good night." I picked up my bag and headed for the front door.

"That was one hell of a demonstration with the bullwhip, Mistress Amazôna." Jesper raised his glass of beer in salutation from behind the bar.

"Pantera is my name," I shot back, anger flashing in my eyes.

"Of course. Of course. Pantera is *who* you are. Mistress Amazôna is *what* you are, or what you have become." Jesper smiled and winked at me. "Flooow at your service. Always."

8

Letter to All T.E.R.F.s[20]

Journal entry # 2252$
Rotterdam, Jun 2019
🎧 Lady Gaga – Born This Way

T.E.R.F.s,

I am a woman not because others have given me approval to consider myself one. I'm a woman because my essence is female. Being transgender is not some freak mistake of nature. Being transgender is by intelligent design. The amazing and brilliant Lady Gaga said it plain, loud and clear: "I was born this way".

---

20 T.E.R.F. stands for Transgender Excluding Radical Feminist

Yes, I am a different kind of woman (I'm a hybrid), but I'm a woman nonetheless. I've never claimed to be a cis woman like you, and I never will. Ever! Doing that would be tantamount to denial of my history and identity.

A trans woman is a lioness with a huge gaping wound on her side, which you are repeatedly stabbing with your poison-tipped knives. You do that with those instruments which you deceptively claim are your creative pens. Although many of you probably consider yourselves as progressive, liberal thinkers, you have knowingly entered an unholy alliance with the zealous forces of the uber-conservative, the ultra-religious and the extreme right. When we call you out, you whine and complain of 'cancel' culture. But who's canceling who? When your goal is to wipe out our entire identity and, by implication, our existence.

T.E.R.F.s, you have inflicted tremendous pain on us, but in due course, justice has a way of prevailing. When that happens, you will be consigned to the rubbish bin of history for the bigots that you've undoubtedly become.

The sad truth is that some of you are lesbians and thus are welcomed with open arms by the trans community to the Rainbow Family of LGBTQ+ peoples. It's all about diversity and inclusiveness – right? So how dare you exclude us from the world of womanhood. To quote Sylvia Rivera: "Y'all better quiet down!"

To the overwhelming majority of women who have supported and continue to support our cause in our hour of desperation and need, a huge warm embrace and a very big THANK YOU from the bottom of my heart. Love you! And I promise you that we will continue to fight for your worthy and noble causes of equality and protection against prejudice and violence; they are our causes too.

To T.E.R.F.s and all the haters like them, the middle finger. Transphobia is not an opinion or an intellectual point of view. Like racism, it's blatant discrimination, pure and simple.

Defiantly,

Zoë van Vixenhoven

''

Jules, a part of me believes that, contrary to general perception in the West, humanity is not on the cusp of a Brave New World of individual freedoms and human rights for all, but rather at the precipice of a dark age of neofascism and populist reactionary doctrine. *The Empire is striking back!* The Rainbow Family's struggle is going to be a very long and grueling one. Let's not kid ourselves – this is not a struggle for decades, but centuries to come.

9

Jeronimo at the Park

Journal entry # 2254$
Park aan de Maas, Rotterdam, Jun 2019
🎧 Christophe Goze feat. Odis Palmer – She Said

I found Jeronimo sitting on a park bench holding a bunch of sunflowers. He was staring at a non-existent squirrel nibbling on a non-existent pinecone. He didn't notice that I had arrived.

"The squirrel – it's gone! It has run away, Jeronimo." I startled him.

"Huh!" Jeronimo sprang to his feet. "Sorry, I didn't

see you coming. These are for you. I remember you telling me that sunflowers are your favorite." He stretched out his right arm to give me the flowers. I sat down on the bench without taking them.

Jeronimo slumped beside me and placed the sunflowers between us. "You're looking good, Zoë. How are you?"

"If I look good, that's no thanks to you, Jeronimo," I snapped back at him. "Do you know you left me with a broken nose and various fractures to my face? Because of you, I had to undergo urgent surgery. Luck would have it that a certain French plastic surgeon, whom I trust with my life, flew to Rotterdam to supervise the reconstructive surgery at Erasmus MC."

"I'm so sorry, Zoë." Jeronimo shook his head and dropped his eyes to avoid my furious eyes burning into them. When he opened his eyes again, they were all teared up.

"I know you are. I read your letter; that's why I agreed to see you." I felt the anger start to ebb away from me.

"What I wrote in that letter, I still feel that way, Zoë. Please find it somewhere in your big heart to forgive me." Before I could respond to that plea, Jeronimo got down on one knee and from his jacket pocket retrieved a dark-blue velvet pouch. He opened the pouch and tilted it sideways. Something shiny gold and red came rolling out onto his open palm. "It's a firebird, a phoenix, made of rose gold and at its heart is a ruby stone. During our second date you told me how much you loved the story of the phoenix. For me, the phoenix is you, Zoë." His hands began to shake. "Please accept this pendant as a token of my repentance and love for you." He extended his right arm to give it to me.

I froze and stared at the pendant – it was nothing short of dazzling. It must have cost him an arm and a leg to buy this. The phoenix with its golden fiery wings and ruby heart called out to me. I love it. Want it. Hell, maybe I should just grab it. Take it. Retribution for the injury he inflicted upon me.

A couple who was passing by hollered at me, "C'mon, miss. Are you blind? Can't you see the lad really loves you. We've been together for thirty-seven years. We know love when we see it."

"Jeronimo, please get off your knees. This is quite mortifying. You're embarrassing me. People are thinking you're proposing to me or something." Reluctantly, Jeronimo succumbed to my request. "I appreciate the gesture, Jeronimo, but I can't accept the pendant you bought for me."

"Why?" He looked dejected.

"Heaven knows that every fiber in my body wanted me to report you to the police for assault and battery. And God knows that that is exactly what I should have done, but something inside me just wouldn't let me. Listen, I don't want to ruin you, and definitely not your parents. They've sacrificed everything to see their son, their only child, become someone they are so proud of. Saddling you with a criminal record would have destroyed them as much as you. I decided I wasn't going to let that happen."

Jeronimo's face lit up. "So, you've forgiven me?"

"Yes, I forgive you. Understand that I'm doing this as much for me as I am for you. I want to move on from this.

And now I want you to go and find yourself a woman who will love you, give you children and a nice home."

"Querida, I want all that, but not with some other woman. I want that with you." His eyes begged me.

"I can't have children. I'm trans. Or have you forgotten already?"

"We'll adopt. A girl and a boy from Cabo Verde. You'll make a fantastic mother. The best, I'm sure," he pleaded.

"No. No. No." I shook my head. "Stop this *querida* shit. You're not thinking straight. This is your guilt speaking. You're confusing a lot of things here. You don't love me. You can't."

"Yes, and I do and I can. Fuck this, Zoë! Could you please stop misinterpreting me?" Exasperation engraved itself on every contour of his handsome face. "I've never wanted something more in my life than to be with you."

I stood up and yelled at him. "You don't get it do you, Jeronimo? The blood stain – it's still on that freaking wall! Please don't follow me!" My eyes welled up; I snatched the sunflowers (why I don't know) and vamoosed the hell out of there.

I came to see Jeronimo at the park to close this chapter and put him behind me, once and for all. Forever and always. Well, I failed. Miserably. All it proved to me is that I still have feelings for him, strong feelings. *Damn you, Jeronimo. If you were to embrace me right now, I'd probably melt like butter in your arms.* I picked up my pace and started running like a cat with its tail on fire… 45, 46, 47, 48, out of the park and into the street. *Run, Zoë, run.* I don't trust me to be anywhere near Jeronimo.

10

Sorry, Ashok

Journal entry # 2257$
Rotterdam, Jul 2019
🎧 Michael Ortega – I'm Sorry

Dear Ashok,

In the past few years, my life has felt like a steampunk contraption which fuses a rollercoaster and revolving door into one crazy, manic experience. I guess you know that I've undergone some pretty profound physical, emotional and social changes. Those changes have been accompanied by multiple surgeries; I've been in and out of hospitals more times than I care to count. That said, with every hospitalization, on some level, I've felt more fragile and that much closer to death. I don't have a lifetime ahead of me anymore. Tomorrow could very well be the last day. Hell, today could be the last day.

With all this weighing on my mind and soul, I want to make amends for the mistakes and regrets of the past. You needed time to process the changes which I was going through, and I didn't grant you that time and space. I was wrong to pressure you into accepting me as trans right away. Now, I know and understand that we all have our own ways of processing change around us.

You were one of the dearests to me, my soulmate of many years, and I cannot let that go without trying one last time to mend bridges with you. I hope you have it in your heart to join hands and hearts with me to repair the once special bond that connected us so strongly.

Love,

Zoë (formerly your BFF Maher)

ı'

P.S. Jules, I don't know why I'm feeling so depressed today. I'm sure I will be my usual optimistic self tomorrow.

11

Holland, I Love You!

Journal entry # 2259$
Rotterdam, Jul 2019
🎧 BLØF – Zoutelande

Dear Holland (or if you prefer, Netherlands),

Once upon a time, I blamed you for all my pain and miseries. I even managed to convince myself I needed to escape you to find peace and a place in this wild world, which I could call home. Today, I know you are my forever home. If it was not for you, today I would be ten meters underground, or more likely dismembered and my body parts dumped somewhere, scorched and godforsaken. For offering me salvation, a safe haven and a future, please accept my eternal love, respect and unending gratitude. Nowhere (in this universe) comes even close to you. You rock my world, and I love you.

Holland, ik hou van jou. Hartelijk dank voor alles!

Zoë van Vixenhoven

12

C'mon Comeuppance

Journal entry # 2263$
Company HQ, Amsterdam, Aug 2019
🎧 Ava Max – Who's Laughing Now

M y project team members started streaming into the meeting room on the ninth floor. There was one member whom I was particularly interested in today. *He better not go AWOL on me today!* When Kurt finally made his entry in his usual bombastic manner, we locked eyes, the way old rivals do.

What an arrogant dog! This guy's not only my nemesis, he's my antithesis. Beloved mother in Heaven, help me pull this off.

"Hey, System Says No (his nickname for me these days), I heard you were in rehab recently. Are you clean now?" he snorted. It was a rhetorical question, of course.

In response, I blew him a flying kiss. "I love you so much, Kurt." The words stopped him in his tracks. He looked genuinely puzzled.

"Are you back on drugs, Shibli?" He swirled his index finger next to his right temple and crossed his eyes. "You must be high today." That elicited a few chuckles in the room.

"Very." I smiled and licked my lips seductively at him. I could see that irked him. *I'm starting to get under your skin, you piece of shit. C'mon, Zoë, you can do this. Push harder.* "Team, please settle down. If you all could take your seats; I have some good news to share with you." Suddenly, you could hear a pin drop in the room.

"Don't look so worried," I tried to reassure them. "At least for most of us, it is good news. May I have a drum roll, please." I looked in the direction of Kurt and gave him an exaggerated smile. "Team, Priority M is no longer a project; senior management has elevated its status to program, and you are now looking at your new Program Manager – yours truly, none other than Ms. van Vixenhoven, herself."

After a chilly silence, the meeting room erupted with cheers and enthusiastic shouts of congratulations. I turned my focus back at Kurt, who was now ashen-faced, and mouthed the world LOSER at him.

"Dear Kurt, it seems like senior management has decided to bypass you. Again." This time, it was me who snickered at him. Perspiration started forming on his fore-head and his cheeks turned a dark hue of pomegranate red. Clearly, he was not finding all this amusing. *C'mon, girl, keep pushing him.*

"Fuck off, Maher. We'll see who laughs loudest," Kurt barked in defiance.

Yes, asshole, we definitely will. He was beyond annoyed, now; maybe even incensed. *Just a little more, and you're toast, you little shit.*

"Team, there's more good news." Like a conductor in a concert room I lowered my hands in unison to signal my colleagues to tone it down a little. "Most of you are well aware that there are colleagues amongst us who have repeatedly tried to undermine our progress. Obviously, that's not something I can tolerate anymore!" *And here comes the biggest bluff of my professional life*: "Luckily, for us, as Program Manager, I now have the authority to deselect the colleagues whom I feel are not contributing in a positive way to the program." I was lying – I had no such author-ity. Team members are exclusively assigned by the com-pany divisions' heads. I was gambling heavily now. "The first person I'm deselecting from the team is Kurt." The room descended into a deathly silence as Kurt and I locked eyes again. "You heard me, Kurt. You're out. Goodbye!" I gestured with my right hand toward the door. *C'mon, you bastard. Take the bait. Go for it. Bite! It's right in front of you.*

"You fucking transvestite bitch! Fake woman, who the fuck do you think you are?" Kurt finally flipped.

Gotcha!

The meeting room door flew open. Marcus Ockermann (head of the air freight division) and Lieselotte Holten (now senior HR manager) came charging in.

"I've seen and heard enough," Marcus yelled at Kurt. "Pack your stuff, Kurt. There's no place for you and your likes in our company. Mister, you're out of Megalaar."

"Smile, Kurt, you're on candid camera." I pointed toward the tiny camera clipped to the side of the TV screen. "Our guests witnessed your overt transphobia live on their laptops in the room next door."

Kurt blew his top. He leapt onto the table and made a violent dash for me. "Devil's child, I will get you!" Luckily for me, there were several colleagues between us who blocked his way and pinned him down. Now horizontal on the tabletop, Kurt kicked and thrashed in sheer futility.

"No, Kurt. If you must know, I'm the child of Pluto," I said as I waved goodbye at him.

"Shibli, I promise you and your kind will burn in hell. 'Let God Burn Them' – that's what LGBT is. Hell. That's where you and your gay filth will end up on Judgement Day." Kurt spewed out more hate and vitriol.

"Enough! Enough of this! Take this freaking zealot out of here and have security escort him off company terrain," Marcus demanded; he was anger, disgust and fury personified.

Later in the day, I thanked Marcus and Lieselotte for their steadfast support – it went above and beyond my expectations. Also, I said a big thank you to Megalaar Logistics for being true to their principles and commitment to Diversity and Inclusion in the workplace.

Jules, the chickens have come to roost. Today, sweet revenge was mine. Actually, bittersweet is a better description of what transpired in that meeting room at work earlier today. Even though I'm delighted with the result, I'm quite sad it had to come to this. I'll expand on that tomorrow. Right now, just let me savor the sweeter notes of revenge a little longer.

13

Raw Poetry N° 3

Journal entry # 2267$
The Hague, Aug 2019

Emergence *by my sister, Nadine Shibli*

A child
Looking into a mirror
Beautiful curls frame its face
Mum's lipstick being applied in not-quite-perfect imitation
Wanting to look just as pretty
The child smiles wide at its reflection
Then a voice yells

The lipstick is snatched away
And a child is left in tears
Not understanding what it had done wrong

~ ~ ~

An adult
Tall and slim
Elegant in dress and manners
A fitted silhouette
The scent of Havana sweetened with a waft of vanilla
Unusual, interesting
These hints of truth
Seen yet difficult to decipher by others

~ ~ ~

A spirit
Trapped
Within a cage of lies
Tormented by endless whispers of disgust and despair
Almost giving in
Dying to be free
Until a glimmer of realization
A spark of undeniable self
Lights a way out

~ ~ ~

A woman
Statuesque and confident
With fire in her eyes
Ignited through anguish
Sustained through courage
She shapes a new existence
Authentic in mind and body
Honest and uncontained

Learning to love and adore with abandon
All that brings her joy
The woman looks into her mirror
Lips shining Rosso-Corsa red
And smiles

14

It's Time

Journal entry # 2269$
Amsterdam, Sep 2019
🎧 Mariah Carey – Almost Home

"It's time, dear Zoë, for me to let you go." With his kind blue eyes, Johan looked at me like a proud father would at his own daughter.

"But can't we meet just once or twice a year?" I protested.

"No, Zoë." Johan shook his head. "To use the analogy of the train, which you are so fond of using – when your train reaches the terminal station, you do not stay seated on the train. You step out onto the platform, and you exit the station into the city and the world beyond that. Your transition, medically, physically and psychologically speaking, is complete. As for the emotional and social dimensions, well, those are lifetime commitments for you to work on."

There was such a decisive finality to Johan's words. They not only indicated the conclusion of my time with him but marked the end of my transition as well. I knew this day would come and yet when it finally arrived, it clobbered me like an emotional sledgehammer. Try as hard as I could, I still couldn't stop my emotions from pouring out. First, a few teardrops trickled down my cheeks and then the floodgates opened. Tears of happiness intermingled with tears of sadness.

Jules, for the past five years, I've known only one life and that is the life of transitioning. I lived from one medical appointment to the other. As tiresome, nerve-racking and heavy as that may have been, it still provided me with a clear structure, direction and milestones. Within that structure, Johan was my trusted guide and coach. Now all that has come to a definitive end. From now on, I am captain and navigator of my life. I'm blessed. There's a new life for me to lead, discover and explore. Thank you, Johan, for everything. You will always be a treasured part of me. Still wish you were the godparent I never had.

15

Terminal
Station / Exit

Journal entry # 2270$
Rotterdam Central Station, Sep 2019
🎧 Seal – Let Yourself
George Michael – Free

With some considerable delay, the train finally pulled in at platform 9 at Rotterdam Central Station. So, Zoë, this is it, this is the terminal station. The *end of the track*, literally and figuratively, of your transition. A conclusion to this remarkable phase of your life. It's been a rollercoaster five years. You've been to a zillion consultations with an army of psychologists, therapists, endocrinologists, surgeons, nurses and anesthetists. After what feels like thousands of blood tests, four surgeries and more than nineteen hours on the operating table, with every facet of your existence turned upside down and inside out, your transition is complete. You have crossed to the other side. Bravo, girl. You've made it! You're a woman now, wholly, and an attractive one at that, if I may say so myself. BLUSH BLUSH. You've made the transition from barely surviving to fully living. From the ashes of a disintegrating man, an *Amazôna* of a woman has arisen.

Jules, I made it! I really made it. I've healed those deep wounds within me. I am a proud trans woman, and I promise to always be true to the 'T' in my identity. I am an enigma to many and probably an anathema to some. Frankly, so be it. That's just who I am and the way it is. It is what it is. Time to move on. *So, what's next for you, Zoë van Vixenhoven?* Life, in its entirety, I assume. For the longest time, I hated the present and could only live for the future. Now that future has arrived, I can live in the present. Now that I'm one with my body, it's time for me to discover my *ikigai*. Relearn to dance the Tango, from a woman's perspective, of course. Perhaps it's even time to take the night train?

Zoë took the headphones off and packed her stuff in her red shoulder bag. As she stood up to leave, a young man across the aisle smiled at her. She smiled back. Maybe for the first time in her life, she actually smiled at a total stranger. Without further ado, Zoë stepped out of the train and walked the short distance to the escalator at the center of the platform. One of several dozen commuters, she started the descent down into the station's belly.

In the station's magnificent and minimalistic main hall, dozens of individuals became hundreds; hundreds multiplied into thousands. With serenity and grace, Zoë waded through the phantasmagoria of faces, bodies, limbs, lights, colors and reflections. Out of the station and into the wider world of humanity, she *disappeared*.

AFTERWORD

A big THANK YOU to Chrissy, Kostis, Julie and Louise for your contribution.

A very special thank you to you, the reader, for coming with me on this journey. I hope this novel touched you in some way. Zoë's transitional journey is inspired by real-life persons and events, primarily my own.

If you're a melomaniac like myself, I hope you also enjoyed the accompanying music playlist on Spotify. I believe music has the power to enrich and enhance any experience including the reading experience. Hopefully, some readers will duplicate the playlist on other music streaming platforms.

It's time for me to say goodbye. Take good care of yourself. Who knows – through Zoë the future might reunite us again, one day?

Love,

Alice Xavanéro

Printed in Great Britain
by Amazon